A CURSE OF BLOOD AND BONE

THE OZERO CURSE

NICOLETTE ELZIE

Hardcover ISBN: 979-8-9872869-2-0

Paperback ISBN: 978-1-0881-3917-2

E-book ASIN: B0BXQ9PY4Z

For more information, address:

nicolette@nicoletteelzie.com

CONTENTS

Dedication   V

Author's Note   VI

1. A Family Affair...Sort Of   1

2. Intruders Don't Knock   8

3. Birds, Bees and Eyrie Secrets   20

4. Monstrous Confessions and Romantic Tensions   28

5. Nightmares, Demons, and Disbelief...Oh My!   36

6. Sex Talks and Emotional Walks   45

7. Not Every Dinner Ends Well   53

8. Overheard and Overwhelmed   63

9. When Love and Blood Don't Mix (But Maybe They   68
    Should)

10. Solidarity in the Midst of Crisis   74

11. Vulgar is the New Romantic   83

12. The Difference Between Desire and   88
     Distraction...There is None

13. Cryptic Clues and Confused Minds   96

14. Spies Get No Goodbyes   104

15. A Little Romantic Chemistry   112

16. Secrets, Lies, and Mate Bonds   119

17. Breaking the Bond   131

18.	Midnight Bonding	142
19.	Intelligence is Not for Prying, or You'll End Up Crying	149
20.	A Lovers Duel	157
21.	Sealed with a Kiss	164
22.	What a Yawn	173
23.	Brotherly Love	177
24.	Secrets Always Come Back to Bite	185
25.	Traipsing in Foreign Territory	196
26.	Right in the Ego	205
27.	Blood Trails Never Fail	211
28.	Healing Woes	217
29.	A Wild Proposal	224
30.	Healing Bliss	232
31.	Only Fools Rush In	241
32.	Caught in the Talons	251
Also By Nicolette Elzie		262
Acknowledgments		263
About the Author		265

For the bravest among us, who embrace the darkness and find the beauty within.

AUTHOR'S NOTE

A Curse of Blood and Bone is a dark, fantasy romance inspired by the Mexican folktale of The Bear Prince. **It is not a retelling.**

///

A Curse of Blood and Bone contains mature and graphic content not suitable for all audiences. Dark romance isn't black and white. What some readers may consider "light" may be "dark" for others. I HIGHLY prefer for you to go in blind, but if you would like a detailed trigger warning list, you can find it at https://nicoletteelzie.com/content-warnings/

CHAPTER ONE

A Family Affair...Sort Of

Luna

The courtyard was alive with music and laughter. People swayed to the beat, their hands thrown in the air as they sang along. Calls of joy echoed through the space as mariachi bands provided the soundtrack. Energetic dancers spun and twirled as people swung from partner to partner in a colorful blur of swishing skirts.

The crowd unashamedly raised glass bottles into the air and drank straight from them, the amber liquid splashing onto cobblestones and clothes alike. No one seemed to mind, as they were all too caught up in the moment to care.

Luna's gaze trailed to Turi, who was surrounded by a group of young men — his cousins, she presumed. They were laughing and talking, gesturing wildly in the air and slapping each other on the back like old friends.

Her heart ached at the sight of their camaraderie and love. She took a deep breath and shook away the pang of jealousy that had risen in her chest. She should be happy for Turi to experience this kind of family bond — it was something she had only ever dreamed of.

The sounds of laughter and joyous singing drifted into her ears as if the world were blessed with a new start. She scanned the people around her, taking in their bright smiles and hugs of celebration. Yet, the more she looked, the more she felt out of place in this new world.

Her heart sank; she could feel the icy grasp of fear clenching at her chest and the chill running through her spine. She tried to shake it off and bury her anxiety, but it seemed like no matter how far she traveled, her fears would still follow.

Luna slowly pushed her way through the packed courtyard and out towards a door leading — she hoped — to somewhere quiet. As she opened the door, the fresh night air hit her face, and she breathed in deeply. The sound of laughter and chatter from the inner courtyard faded as she walked towards a set of stairs that led down to a small landing. She sat on the top step, feeling the cool night breeze on her face, and carefully smoothed out the wrinkles in her Healer Corps apron.

Then she heard a cough, followed by a clearing of someone's throat. She slowly turned her head toward the direction of the noise.

Aurelia stood a few feet away, her shoulders hunched and her face obscured by her long, dark hair. Her toe scuffed at the ground, stirring up small clouds of dust as she absentmindedly kicked at a pebble in the dirt.

Luna's stomach twisted into a knot as soon as she recognized the smuggler. She felt her shoulders tense as their gazes locked, and she pursed her lips together, trying to ignore the dread rising inside her. Aurelia was the last person she wanted to see, let alone speak to.

"What do you want?" Luna said, her voice tight with restrained rage.

Aurelia pressed her palms together in a pleading motion. "I just wanted to say that I'm sorry. I should have told you I was in a little trouble — "

Luna's lips twisted into a thin, angry line as she crossed her arms over her chest, shielding herself from Aurelia's apology. "A little trouble? Those men were thugs. That man — Tomás — he had his hands all over me and that smile on his face — " Her voice faltered as tears welled up in her eyes, and she shook her head, unable to finish the sentence.

Aurelia nervously ran her fingers through her tangled hair and scratched her scalp. "I know. I screwed up. I panicked. When he held that blade against your throat, all I could think to do was offer Kiks and Sol in exchange for your safety."

Luna stared at Aurelia with a glare, and a surge of nausea rose from her stomach. "The fact that solution came to you so quickly and so easily... It's just... it's disgusting."

Aurelia dropped to the ground and scrambled forward, her knees crunching against the gravelly ground. She bowed her head in front of Luna, her voice trembling with regret. "You're right. I'm so sorry. I said it without thinking... I was so scared of him hurting you." She reached out and tenderly took Luna's hands in her own, her fingertips brushing gently against the rough surface of Luna's calloused hands.

Luna's body went rigid, and she pulled her arms away from Aurelia's grasp. Her voice shook as she spat out her words. "Hurt me? Do you want to know who hurt me? You did. We were awake until dawn talking about our pasts and our dreams. I shared with you things that I never even let Kiki know. I believed you when you said you cared, but I was wrong. All those hours, all that trust," Luna murmured, her head shaking slowly in disappointment.

She kept her lips shut tight, her heart pounding in her chest, refusing to admit — even out loud to herself — what she had started to feel for Aurelia. After all that time spent talking, laughing, and sharing secrets, after feeling like she'd found a connection with the girl with silver eyes, it had all turned out to be a lie.

Luna's lungs heaved for breath as her voice quivered and her words came out in a rush. Her eyes were wide and haunted, mouth set in a grim line. She could feel the anger growing in her chest, the pain radiating out of her like heat waves. "You told me you smuggled food, and so I accepted it — my own people are starving, after all. So I understood that. But weapons? Weapons that cost lives? Weapons that could have been used to defend the Wall? Weapons that are the difference between someone bleeding out in my infirmary or seeing another sunrise? That I cannot forgive. And that is something I can't forget."

Aurelia shook her head and nervously ran her fingers through her long brown hair. "If Tomás hadn't caught up to me, would there have been a chance? For us, I mean," she said, her voice soft and uncertain. "Was it just me, or did you feel it too?" She looked away, struggling to keep her emotions in check.

Luna's heart clenched at the sight of Aurelia's soft features, illuminated by the moonlight, twisted with pain. She squeezed her eyes shut, refusing to meet the gaze of the girl who still made her heart flutter. She clenched her jaw, willing the tears away, and spoke with a wavering voice. "Go away, Aurelia," she whispered. "Please don't talk to me again."

Aurelia's voice shook with emotion as she said, "I just want to know. Please. Did I screw everything up? Did you feel anything for me? Do you still?"

Tears welled in Luna's eyes at the desperation that had crept into Aurelia's words.

Luna's insides twisted with guilt and sorrow. A part of her did still have feelings for Aurelia. The smuggler had seemed to understand Luna's deepest fears, never judging her for her mistakes or telling her she could have made a better choice.

Luna felt a twinge of remorse, realizing that Aurelia had empathized with her because she had done horrible things herself.

Tears welled in Luna's eyes, and her throat tightened. Somehow, she found the strength to look up and murmur, "Please, just go."

Aurelia stepped forward before suddenly jerking back as a large figure seemingly materialized from the shadows. "Marui! I didn't see you there," she stammered.

Mauricio stood an intimidatingly tall figure, his frame was powerfully muscled and his arms crossed firmly across his barrel chest. He stared down at Aurelia, his dark eyes glinting in the dim light. "She said to leave her alone. I suggest you listen for once in your life."

Aurelia's face suddenly shifted from guilt to anger. Her lips twisted into a sneer, and her silver eyes flashed with defiance. She took a sudden step forward, her hands clenching into fists at her sides. "So, the dog is off its leash and thinks it can boss me around, does it?" she spat. "We'll see who's in charge when Erasmo returns — "

"That's enough!" Mauricio's chest rumbled with a low, threatening growl as his words lingered in the air. His eyes were slits, and his lips pressed into a thin line. "Our cousin only tolerates you because of what you bring to the table," he said coldly. "Don't mistake his loyalty for affection. If your service could be replicated, trust me, he'd put you and your gifts out on the street without a second thought."

Aurelia winced and shrank back at his scathing words. "You're a bastard, Mauri," she spat, her fingers curling into fists and her jaw clenching in anger. "A yappy dog that trails after Erasmo's every step. You have no original thought in that empty head of yours. Why don't you run off and go do what dogs do best, sit at the gate, and wait for your master."

Mauricio stepped forward until he was just inches away from Aurelia, the air crackling with electricity. His shoulders were outlined with a darkness that seemed to seep from his very pores and curl around him like a cloak.

His hand clapped down on Aurelia's shoulder, and Luna didn't fail to notice the smuggler's throat bobbing. Mauricio's claws extended from his fingertips, and Luna could see their razor-sharp points pressing against Aurelia's neck.

"Insult me all you want," he growled, "but you'll be leaving this woman alone, or you'll have to answer to me. I won't be telling you again, cousin."

Aurelia's wide brown eyes filled with desperation as she tried to tear away from Mauri, but he held fast. When she finally gave up, her shoulders slumped, and her fists tightened into tight balls. Without looking back at Luna, she walked away slowly; her head bowed in defeat.

Luna sighed and shifted on the step, tucking a lock of curly black hair behind her ear before she propped her chin up with her hand. "Thanks for that," she whispered, shame curling around her chest.

Mauri slowly turned towards her, and his gaze lingered over her face, the corners of his lips quirking up in a small smile. "Don't mention it," he said softly.

He took a step back and turned as if to leave when Luna spoke up. "Thank you for earlier, too, by the way," she said.

His body froze, his foot suspended in midair, then he rotated reluctantly to meet her gaze. His brows were furrowed, and his jaw clenched. "Aurelia was right," he growled. "I am a bastard. Don't think for one moment that just because I helped you, I'm some kind of hero. I'm a killer, and I'll do anything to protect what's mine. That's the end of it."

Luna pursed her lips and sighed. "But you did rescue me; that has to be worth something."

Mauri crouched down, resting on his haunches, so he was on her level. His dark brown eyes were hard like stones, and he ran a calloused hand through his disheveled black hair. "My ledger is filled with too much red, *chiqui*. One kind act won't erase all the lives I've taken."

Luna's mouth curved into a half-smile. "No, but it's a start," she said with a shrug.

Mauri stood in a rush and turned away from her, but before he disappeared, he stole one last glance behind himself, and their eyes locked. Tension heated the air between them, and Luna held her breath, afraid to disrupt the moment. Mauri's jaw clenched, and his fists tightened at his sides before he strode away without another word.

Luna watched as the large man stepped back into the shadows, his form becoming invisible against the darkness. But she could still feel his eyes on her, and it brought a strange sense of comfort. He was like a guardian, keeping watch.

She curled her body into a tight ball and hugged her knees close to her chest. She was thankful he was watching over her, no matter how far away he was.

CHAPTER TWO

'INTRUDERS DON'T KNOCK

SOLANA

S olana was jolted awake by a thunderous crash. She opened her sleep-heavy eyes and blinked at her unfamiliar surroundings. The soft, mint green paint of her bedroom walls was illuminated by a shaft of white moonlight that cascaded through the window. Flickering orange and yellow flames crackled in the fireplace, barely throwing off enough heat to take the chill out of the air.

Bernat lay beside her, his breathing shallow and steady as he slept. The thin pillow propped under his head muffled each exhale, and the log in the hearth snapped and hissed in the silence.

The clang of metal against metal echoed through the air, and she surveyed the bedroom, looking for the source. She cautiously pulled the fur blankets off when it stopped and stepped onto the frigid wooden floor.

She grabbed a large fur blanket from the nearby chair and draped it around her bare shoulders before making her way to the window. She peeled the curtains aside and peered out into the night. The snow had started to pile up, and a strong wind rattled the window panes.

As Solana heard the metallic sound again, she whipped her head around and quickly rushed to her bedroom door. Her heart raced as she slowly opened the door a crack and peered out into the dark hallway.

The only light source came from the faint glow of the flickering candles, casting eerie shadows against the walls. Not a single sound could be heard as everyone in the manor house had gone to bed for the night.

Solana heard the same metallic echo as before, but this time it was followed by a voice — low, muffled, and hushed like a whisper. She held her breath, hoping that if she calmed the pounding of her heart, she'd hear better. Whoever was lurking around the house was most certainly up to no good.

She shut the door to her bedroom behind her, careful not to make any noise. Her eyes darted to the crumpled pile of black leather in the middle of the floor. Gripping the soft, black leather pants and jacket, she peeled them from the pile and put them on quickly. The soft material slid against her skin like butter, and the buckles clinked as she carefully fastened them around her waist and arms.

She dropped to her hands and knees and scanned the floor for her boots. They were half-hidden under the bed, their laces askew and tangled. She slowly pulled them on, every movement seeming too loud in the stillness of the night.

She was about to stand when she heard Bernat's low, sleepy voice come from the bed. "What are you doing awake? Come back to bed, Sol." Her heart skipped a beat as she froze, caught in the act.

So much for not waking him.

She worked at the knot in the laces as she said, "There's a weird noise downstairs, and I'm gonna go check it out."

Bernat groaned and rolled onto his back, his hands pushing away the sheets twisted around his body as he shifted on the mattress. The light in the room cast a faint glow across his chiseled frame, highlighting the tight muscles of his torso and the ridges of each defined ab.

His voice was thick with sleep as he asked, "What did it sound like?"

Solana shrugged. "If I had to guess, it sounded like someone had broken a lock. Like someone banging on metal until it cracked."

Bernat eased himself up from the bed, which creaked in protest, and Solana's eyes widened in surprise. He rolled his shoulders back, firmly planting his bare feet on the solid wooden floor.

"What are you doing?" she asked him.

Without hesitation, Bernat replied, "Where you go, I go."

A warm sensation spread from her chest outward as Solana listened to his words. She felt the corners of her lips turn into a smile; she had tried to push away these feelings only hours before, but now, with him standing right in front of her, she couldn't deny them any longer. He was her rock in a storm, her lighthouse in the middle of a hurricane.

Bernat pulled his pants up from the ground and hastily buckled the belt. He began walking in a tight circle, eyes darting around the ground. "Where are my boots?" he murmured, looking around with growing concern.

Solana's eyes sparkled with amusement as she spotted the scuffed leather boot next to her foot. She grabbed it and flung it in the air. It soared towards him, and he grabbed it out of the air with lightning-fast reflexes. His grin matched hers.

"Where is the other one?" he asked, a blush already forming on his cheeks.

Solana pointed towards the bed, and he dropped to his knees to check beneath it.

A few moments later, he pulled out the missing boot and stood, a sheepish expression on his face.

He scooted to the edge of the bed and slid his feet into his boots. Standing up, he stepped closer to Solana. His hands were warm and smooth against her skin as he cradled her face in his palms.

His deep blue eyes sparkled as he looked into her own, and his thumbs moved in gentle circles along her cheeks.

Solana felt her breath hitch as his eyes slowly traveled over her face, lingering on her lips. A wave of heat rushed through her body. His brilliant azure eyes caught hers, and a small, playful smile appeared on his face.

"Why are you looking at me like that?" she asked, her voice barely more than a whisper.

He stepped closer to her, close enough that she could feel the warmth radiating off his body. "I'm still finding it hard to believe that all of this is real," he said after a beat, "That I'm not dreaming. That you're here with me."

Solana closed her eyes, savoring the smell of his skin – a comforting blend of smoky campfires and worn leather. His scent evoked a sense of home as if it was always meant to be hers. She lifted her hand to place it over his, feeling the warmth of his touch.

She felt her heart swell with emotion as she looked upon him. His presence was powerful, and his eyes sparkled with a kind of devotion she hadn't encountered in any other man. He had been her rock through the toughest of times, and she was comforted by the thought that he would never desert her.

Solana shook her head in disbelief, her eyes staring off at the dwindling fire in the mantle. She shuddered as she remembered the latest horrific events: their people being kidnapped from their base camp in Norcera, Kiki and Yari vanishing without a trace, and the curse that seemed to have befallen all the males of the Ozero line, including Bernat.

She focused her attention back on Bernat. Her friend. Her savior. She allowed herself to believe that something good might come out of this. He was the only bright spot in this living hell.

"I can't really believe it either," Solana admitted. "But there's no way anything that's happened to us is just a dream. We're living in an absolute nightmare." She reached for his arm, and her voice softened. "The only thing that makes any of it bearable is you."

Bernat held her face in his hands, fiercely searching her gaze before lowering his mouth to meet hers. His lips were tender on hers, and a timid flutter of anticipation raced through her chest. He coaxed her mouth open and tenderly explored her with his tongue. His hands cradled her face as the kiss intensified, and his tongue moved with more urgency.

Solana felt the heat rise within her, an overwhelming urge to give in to the moment, but the mystery of the strange noise looming in her mind held her back.

Grudgingly, she pulled away, her head spinning and her body aching for more. She looked into Bernat's eyes, wishing desperately for just one more moment of bliss before reality set in. "I'm sorry," she said softly, "but we still have to figure out who is sneaking around the house."

Bernat heaved a deep sigh and reluctantly stepped back, his eyes lingering on her face. "You're right. I just wanted to take a moment and pretend that we didn't have to go back out into the real world."

She looked down at the floor and echoed his sentiment before meeting his eyes. "Me too. But for now, we have a bigger problem to deal with."

Bernat finished lacing up his boots and stood, gesturing to the door. "Ladies first."

Solana tiptoed past him, opened the door, and stepped into the dimly lit hallway. The air was thick with anticipation and the smell of wax. In the darkness, she could make out several doors, illuminated by the faint glow of fluttering candlelight, their waxen spikes almost completely melted away.

The sound of a door creaking shut reverberated up the stairs. Solana's head snapped up. Adrenaline surged through her veins. She scrambled down the stairs, her fingers grasping the railings. The pale yellow moonlight spilling in from the window illuminated the hallway. It was empty, but in the corner of her eye, Solana saw a figure dart out of sight. Taking a deep breath, she quickened her pace and followed.

Reaching the bottom floor, Solana's eyes darted around, searching the shadows for any sign of movement. She held her breath, straining her ears for any sound beyond her own pounding heart.

Bernat watched her intently and whispered, "I don't see or hear anything, Sol. What next?"

Solana's nostrils flared as she pointed to the southern end of the manor. "We should split up and look around. Stop them for further questioning if you spot someone who looks out of place."

Bernat followed her gaze turned back to Solana, and shook his head softly. "With so many people living here, it could be easy for someone to slip past us and just be getting food from the kitchen."

Solana's eyes narrowed as she planted her feet, her hands firmly on her hips. "Or it could be somebody doing something they shouldn't be. This may be your family's ancestral home, but that doesn't mean you don't have enemies here. We still don't know why demons are abducting our people, where Kiki disappeared to, or what happened to your brother. There's something going on here, and I don't like it. I don't trust these people."

Bernat held his hands up, palms outward, in a sign of surrender. "Alright, I get it. I'll go investigate the kitchen and dining room. What about you?"

"I'm headed for the inner courtyard and the gardens behind the manor house. Let's meet back here in half an hour."

Bernat nodded and headed toward the kitchen. Solana watched him go, then quickly pivoted on her heel and moved stealthily through the house.

When she arrived at the door leading to the courtyard, something caught her eye: a thick, dark substance smeared across the handle. She reached out to touch it and felt a familiar stickiness. She gingerly brought her fingertips to her nose and inhaled deeply, her senses instantly assailed by the unmistakable aroma of fresh blood.

That couldn't be good. Whichever way she looked at it, either someone was a victim or the perpetrator. Either way, blood had been drawn.

Her heart raced as she pushed the door open and stepped out into the cold night air. A chill wind brushed against her face, stirring up the fluffy layer of snow that coated everything in sight. She saw a set of footprints leading from the house, through the garden, to the well-house in the farthest corner of the grounds.

Solana ground her teeth in frustration, taking care to step into the footprints so she would not leave a trail of her own. Her feet dwarfed the small tracks, confirming that the suspect had to either be a child, unlikely, or someone unusually short.

She followed the tracks to the well-house and skirted along the outer wall, keeping her eyes trained for any movement. When she reached a window covered in creepers and ivy, she pressed closer to see what lay within.

Solana held her breath as her ears caught the sound of a soft whisper in the darkness. Peering through the leaves, she spotted a figure wearing an emerald cloak and a hood that concealed their face. The figure was standing by the window sill, their hands fidgeting with something that resembled a small wooden box. Solana leaned closer, trying to make out the words they were murmuring.

The person's voice was firm as they said, "Now you tell him that I need more time. Tell him the situation has become more complicated, okay?"

A squawk answered the request, and glossy black feathers shimmered in the moonlight.

A raven? Solana's brows drew together as the speaker continued to talk to the bird. The raven cocked its head and began to reply in strange beak clicks as if engaged in a two-way conversation.

"Don't be rude. I'm doing the best I can," the intruder hissed.

She dared to take a step closer, pressing onto her tiptoes to crane her neck further. A mop of silky black hair was just visible from where she stood, and if she could get another inch or so, she'd get a glance at the person's profile.

But just as Solana was about to get a good look, snow from the window sill fell to the ground, startling Solana and sending her back into a crouch.

The sound caught the speaker's attention, and they jerked their head in Solana's direction. "Someone's here. You have to leave." The speaker glanced around nervously and lowered their voice, "And next time, don't keep lurking around. You draw too much attention."

With a croaking cry, the raven spread its wings and took off into the inky night sky. A gust of wind ruffled its feathers as it soared into the darkness.

Solana spotted the intruder dashing through the back entrance of the well-house and gave chase. She bellowed a warning for them to stop, but it only spurred them on, their cloak billowing out behind them like a green sail.

Solana pumped her arms and legs as fast as possible, but the cloaked figure stayed ahead. She careened around a corner, barely maintaining her balance, and slammed into a brick wall over twenty feet tall. Her breath came in gasps, and her mind raced; the cloaked figure had been ahead of her. There was no way they could have vanished.

She stepped forward and ran her calloused fingers over the cold, rough texture of the brick wall, her gaze scanning for any hint of a crack or break in the mortar. She thought she felt a slight give in the bricks for a moment, but nothing came of it. She huffed in frustration and placed her hands on her hips, pondering the mysterious disappearance of the cloaked figure.

Solana's gaze was trained on the wall, but the sound of crunching snow caught her attention. Tlazon in hand, she spun around, ready to fight off whatever danger lurked in the shadows. But, as the light of a sputtering torch fell on Bernat's face, she released a sigh of relief and lowered her weapon.

Bernat's hands shot up in surprise as he stepped into the clearing. "Whoa, it's just me," he said, taking in Solana's grumpy expression. "Did you find anything?"

"Yes," Solana replied curtly. "But they disappeared."

Bernat's eyebrows rose, and a half-smile spread across his face as he said jokingly, "Someone got the better of you? That's rare." His smile quickly faded as Solana pinned him with an annoyed gaze. He cleared his throat and looked up at the sky as if it was suddenly very interesting.

"What about you?" Solana asked, her eyes still searching the wall. The person she'd seen had vanished as soon as they had rounded the corner. It was impossible, but how else could they have disappeared so quickly?

She knew that anything was possible — she had seen more than enough of it in recent days. Demons, curses that turned men into bears, magical totems to protect them during daylight hours, and a special pair of silver eyes that could see what most people couldn't. If all of those things were true, then why not the possibility that the person used magical means to disappear?

"Nothing," Bernat confirmed with a frown. He then brightened, a mischievous glint in his eye as he said, "Though, I did find some sangria in the kitchen." He pulled out a dark bottle from the folds of his fur-lined cloak and flashed a smile at her.

Solana shook her head in refusal. She didn't like her head feeling fuzzy. It was enough that her heart beat rapidly against her ribs whenever Bernat was near. That was all the distraction she was willing to permit herself.

Bernat let out a deep sigh and said, "Suit yourself." He lifted the lip of the cold bottle to his mouth. His eyes closed as he savored the contents of the bottle, and his lips curved into a mischievous grin after he had taken a long swig. "I'm never going to tire of the drinks here. It's sweet. Like actually sweet," he said as he looked at Solana and pulled her closer to him. "Want to taste for yourself?"

Solana's eyes burned with intensity. "No. I want answers. Where is your cousin, the one who brought us here? His name was Marco or something like that."

Bernat ran a hand through his hair. "His name is Mauricio — or Mauri. It's late, Sol; he's probably asleep." He reached out and gently curled his fingers around hers. "Come on, let's get some rest ourselves."

Solana's gaze dropped to her and Bernat's fingers, still interlocked like keyholes. Her mind raced with the possibilities of how someone was sneaking around the estate. "Do you think the estate keeps ravens? To send messages?"

Bernat frowned, his dark eyes scanning the trees for a sign of the birds. "I can't be sure. I haven't seen any flying about. But we haven't been here long."

Solana chewed her bottom lip in thought, and Bernat immediately reached out and grabbed her chin. "You're going to be the death of me if you keep doing that."

Solana's breath hitched in her throat, and a shiver of pleasure ran up her spine. Bernat's pupils were blown wide as if he could swallow her whole with his eyes alone. The look in his eyes was enough to make heat pool in her pussy at the promise that lurked within his gaze.

Bernat groaned as he traced a finger down her cheek and rubbed her bottom lip with his thumb. His chest rose and fell in ragged breaths. "Do you have any idea what you do to me?" he asked, his voice a pained whisper. "The things I want to do with these lips," he added as he bent his head closer, his breath kissing her skin.

Solana's breath caught in her throat as fire raced up her spine and heated her cheeks. "You're trying to distract me from the problem," she said, her mind heady and swirling with the memory of their lovemaking just hours before.

Bernat's lips curled as he grinned. "Is it working?" he asked, his voice husky.

"Yes," Solana admitted, letting him pull her closer, wrapping his arms around her and pressing against his solid body. "But a part of me still wants to get to the bottom of this. If there is a traitor in our midst, we have to root them out. Your cousin may know something, and if he doesn't, then he needs to know right away."

Bernat's eyes softened, and he angled his lips to hers. He stopped a hair's breadth away and said, "Sol, you're my number one priority. Nothing and no one else matters to me but you. I promise we will get to the bottom of this. If so much as a hair is harmed on your head, the person responsible will die a very slow and painful death."

"I don't need you to babysit me," she snapped, placing her hands on his chest to shove him away.

But his arms around her tightened, not letting her escape. "All I've ever done is look out for you. I'm not changing now."

His words melted the ice forming around her heart, and she asked in a choked whisper, "Why me? You're so kind and compassionate. Everyone loves you as soon as they meet you. I'm none of those things. I'm — "

He slid his fingers along her cheek as he said, "You are those things. You don't like anyone seeing those qualities unless you trust them. You carry the weight of responsibility on your shoulders. Always have. But you don't have to do it alone. Even if I'm the only person you let see the real you, I want you always to be honest with me."

Solana let herself enjoy his touch for a moment before her anxiety spiraled out of control. "In the spirit of being honest, I'm worried. If we can talk to Mauri — "

"We will," Bernat urged, pressing his forehead to hers. "In the morning. Let him sleep. Did you see him at the party? He looked like he'd eaten a rotten egg."

Solana scoffed. "He looked like he wanted to swallow Luna whole."

Bernat gave her a meaningful look. "He wasn't the only one."

Solana nodded. "Aurelia. That conniving little snake. Luna will never forgive her."

"No. Probably not." He laced his fingers in hers. "Come. We'll tackle all of this in the morning. After we've gotten rest."

Solana closed her eyes, admitting defeat. "I'm not tired anymore. I'm too amped up now."

Bernat's smile widened, and the sight made Solana gape in awe. He was a devastatingly handsome man. His black hair, azure eyes, and tanned skin made a heartstopping combination. But it was his smile that melted her heart. When he smiled, it was as if she were the only person in the world. The adoration and joy she saw in his eyes when he looked at her made her heart leap.

Bernat pressed his lips to her jawline and continued down the side of her neck as he whispered, "If you're not tired, I can think of over a dozen things we can do in that bed upstairs, and none of it involves sleep."

His words stirred heat in her pussy, and she pressed her thighs together to staunch the burning need building there. "Lead the way, Captain," she whispered back.

Bernat's eyes widened, and he crashed his mouth to hers. His lips were punishing, and his tongue pressed against the seam of her lips, demanding entrance. She opened her mouth to him, and his tongue assaulted hers with a frenzied pace. His large hands gripped her thighs and he hoisted her up, wrapping her legs around his waist.

Solana broke away from the kiss breathlessly. "What about the room?"

Bernat growled low in his throat and curled his hand around the back of her neck. "No one's awake to notice us," he said, pulling her face to his.

"It's freezing," she protested weakly, letting him draw her mouth to his.

"I'll warm you up," he whispered against her lips.

If there was one thing about Bernat. He kept his promises.

CHAPTER THREE

BIRDS, BEES AND EYRIE SECRETS

KIKI

K iki's boots sank into the pristine white snow, a dazzling landscape with no end. With each step, she gathered her strength to bravely march forward, her breath a cloud of fog in the cold winter air. Her eyes determinedly scanned the horizon as if looking for something more than the path ahead.

"How many days until we reach the eyrie?" she called ahead, the thick layers of snow muffling her words.

Erasmo spun around, seeming to have no trouble hearing her. His long dark hair billowed in the breeze. He cupped his hands around his mouth and shouted, "A few days on foot. We'll pick up my horse in a nearby village and then make good time from there."

A shiver of pleasure rippled down her spine as she took in the sight of him: tall, broad-shouldered, captivating blue eyes and delicious caramel brown skin.

A few days. She could make it through a few days. No matter that every fiber in her being wanted to scurry up him and ride him as if her life depended on it —

She could resist. She had to. Anything less than finding Yari was a failure.

That's what she told herself as she continued trudging through the snow. Yet no matter how much she tried not to think about it — of his arousal this morning and her body responding in kind — the memory of it clung to her, tempting her.

"What were you doing out here?" she asked, her dark gaze full of suspicion. "How did you end up getting captured?"

His eyes dipped to the white-powdered ground, and he cleared his throat before grunting out a response. "I was looking for Aurelia. I had something to ask her. But before I could find her, Tomás found me first."

Kiki's heart thudded against her ribcage, a million questions running through her head. What was so important that he'd take such a risk? Why travel alone? And why Aurelia, of all people?

Kiki's stomach twisted into a knot as thoughts of Aurelia crept into her mind. Fury and helplessness surged through her veins like molten steel.

At first, Kiki had been relieved when a group of soldiers swooped in and scattered Tomás and his men. But her victory was short-lived when Luna was taken for ransom. Kiki threw herself into the chaos, and while she had managed to free Luna, she'd gotten herself captured in the process.

Somehow, everything had a way of coming around and pointing back to Aurelia. Thanks to the smuggler's self-serving machinations, Luna had been taken as ransom in the first place. If only Aurelia had paid her debt to Tomás instead of trying to wriggle out of it, then Kiki wouldn't be in this mess.

Kiki's voice was full of venom as she spat her words, "Why did Tomás capture you? I assume you owe him a debt too?"

Erasmo's expression shifted to a dark scowl, his gaze narrowing. "I pay my debt. Aurelia's too. I don't like loose ends."

Kiki scoffed, unable to contain her disbelief. "So, you mean to tell me that when that thug was trying to terrorize my friend, he had already been taken care of?" Her voice was a mixture of disbelief and outrage.

Erasmo's features darkened, his jaw set in a firm line, and his knuckles turned white as he curled his hands into fists. His usually soft blue eyes now glimmered with a vengeful light, and his voice was laced with determination.

"I swear on my life, Tomás will pay for what he did to you and your friends," he said, sending a wave of surprise through her at the conviction in his eyes.

But she was still baffled. "What did Tomás want with you if he'd already been paid?"

Erasmo's shifted, his blue eyes narrowing as the danger in his voice dropped to a dangerous whisper. "I'm still trying to figure that one out."

She could no longer ignore the feeling that he was holding something back from her.

"You're hiding something," she accused, her words dripping with venom.

He took a deep breath and looked up towards the heavens, his face contorting in anguish. His fists curled into tight balls, and his jaw clenched, each word hissing through his gritted teeth.

"I need to know everything before I draw a conclusion. I don't jump to assumptions."

Kiki swiveled her head to meet his gaze, her lips curving into a sly grin. "Why not?" she taunted. "I make a habit of it."

He slowly shook his head, his gaze narrowing as he studied her with a curious intensity. "Let me guess — that's how you ended up inside the dreaded Cicatrix?"

Kiki shrugged indifferently, her dark eyes twinkling mischievously. "Perhaps."

He furrowed his brows, inspecting her from head to toe. "Speaking of — why are *you* here? I didn't get around to asking last night."

She snorted, her eyes sparking with fury. Not because he'd asked her a simple question. No. Because his question was a reminder of her failure to find Yarixa. "My best friend was taken by a demon. It dragged her into the Cicatrix, and I had to save her. So here I am."

"How did you end up with Aurelia?" Erasmo asked, his voice laced with caution.

Kiki's stomach tightened at the mention of Aurelia — again. Her cheeks grew hot with shame and guilt as she recalled the night she'd met Aurelia — the night she'd been caught trying to leave the Demon Corps after Yari's abduction.

She cleared her throat and tried to sound nonchalant. "That's sort of a longer story."

Erasmo sighed heavily; disappointment scrawled all over his perfectly sculpted features. "It always is when it comes to her."

He wasn't wrong.

They continued in silence when Kiki arched an eyebrow and crossed her arms. "You still haven't answered my question."

"Which one?"

She stared at him, wondering how long he would milk this dumb and cute act. When he didn't offer up the information, she sighed heavily and asked again. "Why were you out here alone? Without any backup?"

The silence that followed was louder than any response could have been. The way he gulped said it all. After a moment, he finally uttered, "I told you, I was looking for my cousin."

Kiki's jaw tightened as she glared at Erasmo's back. "And yet you still haven't shared why you were looking for her in the first place."

"You're right. I didn't," he replied, a glimmer of amusement in his voice.

Kiki pressed her lips together into a tight line, her brows furrowing. "Well? Are you going to tell me or not?"

Erasmo let out a low chuckle — the sound echoing with a mocking edge. "If I wanted to tell you, then I would have."

"You're infuriating," she spat, her fingers coming to grip her cloak tightly as she imagined it was his neck she was wringing instead of the fur trim.

The corner of Erasmo's lips quirked up in a cocky smirk. "I do try," he drawled. "It's one of my better traits."

"That wasn't a compliment, you idiot."

"I take my wins where I can," he smirked. "Come on, we better pick up the pace before more questions pop up in that head of yours," he said, shooting her an amused look like he knew that wasn't going to happen.

Erasmo's strides grew longer and longer as if he were purposely trying to leave Kiki behind.

Each time Kiki fell too far behind, she was forced to jog to catch up. After the fourth time falling behind, she decided she was done playing his game.

"Can you slow down, please?" she snapped. "I don't have horse legs like some people."

The prince whipped around with a devilish smile.

He'd done it on purpose! She knew it!

A deep chuckle rumbled from his chest. "I was wondering how long it would take you to ask me to slow down," he quipped. "You lasted longer than I thought."

Kiki's voice was like a blade as she sneered, "You're such an ass." She continued, her bitterness clear. "You're nothing like your brother; he never leaves me behind. He always looks over his shoulder, making sure I'm okay."

Erasmo's body tensed, his playful expression melting away like snow off a roof. His gaze was guarded when he asked, "Which brother are you talking about? Arturo or Bernat?"

"His name is Turi," she spat back, her mocking tone ringing in the air.

He rolled his eyes, waving his hand in the air with irritation. "Fine. Turi. How long have you known him?"

Kiki sighed a heavy breath, her hands moving to clutch the twin bandoliers strapped across her chest. "Pretty much my whole life," she spoke quietly, her gaze drifting to the track marks in the snow. "I joined the Demon Corps when I aged out of the orphanage. I've known Turi ever since."

He broke the silence with a gentle but pressing inquiry like a feather brushing her skin. "How old were you when you joined?"

The question was soft and gentle, yet Kiki's answer was hard and unyielding.

"Nine," she answered, her voice cold and hollow.

For Kiki, the Demon Corps had been her home since she had aged out of the orphanage, and in those twelve years, it had become her entire life.

Turi had been a part of it since the very beginning, an unwavering companion and friend.

Erasmo's jaw tightened as if he were biting back words. "That's very young to start training to become a warrior."

Kiki let out a cynical snort. "You think I had a lot of options? It's either the Corps or working in the brothels. And, yes, that applies to males too. The Cicatrix didn't only carve the kingdom in two, it quite literally gouged out its heart as well, leaving it nothing more than a cold and empty shell of itself."

Kiki's eyes flickered over Erasmo's face, noting how his skin was dusted with a crimson flush. It was almost as if he cared. But that was stupid. Why would he? These weren't his problems.

"What do you and my brother do in the Demon Corps?"

She hardened her tone, determined to give the abridged version. If she kept talking about the Corps, the guilt that she'd abandoned, it would rise back up, and she couldn't afford to be weak.

"Technically, I'm a Slayer, but I didn't really get to enjoy the title much because Yari was kidnapped the night of my graduation. Turi is a supply officer, but his talents are wasted there. He should be in the Engineering Corps, but he says he likes where he's at. Bernat is a Captain and is Solana's second in command."

"Solana?"

Kiki gritted her teeth together as she thought of Solana Ramirez. The Commander who'd made her life a living hell with strict rules and even stricter punishments. "Yeah, she's the other person in my group. She was my Commander, and she came after me," Kiki bit out.

Erasmo scratched at the black stubble along his chin as he thoughtfully, "Wow, she must care about you a lot."

She scoffed. "Please. She chased after me so she could drag me back to the Corps for a court martial. That, and apparently, there were more disappearances after Yari, so she wanted to investigate."

The words had barely left her lips before Erasmo stopped walking, shock written all over his face. "More disappearances? What do you mean?"

She tapped her foot impatiently in the snow, already tiring of his questions and not wanting to revisit all of the awful things that had happened of late.

"It's what it sounds like," she quipped. "Yari wasn't the only one kidnapped. She was just the first. More of our people were taken the following night."

Erasmo inhaled deeply, his eyes far away. "This is news to me. I haven't received news of increased activity around the border."

Kiki's jaw dropped in disbelief. "Really? Nothing strange has happened in the Cicatrix recently?"

Erasmo laughed humorlessly. "Strange? Yes. All the time. Out of the ordinary? No. No mass disappearances."

Kiki threw her hands up desperately and released an exasperated sigh. "Awesome. I love knowing that I came all the way out here to find you for nothing," she spat. "That's the whole reason I let Aurelia convince me to come to find you first. She said you could help. Which, apparently, was a waste of my time."

Erasmo growled, his eyes flashing fiercely. "I said I had no knowledge of it, not that I couldn't help."

"Fine. Don't get so defensive." She climbed over a fallen tree limb, her movements powerful and effortless. At least there was one good thing about all the walking she'd been doing. She wasn't losing any of her strength. "So, how far until we get to your horse?"

"We should get there before nightfall."

A heavy sigh escaped her lips as she spoke, "Good, I could use a bath." The tension was already leaving her shoulders at the promise of washing the grime, blood, and demon ichor off her skin.

"I'm sorry, what?" he sputtered.

"I don't know about you, but where I'm from, people bathe when they're dirty," she spat back with a smirk.

"Thanks, smartass. I meant, when are you going to find time to bathe?"

Kiki quirked her head at him, her eyes narrowing. "At the village. I assume there must be an inn there or something. When we stop for the night, I'll take a bath."

Erasmo let out a throaty laugh and looked down at Kiki, his azure eyes burning with something she couldn't name. "We're not stopping for the night. You'll just have to wait until you get to La Aguilera."

Kiki scoffed. "We can't ride through the night. What about the demons?"

He stopped and stepped closer, his eyes like two burning sapphires. "I'm the worst monster in these woods," he murmured, his hot breath fanning her face.

She sucked in a sharp breath, her heart hammering against her ribcage. She told herself that her reaction was because of what Erasmo had just said because it couldn't be for any other reason.

She swallowed the lump in her throat. "Right...how could I forget?"

CHAPTER FOUR

MONSTROUS CONFESSIONS AND ROMANTIC TENSIONS

ERASMO

E rasmo couldn't get Kiki's words out of his head. She had known his little brother, Arturo — or Turi as she called him — since she was nine. He should have been more concerned about the disappearances she mentioned, but he couldn't get the image of her knowing his brother so well out of his head.

Pain ripped through his chest at the thought of her with someone else. He had to know just how well she knew Turi.

"So you said you know my little brother well?" he asked, struggling to keep his voice even.

All he wanted her to say was that she didn't know Turi well. That they'd been acquaintances, nothing more.

"I mean, sure, as well as you can know anyone you date, I guess," she said with a shrug.

Jealousy coursed through his veins like wildfire. They had dated? His fingers curled into his palms and dug in until he felt the warmth of his blood seeping through.

"I see. So you're still together, then," Erasmo spat out the words, his fists clenching involuntarily at his sides. The words tasted like ash on his tongue, but he had to know.

Kiki shook her head. "No. Not anymore."

Her silence grated at him like rocks scratching across glass. That wasn't a good enough answer. He needed more.

"What happened?" he prodded, trying not to seem too eager but needing to know all the same.

It killed him that she'd dated someone else. Let alone his own brother. She was his mate. Not that she knew that. Nor had he figured out a way to tell her.

How did anyone tell another person they had just met that the two of them were destined to be together? There weren't exactly grimoires full of this kind of information.

Of course, he couldn't blame her for living a life before him. Without him. But the beast within wasn't happy and thrashed against Erasmo's ribs. The beast possessed no logic and for a moment neither did Erasmo. Still, he didn't begrudge her for finding solace in another person.

Kiki heaved a sigh. "Well, it's sort of my fault," she muttered. "Turi is a great guy. But I couldn't afford that kind of distraction. I have Luna and Yari to look out for. I can't even think about taking care of someone else. Before crossing into the Cicatrix, all I knew was slaying demons, watching out for demons, and starving in the cold. Now, I've lost Yari. I can't afford to think about something as trivial as being in a relationship."

It felt like he'd been punched in the gut. He didn't know anything about the life she'd led before crossing. All he had felt over the years were various feelings through the mate bond. He'd hoped she was well and cared for. Hearing that the opposite had been true stoked the fire in his veins. He wanted to punch something.

"I also couldn't afford to get pregnant," Kiki added grimly. "The Corps has a hard enough time providing enough food for everyone. Let alone providing enough medical supplies. Contraceptives were the last thing on the Corps' supply list. A pregnancy can end a Slayer's career faster than any demon can."

And just like that, his earlier rage rose to the surface and boiled over. His mate and his brother. Together. Intimately.

The thought made him sick to his stomach, and the urge to punch something grew into the need to spill blood. Anyone who touched his mate deserved to die. Slowly. By his bare hands.

Kiki cleared her throat, startling him back to reality. She gave him a wary look. "Are you okay? You look like you've seen a ghost."

He could picture Kiki and Turi together, and the images playing in his mind made his jaw clench so tight that it ached.

Without thinking, he slammed his fist into the nearest tree. "Damn it!" he bellowed, the rage he had felt since sensing Kiki through the bond and learning she was in danger finally boiling over.

His hand throbbed from the rough bark embedded into his skin, but he hit the tree again and again, roaring out his fury with each strike. Sweat trickled down his brow as the anger slowly dissipated.

"What's wrong with you?" Kiki demanded as she yanked him away from the tree, her face scrunched up in confusion.

Erasmo wanted to confess to her — that she and he were mates. The thought of her with another man made him want to kill, rip out throats with his fangs, and slash flesh with his claws. But he couldn't bring himself to say it, fearing that speaking would only drive her away.

"Erasmo?" Kiki asked quietly, her hand still gripping his arm.

He shut his eyes, inhaling a deep breath as he willed the beast within to settle. He kept his gaze firmly ahead, his line of sight vanishing into some far-off place. "I just can't stand that you had to live like that. The darkness did more than divide the kingdom. It ruined lives."

Kiki spun him around, her lips forming a tight line and her free hand settling on her hip in a defiant gesture. "We still have hope, though, right? The darkness was created by a spell — a curse your mother made. So there must be a way to put an end to it."

Yes. There was a way, in theory. The spirit woman had given his brother a prophecy years ago, providing the means to end the curse. But the method was unthinkable.

Even then, Erasmo could sense his mate. He had felt her every emotion. Her every joy and triumph echoed in his soul, and he celebrated with her from afar, not knowing why she felt such things but content that she at least seemed happy.

The solution given in the prophecy was too great a price to pay — the life of his mate in exchange for his freedom from the curse.

Kiki didn't wait for him to respond. "Look," she began. "I'll make a deal with you. If you help me find Yari, I'll do whatever I can to help you break this curse."

His eyes winced shut at her offer. That's what he was afraid of. "I'm willing to help you find your friend, regardless," he said gruffly. "You don't need to trade with me."

Kiki snorted, flicking her wrist dismissively. "I take nothing in this life if it's offered for free. Besides, Turi is affected by it too. I owe it to him to at least try."

As they continued walking through the snow-covered landscape, Kiki filled Erasmo in on her life in the Demon Corps.

Her words painted a picture of poverty, with training from dawn to dusk, minuscule meals, and frigid winter nights. He struggled to keep his temper under control. He'd assumed she was doing alright but had felt no strong negative emotions through their bond. Despite her harsh circumstances, she persevered — inspiring him with her strength. His perfect partner.

Suddenly, the conversation shifted to her old Commander, and she had been ranting ever since.

" — and that's why I can't stand Solana Ramirez," Kiki grumbled. "I don't understand what Bernat sees in her."

"Actually," Erasmo countered, "from my outsider's perspective, it sounds like the two of you are more alike than you care to admit."

Kiki glared at him menacingly. "You had to go there, didn't you? Just when I started to like you, you had to go and say something like that?" She crossed her arms over her chest. "I take back all the nice things I said about you."

Erasmo chuckled. "What nice things?"

Kiki gave a small shrug. "I'm sure there was something."

Erasmo held back a laugh, keeping his lips firmly closed. If it was possible, she was even more attractive when she was mad.

They crested the top of the hill, and in the valley below sat the village Erasmo had left his horse, Ocaso, to rest. The sun was slowly descending in the sky, casting the world in hues of orange and pink.

"See, I told you we'd make it before sunset," Erasmo said with a triumphant grin.

Kiki rubbed her arms with her hands and shivered. "Good, because I could use a hot meal and a warm fire. I think my toes fell off."

They trudged down the hill and came up on the village. Not a single soul stirred outside of their houses. No one bustled from shop to shop. It was as if the town had been frozen in time.

This was not the way Erasmo had left this place. His eyes scanned the empty snow-filled street. An eerie silence hung in the air, and Erasmo's skin prickled with goosebumps.

Kiki swiveled her head back and forth as she peeked into empty shop windows. "Where did everyone go?"

Erasmo's brows knitted together, and he prepared himself for the shift if he should need it.

A loud crash came from the outer edge of the village, and Kiki drew her machete from her belt faster than he could blink.

She became all business the second her weapon was free, and he felt his mouth drop open at such a sight.

Seeing his mate with a weapon in hand did something to him that took his breath away. Feeling his pants get tighter, he adjusted himself so she wouldn't see what the mere sight of her had done to him.

"I'm going to go check it out," she whispered as she inched forward on light feet.

The air in his lungs seized at the thought of her in danger, and without thinking, he pulled her back by her arm. "No, you stay back. I'll go look."

Her eyes flashed as she looked down at his hand, and he instantly regretted his decision to hold her back. If looks could kill, he'd be a dead man. "Or, not. I'll watch your back."

She gave him a brisk nod before shaking her arm out of his grasp and taking the lead.

The smell of fresh hay reached his nostrils as they approached the source of the sound. They rounded the corner and were met with a loud neigh.

"Ocaso!" he shouted as he rushed forward to embrace his horse. "What happened, boy? Where did everyone go?"

Kiki re-sheathed her machete and propped herself against a wooden beam. "You know he can't talk, right? Or does the curse affect your mind too?"

Erasmo cast a mocking glance back at her. "Clearly, you've never ridden a horse. They're very sensitive creatures," he purred, stroking his horse's muzzle. "Don't listen to her, Ocaso. It's not you. She's always like that."

"Excuse me. Like what?" Kiki huffed.

A grin tugged at the corners of his mouth as he glanced over his shoulder again.

Kiki stood with both hands planted firmly on her hips and a scowl on her ridiculously beautiful face. Damn. This woman would surely be the death of him. Those ebony eyes burned with an inner fire. Those full lips. Her perfect curves were showcased in that supple leather, radiating an almost unnatural beauty.

Kiki threw her hands in the air and whirled around on her heel. "You know what? I don't care what you think about me."

Oh, but he thought the world of her, and his expression softened.

Kiki continued on her rant. "The sooner we get to the eyrie, the sooner I can be rid of you and the sooner I can find Yari."

"I thought you were hungry," Erasmo replied, cocking an eyebrow.

"I am. But in case you haven't noticed, there's nobody here," she said bluntly.

"I can cook for you and get a fire going while you wait. I'm sure the kitchen is stocked at that inn over there," he offered.

Kiki chewed her cheek as she pondered. "What about a bath?"

He chuckled. "I'm sure I can figure something out," he assured her.

She narrowed her eyes skeptically. "I thought you said we wouldn't stop for the night."

He shrugged casually. "I changed my mind."

"I don't know how I feel about staying here. We still don't know what happened to all the people," she pointed out, the apprehension clear in her voice.

He ran a hand through his hair in thought. "Didn't you say some of your people were taken by demons from your base camp?"

Kiki circled around, her eyes darting around the village in assessment. "Yes, but there are no signs of a struggle here. No drag prints through the snow. No blood. It's like they just vanished."

He shook his head, a look of bemusement crossing his face. He couldn't help but admire her tenacity. "That's the best theory I've got."

"If we go with that theory, what if the demons come back?" Kiki asked hesitantly. "I'm short on weapons," she added, motioning to the empty bandoliers strapped across her chest.

Erasmo couldn't help but smirk. She'd forgotten who she was with.

"What are you smiling about?" Kiki hissed. "This is a serious problem," she scolded.

Erasmo's smirk stretched wider as he replied, "I already told you — I'm the worst monster in these woods."

Kiki's mouth parted slightly, and she swallowed hard. "I don't know if you're trying to comfort me or scare me," she mumbled.

Erasmo crossed the distance between them in three long strides until he was just inches apart from her.

She dropped her head back to look up at him, and his mouth watered at the sight of her lips so near. He lifted his hand and gently grabbed her chin between his thumb and forefinger.

"Maybe it's a little of both," he said, his voice rough and full of longing.

Her breathing hitched, and for a moment, he thought he saw desire flare in her eyes. Did she feel the bond between them? That string that pulled them together?

She swatted his hand away as if regaining her senses and stepped back out of reach. "Stop messing around. I thought you said you were going to make food."

"Your wish is my command," he said, faking a bow. He brushed past her and led the way to the inn.

Chapter Five

Nightmares, Demons, and Disbelief...Oh My!

Yari

"Where am I?" Yari asked to no avail, her voice a mere whisper in the thickly wooded forest.

A chill wind passed through the trees, carrying with it an arctic chill and the ghostly notes of frozen pine needles. Snowflakes descended from the sky, their white hues contrasting starkly with the black shadows that cloaked the trees in gloom.

A faint smell of decay lingered in the air, and Yari shivered as she tried to make sense of her unfamiliar surroundings.

Yari's skin was covered in goosebumps as the frigid air cut through the thin white nightdress she'd worn to bed. Her toes curled against the frozen ground, numbed by the cold.

Above her, a flock of black ravens perched atop the naked trees, their raucous cawing echoing through the clearing like a death knell. Yari swallowed hard, feeling a dread grow in her chest like an icy chill.

In the distance, the wood-shingled roof of a cabin shone through the moonlight.

Gritting her teeth, she made her way to the cabin and its weathered walls, the paint splitting and chipping, the timber barely holding together. She could see a thick black moss had taken over the roof, ivy snaking through the window frames like steel bars, and a few crows hopping from branch to branch.

The icy wind bit at her nose and cheeks, making them burn. She raised a heavy fist to knock on the door, gnawing at a cuticle as she waited for a response. But nothing came. The longer she stood there, the more certain she was that no one had been here in a while.

Still, she didn't want to be rude and barge in. Peering through the window, she saw that the inner room was undisturbed. A single candlestick sat on a table near the window, the wick covered in dust.

The knob of the door felt icy against her skin, sending a chill up her spine. She paused a moment, her heart pounding in her chest, and silently asked for forgiveness. Taking a deep breath, she pushed the door open just enough to peer inside, her knuckles white on the knob.

"Hello?" she whispered into the darkness but was met with nothing but silence. Taking a small step, she entered the house and immediately felt the wind push the door shut behind her. Fear and anticipation clung to her like a heavy cloak.

Now that she was inside and out of the biting winter wind, Yarixa cautiously peeled her hands away from her arms, breathing in the stale air of the room.

She cleared her throat and called out a greeting again, hoping that someone would respond. Nothing but silence welcomed her. Sighing in resignation, she moved to the seating area in front of the hearth and began gathering wood to build a fire.

"I'm going to get a fire going if that's alright," she called out again, feeling foolish for talking to nobody but doing it anyway; she reasoned it was only polite. At the very least, it eased her guilt just a fraction for having barged in uninvited.

She found flint and stone and stuck them together with a few determined taps, sparks catching on the dried wood. In a matter of moments, a tiny flame sparked to life.

Yari watched it grow and felt a wave of relief wash over her.

But then, suddenly, there was a loud crash from somewhere inside the house, and Yari's heart stopped. She jumped up, eyes darting around the room as she searched for whatever had made the sound.

"Who's there?" she called out timidly. "Is someone home? I'm sorry I came in — " she started to say when she heard another dull thud from somewhere close by.

Her heart leaped into her throat as she followed the sound to the corner of the room, where it seemed to resonate from beneath the floorboards. As she knelt down and pressed her ear against the woodgrain, the faint clatter grew increasingly louder.

Yari stumbled into the kitchen, her eyes darting around until she spotted a small cellar door tucked away in the corner. She pushed it open cautiously, a chill rushing up to greet her.

She took a few steps down and called out, her voice lost in the damp air of the cellar. Goosebumps prickled across her skin, and she shivered, realizing how frigid it must be down here. If someone were down here, they'd be freezing.

She ran back to the living room and snatched a thick woolen throw from the armchair, then descended again, holding the blanket close to her chest.

A bead of sweat trickled down her forehead as she called out into the dark, her voice echoing against the walls. She swallowed hard and tried to keep calm.

"I'm going to help you," she shouted into the void before her, wishing she had brought a candle with her to illuminate the way. Just as she was about to turn around and go back for one, something cold touched her arm, causing her to jump back in alarm.

Yari gasped as an impossibly tall figure materialized from the shadows, its body an indeterminate mass of inky blackness surrounded by an eerie blue light. She could make out two glowing blue eyes that seemed to pierce her soul and a taloned hand that stretched out towards her. As the beast grasped her throat, her scream died in her throat, her heart pounding in her chest.

Yari jolted upright, the scream of terror trailing off as the fog of sleep dissipated. Her chest heaved as she tried to catch her breath, and her forehead was slick with sweat.

It had been a nightmare, nothing more.

As she lay back down, her hands trembled against the tangle of blankets. She rolled over to find the other side of the bed empty, and she trailed her hand along the cold sheets, reaching out for comfort that wasn't there.

"Where are you?" Yari whispered into the silence of the bedroom she shared with Arlando.

Her heart began to beat faster, and warmth spread through her body as images of their lovemaking flooded her mind.

"Arlando?" she called out softly, hoping the sound of her voice would bring him running back to her side.

But there was no answer.

She pushed the heavy blankets off her body and shivered as the cool air met her skin. Padding across the cold granite floor, she searched for her nightgown, her heart racing as she pulled it on and grabbed a fur blanket from the bed. With one arm, she wrapped it tightly around her shoulders and set off in pursuit of her love.

She stepped out of the room and looked down both ends of the hall. The hallway was illuminated by tall, dripping candles that cast flickering shadows against the cold stone walls. She could feel a cool breeze wafting through the castle, stirring the flames and setting her skin alight with goosebumps.

With a sigh, she descended the grand staircase and found the dining hall cloaked in stillness and gloom.

Yari spun around, her eyes darting in every direction. A flutter of movement caught her eye, and she thought she glimpsed a familiar figure. "Arlando?" she cried out, squinting into the night.

Taking off at a sprint, her heart racing, Yari chased after the figure. She darted through the kitchen until she reached a pair of glass doors that opened into the castle's inner courtyard.

The wick of the lanterns outside sputtered in the violent gusts of wind, casting strange and distorted shapes on the statues of deer and coati that speckled the perfectly sculpted grounds.

A chill ran through her body as she opened the heavy glass doors and stepped out onto the veranda, her bare feet crunching against the newly fallen snow.

The silent courtyard was blanketed in white, with a fountain at its center encased in a sheet of pale ice. Hedges of perfect white drooped around the edges, each branch glistening with a thin film of frost.

The courtyard was breathtaking in its pale beauty, as was much of Arlando's estate. She often wondered what it would look like in spring. She imagined rows of fragrant flowerbeds lining the winding pathways and the sun setting behind the trees casting a golden glow on everything. But that wasn't the sight before her now.

She inched forward, her pulse beating wildly as a large, menacing silhouette appeared in the darkness behind her. She could hear its snuffling breath and feel its hot, fetid breath on her neck.

She spun on her heel, and a towering beast twice her height loomed before her. Its frame was cloaked in menacing darkness, and its glowing blue eyes pierced through her as she stumbled back and landed hard on the ground. She scrambled up just in time to see the creature's razor-sharp claws coming straight for her.

Panic welled up inside her chest, and her throat closed, preventing any cry for help from slipping past her lips.

The beast stepped out of the shadows, and a chill ran up her spine. Its silver fur shimmered in the moonlight, and its cold blue eyes glowed like sapphires. Its massive paws slapped heavily against the frozen ground as it advanced.

This wasn't just any bear. She recognized this beast — it was the same one that had attacked her two years ago, nearly killing her.

She reached for the bear tooth necklace she wore around her throat, a reminder that she had survived. But her hand came back empty. She always seemed to forget that she had lost it the night the demon had kidnapped her and dragged her into the Cicatrix.

The beast's hulking frame caused the ground to shake with each step, and as it approached, its jaws opened wide, releasing a gut-wrenching roar. Rows of jagged black teeth glistened in the moonlight, and its tongue flicked out, coated in thick, smoky saliva.

Her body froze in terror as she let out a shrill, bloodcurdling scream that felt like a thousand stabbing knives cutting through her throat.

The beast let out a roar of surprise, and she seized her chance, springing upright and sprinting away. Her heart thundered as she raced through the winding lines of white hedges, searching for a hiding place. But no matter how fast she ran, the bear's thunderous paws never seemed to draw any farther away.

She didn't dare look back and see the demon hot on her heels. She darted down the paths, and every now and then, she heard a roar from behind her, pushing her to run even faster.

She made one wrong turn and ended up at a dead end, forcing her to retrace her steps. All of a sudden, she burst out of the maze and back to where she had started. She raced through the glass doors and slammed them behind herself, not caring if they shattered in her wake.

Her feet pounded against the cold tile floor of the dining hall as she ran, her heart pounding in her chest. She threw open the door to Arlando's room and fearfully shouted his name, her voice echoing off the stark walls. Nothing but silence greeted her in response.

Sweat beaded on her forehead as she scanned the room desperately. Her eyes darted back and forth, trying to find something, anything, that could be used as a weapon.

She knew in her heart that she had no chance against the demon bear, not without her jade or obsidian blades, but she wasn't ready to give up. She would fight until the very end. That's what Kiki would do if she were in this situation.

She scanned the room, her gaze landing on a heavy silver candlestick. Her hands shook as she reached for it, hefting the weighty object in her grip and holding it in front of her as if it were the sharpest machete she'd ever been issued.

Heavy darkness settled over the open doorway like a curtain pulled across the night sky. She felt her muscles tense as an imposing figure moved into view, framed in the cold silver glare of moonlight. A sudden surge of determination rushed through her veins, and she darted forward, a strangled battle cry erupting from her lips.

But as the figure stepped into the moonlight, she recognized him. Her initial fear turned to surprise as she saw his face, and her plan to fight quickly evaporated. She stumbled mid-stride, her strangled battle cry dying in her throat.

"Arlando?" she asked, breathless.

Arlando stood in the doorway, his white pants offset by a luxurious fur-lined overcoat. When he caught sight of her, his eyes went wide with surprise, and his head quirked to one side.

"Yari? What's going on?"

"Did you see it? The demon? The bear?" she asked in a rush as she pulled him into the room and shut the door behind them. "Where is it now?" she asked, her heart racing so fast she felt like she was going to faint.

"You saw a demon?" he asked, his face twisting in concern. "Where?"

"The courtyard. I was looking for you. And — "

"You mean there is a demon here? On castle grounds?" he asked, grabbing her by both arms and forcing her to look up at him.

She nodded her head so fast that her teeth clattered together. "Yes. And it was chasing me."

Arlando breathed out a sigh of relief as he pulled her into a bone-crushing hug. "I'm so glad that you're safe, that you're okay."

"But the demon," she cried, wiggling out of his grasp.

He redirected her gaze to the window that overlooked the towering castle walls, proudly standing against the night sky.

"Demons can't get in," he said confidently. "The wards around the perimeter are strong enough to keep them out of the grounds, and every stone in this castle is warded too. His voice dropped to a whisper as he added, "You're safe here."

Yari's face was a mix of confusion and surprise as she pointed toward where she'd seen the demon. Her brows furrowed in disbelief, and her voice grew louder with each syllable as she asked, "But how did it get here then? I saw it right in front of me!"

Arlando's eyes took on a deadly sheen, his hands like a vice grip on her arms. "I don't know, *amor*. But I assure you, I will find the demon and exterminate it. I won't let anything happen to you," he growled.

His words were heavy with the promise of retribution, and as he pulled her close, clutching her tightly against him, a tremor of fear rippled through Yari's chest. He pressed a gentle kiss to the top of her head and she forced herself to relax in his embrace.

As Arlando's strong arms tighten around her protectively, she felt the tension in her body melting away. Closing her eyes, she inhaled the woodsy scent of his soap and clung to him for a moment before he pulled away and looked deep into her eyes.

His voice was like steel as he declared, "Go back to sleep. I'm going to find out who is responsible for the breach and make them pay for it dearly."

She opened her mouth to protest, not wanting anyone to be punished because she had gone wandering around the castle in the middle of the night. In all fairness, she should have known better. They were in the Cicatrix, after all. The home of demons. It had been foolish of her to go off without some form of protection.

But Arlando was already out the door, the sound of his hurried footsteps fading away. She slumped onto the bed, her head heavy with disappointment and shame.

Tears stung her eyes as she berated herself for being so helpless and foolish. Yet again, proving that she was a useless waste of space. Always relying on others to take care of her.

She wished Kiki was here — her dear friend had always been there to protect her. Now, she had no idea if Kiki was okay. If she was even alive.

Yari wrapped a plush fur blanket around her trembling shoulders and let the tears rimming her eyes fall freely. She wished she knew that Kiki was okay. That her best friend was alive and safe.

CHAPTER SIX

SEX TALKS AND EMOTIONAL WALKS

LUNA

T he house was quiet when Luna wandered out of her room. The hallway connecting all of the rooms to each other was cast in shadows, the meager morning light filtering in through the windows, not yet enough to chase the darkness away.

On silent feet, she padded down the winding stairwell to the bottom floor and walked into the dining hall.

The room was filled with long tables that stretched from end to end, with wooden benches on either side. It reminded her of the mess hall at the Demon Corps base camp in Norcera. Smaller square tables were pushed along the back wall, each with four wooden chairs a piece.

She backed out of the hall and moved toward the kitchens, hoping to find a bite to eat.

Her stomach grumbled as she moved through the kitchen, finding a basket overflowing with colorful fruit. She snatched a bright yellow banana and sniffed it, exhaling with a sigh as she savored the scent.

She hadn't seen a fresh fruit like this in years. She quickly peeled it and took a savoring bite.

She didn't notice someone walking into the kitchen behind her until she heard a throat clear.

She whirled around and came face to face with Mauricio — her silent shadow.

His eyes slowly traced the line of her mouth around the banana, and she quickly swallowed.

Shaking his head as he moved around the counter, he said, "You might want to wrap that up. I have a handful of cousins that are at that age where they want to pound anything that walks. If they catch you doing that, they're going to take it as an invitation."

Did he just say what she thought he said?

She felt her ears redden, and she ducked her head so that her hair fell around her face.

"Good morning to you, too," she said, wanting more than anything to hide in a corner and never be found.

Mauricio leaned his muscular frame against the opposite counter, crossing his feet at his ankles as he tossed a bright red apple in the air. "What, you don't like sex?"

She choked on a bite of banana and caught a smirk forming along the corner of his lips. "No — it's not that — I mean, you shouldn't be asking me that — it's just — "

She stumbled through her words, feeling her chest tightening all the while. Here was this devastatingly handsome man asking her about sex, and she couldn't get her tongue untied.

Mauricio chuckled, "I'm just messing with you. However, I'm serious about my cousins. Look their way too many times, and you'll have a pack of them waiting at your door come nighttime. Unless you're into that sharing thing."

Needing to do anything else, she put the banana down and angled her body away from him, so he couldn't see the flush running across her cheeks. "Are you this crass with all of your guests?"

She felt him draw near, the heat from his body radiating off him in waves. When he was right behind her, he leaned down and brushed her ear with his breath.

"Do I talk about sex with every beautiful woman I meet?" he said, his voice low and dangerous, the feel of his breath along the nape of her neck making her head feel light. He curled a finger around an errant black curl, and his lips were so close to her skin that a shiver ran down her spine. "The answer is no. Just you, *chiqui*."

She felt the breath whoosh out of her, and she whirled around to confront him when a man came striding into the kitchen.

"Good mor — Seriously, Mauri? In the kitchen! I eat here," the newcomer whined as he circled around Luna and Mauri, giving them as wide a berth as possible.

The new man was broad with dirty blonde hair and hazel eyes. He had four scars in the shape of claw marks along the right side of his forehead that traveled down his brow, stopping just above his eye.

Mauricio caged her in with his arms, his hands on either side of the counter behind her. He exhaled a long, suffering sigh and reluctantly withdrew. "Yasir," he growled. "Your timing is impeccable. As always."

The man, Yasir, opened a cabinet and pulled out a carafe and a glass jar of whole black coffee beans.

"Hey," Yasir said, turning to face Luna. "You're one of the girls that came in with Bernat last night. Soledad, right?"

She shook her head. "No, I'm Luna. The other girl with me is Solana."

Yasir snapped his fingers together as he said, "Luna! That's right." He filled the carafe with water and set it on the stove to boil. "That's a pretty name for a pretty — "

Mauricio cut him off with a growl. Yasir cut his gaze to Mauricio, a shit-eating grin on his face. "Nevermind," Yasir murmured as he busied himself with grinding the beans with a mortar and pestle before adding them to the carafe on the stove.

The tension in the air was palpable, and Luna was about to walk away when Yasir spoke. "So, are they heading out to look for Raz today?"

Raz? Her gaze darted between Mauricio and Yasir.

Mauricio ran a hand through his black hair and nodded. "Yeah, Erasmo has been gone for too long. We'll call a meeting after breakfast and split up into groups."

Luna tucked that piece of information away should she need it again.

The carafe whistled, and Yasir plucked it from the stove and poured it over a sieve, hot black liquid pouring into a glass jar.

"Great," Yasir announced. "I'll pair up with the pretty one here while you take the lead," he said, his eyes dancing with mischief.

Mauricio stepped forward, his lips drawn back in a snarl. "She's coming with me."

Ire filled Luna's chest, and she slammed her hands on the counter. "*She* is right here, and *she* will make her own decisions."

Mauricio had the sense to look ashamed of himself while Yasir was grinning at his cousin like he knew something but wasn't going to say it.

A ruckus of noise burst through the manor, and seconds later, a group of five boys rushed down the stairs, elbowing and jeering at each other as they slid into the kitchen.

Luna backed herself into a corner, holding onto the counter behind her to avoid being trampled over.

The boys were all in their late teens, though one of them did look closer to her twenty-one years. All of the boys were arguing with one another, their voices raised as they talked over each other.

An ear-splitting whistle pierced the air, and the room fell silent. Mauricio stood with his fingers in his mouth and a scowl on his face. "Out. All of you. Now!"

The oldest, a boy with brown curly hair that bounced on top of his head, stepped forward. "Come on, Mauri, we're hungry. Just a little snack."

Mauri pointed toward the entryway. "To the dining hall."

"But breakfast isn't for another hour," the boy whined.

"Then be grateful I don't drag your sorry asses to the training yard for the next hour," Mauri growled.

That was all it took for the five boys to scramble out of the kitchen, shoving each other all the way. Mauri's gaze landed on her, and he said, "Are you okay?"

Luna forced a smile onto her face. "I'm fine. I just didn't realize how many people lived here."

He palmed his face and groaned. "Honestly, neither do I most days."

Having siblings wasn't common in the Corps. Seeing so many people related to one another wasn't something Luna was used to. She could see the resemblance many of them bore to Turi, and it was a bit unnerving.

"How many cousins do you have?" she asked, moving back to the counter to retrieve her banana.

"Well, my father had twelve siblings, including Erasmo's father. Nine brothers and four sisters," Mauri explained.

Yasir spoke up. "In case you're wondering, my mother was one of the four sisters. Hence the hair," he said as he motioned to his blonde locks. With a wink, he added, "Dad was from the southern isles."

Luna frowned at him and looked to Mauri for an explanation, but when he didn't offer one, she asked, "The southern isles?"

Yasir glanced between her and his cousin. "Yeah, you know, the sea people, all tan skin, blue eyes, and blonde hair? Best seafood in the world. Known for their pearls and all those other fancy exports people like so much."

She shook her head, feeling like an idiot. She didn't know about any of those things. The Demon Corps maps were of Ozero alone. Luna silently scolded herself for having never questioned it.

Yasir's mouth fell open. "You're joking, right? You're the one that's been living on the other side of the darkness, and you're telling me you've never heard of the southern isles? Mauri, are you listening to this — "

Yasir's words trailed off as Mauricio placed his whole hand over his cousin's face and pushed him into the pantry. Yasir fell back into a shelf before tripping over a bag of flour. He stumbled backward, and a cloud of white powder exploded in the air.

Luna hid her smile behind her hand at the sight.

"Shut your mouth," Mauricio snarled at Yasir. "Obviously, she doesn't know. You don't need to be an ass about it." Turning to her, Mauri said, "Don't mind him. He doesn't get out much."

"I just washed these pants," Yasir whined as Mauricio corralled Luna out of the kitchen and led her to a sitting room.

He handed her an apple and stationed himself by a window overlooking the south end of the eyrie. She waited for him to begin pestering her with questions, but when he didn't, she relaxed on the sofa and bit into the apple.

Several minutes ticked by, and Mauricio seemed content to stand sentinel by the window.

Luna couldn't take the silence anymore, though. "So," she ventured, feeling awkward. "Do you have any siblings?"

A grin tugged at Mauri's lip as he said, "Oh, yes. You met them this morning."

She frowned and then remembered the five boys that he had scared off from the kitchen. "All five of them are your brothers?"

He nodded. "It's a wonder I haven't gone gray yet," he said with a rueful shake of his head.

"What about your parents?"

Mauri inhaled deeply, his shoulders rising and falling as he did. "Dad shifted right away, along with all my uncles. He came back a few times. We thought maybe he'd figured out how to stop the shift. That's how we got the twins," he said. "They were the youngest in the pack you saw this morning."

"Oh," she said uselessly, not sure what to say.

"The last time we saw dad, he shifted and went completely feral. He attacked mom and — " he trailed off, and his features pinched.

"I'm sorry," Luna said, not wanting to force him to say the words.

"Anyway, I've been taking care of them since," he quickly added as he shifted from foot to foot.

Luna didn't know what to say to that. She grew up an orphan and had lived in group homes her whole life until she joined the Corps with Kiki and Yari. They were her family.

"What about you?" he asked, turning to face her.

She shrugged. "My parents disappeared when the darkness came. Kiki, Yari, and I grew up in an orphanage before joining the Corps."

"Kiki?" he said, mulling the name of her best friend over. "That's the one with the short hair?"

Luna nodded.

"She stole my sword," he said deadpan.

A laugh bubbled up from Luna's chest. "That sounds like something Kiki would do."

"She went after you," Mauri added softly.

"That she did," Luna whispered, her heart aching for her best friend. Kiki had rescued Luna from the bandit, Tomás, but in doing so, she had been captured in her stead.

"We'll find her," Mauricio said in reassuring tones. He moved to sit on the low table in front of Luna. "I promise you."

She shook her head. "I'm not worried if she's okay. She can handle herself. I just hope she isn't causing too much trouble. I know her. Kiki will raise so much hell that Tomás might think he is better off just getting rid of her."

Mauri reached out and placed his warm hand over Luna's. She met his gaze as he said, "No. That won't happen. I know Tomás. If he could make a profit, he'd suffer anything for it."

A small measure of hope blossomed in her heart at his words. "Even Kiki," she murmured, a smile tugging at the corner of her lips.

Mauri nodded, his own lips tugging into a smile. Something fluttered in Luna's stomach at his nearness, and she wondered what about this man intrigued her so much.

She supposed that if she was going to be stuck here until they found Kiki, she was willing to find out.

Chapter Seven

NOT EVERY DINNER ENDS WELL

Kiki

E rasmo quickly shuffled around the inn, shoving pieces of kindling and logs into the hearth. He struck flint against stone, and soon smoke curled around the mantle as the fire came to life.

Kiki stumbled into the inn, dropping her pack and throwing off her snow-encrusted boots. She sighed in relief as she set her toes next to the orange-yellow flames. As the flames warmed her icy skin, igniting a tingling sensation from her toes and traveling to her flushed cheeks, she could hear Erasmo moving around in the kitchen.

The clanging of pots and pans from the kitchen broke the silence, and soon a rich aroma began to seep out and fill the hallway.

Curiosity propelled her to her feet as she peeked around the kitchen counter to see Erasmo hard at work, effortlessly chopping bite-sized chunks of meat and vegetables before adding them to a boiling pot. Kiki watched as he stirred a pan of sizzling onions and peppers on the stovetop while still stirring the pot with a ladle.

It was hard not to stare at the man. He had unbuttoned his white linen shirt and rolled up the sleeves to his elbows, revealing a map of intricate black tattoos snaking up and down his muscular arms. His broad shoulders and chiseled jaw were impossibly attractive, and a flood of desire pooled low in Kiki's belly.

She felt something tug in her core, like a thread pulling her toward him. She quickly snapped that cord with a single thought.

Erasmo may be a tall glass of water on a hot day, but he was Turi's older brother. That was forbidden territory. She didn't even want a relationship.

What she told Erasmo earlier was true. There was too much for her to worry about, let alone care for. She couldn't afford to think about adding one more person to her list.

Erasmo shuffled around the kitchen, softly singing a tune Kiki didn't recognize. His low, steady baritone echoed around him, the tune carrying an undeniable trace of sorrow.

Kiki had shared a lot about her life in the Corps, and Erasmo had seemed to genuinely care about her experiences. When he wasn't being a self-absorbed ass, he was also kind of a nice guy — if someone who shifted into a demon bear could be considered nice.

Kiki swallowed hard as she watched Erasmo reach for the dried herbs that hung from the ceiling beams. The fabric of his shirt rose with the motion, revealing the deep ridges of his abs and the v-shaped indent that traced its way past the waist of his pants.

She cursed under her breath. Why did he have to be so attractive? Couldn't Turi's brother have been hexed with something that didn't make him so delicious? That would have made Kiki's life much easier.

Erasmo pivoted in her direction and tensed when his eyes landed on her.

She tried not to blush, hoping that he didn't notice she'd been staring. Clearing her throat, she asked, "Do you need any help?"

He smiled and gestured back to the large pot he was stirring. "Not really. Though I could use your thoughts on this," he said, pointing back to the pot he was stirring.

"Sure," she quipped as she nervously rounded the counter to join him.

He motioned for her to come closer as he dipped a wooden spoon into the soup and blew over the steaming liquid before bringing the spoon up to her lips.

"Tell me what you think," he said as he slowly moved the spoon toward her.

His hand cupped beneath the spoon, keeping any hot liquid from dripping onto her as she leaned forward and took the spoon into her mouth. An explosion of flavors burst on her tongue, and a soft moan escaped her lips as she swallowed. "Is that real meat in there?"

"Do you like it?" he asked, his brows lifting as if he were bracing for her rejection.

"Are you joking? I love it!" She leaned over the spoon and took the rest into her mouth. "That's the best soup I've ever tasted."

"Good," he smiled, and her heart stopped at the sight. He was such a devastatingly handsome man. "I'm glad," he added sheepishly.

"Who taught you to cook like that?"

Erasmo shifted from foot to foot and went back to stirring the soup. "I have a lot of picky eaters in my family," he said, his lips forcing a smile.

She stayed quiet, waiting for him to elaborate.

"After my mom sacrificed herself to put the curse in place, most of the males in the family were taken by it and shifted immediately. They didn't turn back into humans at sunset, and I have a lot of cousins. It sort of fell to me to care for them."

Guilt instantly washed over her. Here she had been complaining about the Corps when Erasmo had been left to basically run an orphanage.

"I'm sorry," she whispered. "That sounds like a lot of responsibility."

He shrugged and forced a tight-lipped smile. "It's okay. The curse affected us all, right?"

She nodded, feeling a connection to him that she hadn't felt before. Something that knit them together. They both knew what it was like to carry the burden of others' welfare before their own.

He pointed to a large pot hanging over a fire. "That's for you," he said. "I added a few pots to a bath in the room down the hall. One more should do it."

Gratitude filled her chest so much that water lined her eyes. She quickly gulped down the lump in her throat. "Thank you," she whispered, and she truly meant it.

He turned his face toward her again, and she swore there was a softness in his eyes that she hadn't noticed before.

"I set some fresh clothes by the bath. Figured you might want to wash your leathers and let them dry by the fire overnight."

"Thanks," Kiki whispered. "That's really considerate of you." Before she could make a fool of herself, she left to go check out the bath.

A small fire crackled in the bedroom where a large pewter basin had been half-filled with steaming water.

Footsteps down the hall announced Erasmo's approach, and she turned in time to see him lugging the pot in front of him. He walked to the basin and poured the water inside.

Setting the pot down, he dipped his hand into the water and stirred it around. "That should be good. If it's too hot, let me know."

She felt her cheeks get hot at the attention to detail he'd paid to setting up her bath. No one had ever catered to her in such a way before. She wasn't sure what to do in response.

"Thanks," she mumbled.

"The potatoes will take a while to cook all the way through, so take your time," he said before he left the room and closed the door behind him.

Kiki felt his absence as if a piece of her had walked away. She quickly dismissed the feeling, knowing it had something to do with the care he'd taken to set up a bath and for cooking a delicious meal. It was nothing more than that. It couldn't be. She couldn't let it.

Without letting herself think about the whole situation too much, Kiki slowly peeled off her leathers and set them off to the side, folding them carefully as she'd been taught in the Corps, the habit too ingrained to break.

A Slayer's leathers were an honor to wear and should be cared for accordingly, even if they were covered in demon ichor.

Turning to the bath, Kiki swung her leg over the hip-high rim of the basin, and a moan escaped her lips as the hot water soaked her toes. Swinging the other leg in, she slowly lowered herself into the tub, savoring the feel of hot water. This was a luxury she wasn't used to.

She did as Erasmo suggested and took her time. She washed the grime from her hair and scrubbed her nails until all the blood and dirt caked beneath them came out. When the water had cooled enough to start to feel like the showers in the barracks, she slipped out and wrapped a towel around her frame.

Steam rose from her skin as she toweled dry her short hair and tugged on the pile of clothes Erasmo had set out for her. A simple pair of brown pants and a soft linen shirt. She grabbed her leathers and set to wiping them down with a damp cloth, taking care to remove the dried blood.

When her leathers were soft and supple once more, she opened the door to the bathroom and was greeted by the alluring scent of cooked pork, cumin, and chiles.

Her mouth watered at the scent, and her legs moved on their own, taking her to the kitchen in a trance.

Erasmo ladled soup into a pair of bowls and took them out to the dining area of the inn. She watched him carefully look around the room as if he were trying to determine the best possible spot. He settled on a small round table with a pair of wooden chairs that were closest to the fire.

Watching him stirred something in her chest. He was a man full of surprises and mystery. She felt drawn to him in a way that she had never been drawn to another person before. But she couldn't let herself fall for it. Those feelings were temporary. She was hungry and tired and merely grateful for a hot meal and a warm bath. Nothing more. Those feelings were gratitude. That's all.

She stepped out of the shadows and walked to his selected table.

"That smells even better than before," she said, pulling a chair out and sitting, her eyes widening as she saw the rest of the spread he'd laid out.

In addition to the soup, Erasmo had whipped up some tortillas and wrapped them in a towel to keep them warm. On another plate, he'd found some plantains and fried them up, their outer edges crispy, just how her *wela* used to make them. The best part was a small square of flan, its golden-brown top perfectly toasted.

She pointed to the flan as she said, "Please don't tell me you made that from scratch as well."

Erasmo chuckled, and she felt a rush of heat run down her spine at the sound. "I can't take credit for it. I found it in the icebox. Seemed a shame to let it go to waste."

She hadn't seen food like this in years and definitely not all at once. Her mouth watered, and she didn't hesitate to grab a tortilla and stuff it into her mouth. A moan slipped past her lips, and she added a spoonful of soup. She shoveled bite after bite into her mouth, all the while savoring each morsel.

Erasmo ran a hand over his face and groaned.

She looked up and saw that he had a pained expression. "Is everything all right?" she asked around a mouthful of food.

He leveled his bright blue gaze at her, and she felt her heart leap in her chest. There was something feral in his eyes that beckoned to the wildness within her.

"Can you stop making those little noises, please? They're very distracting."

She blushed hard at realizing she'd been moaning during the whole meal. "Sorry," she mumbled, grabbing a plantain and shoving it into her mouth to hide her embarrassment. "I just haven't had food like this in — well — ever."

His features softened, the corners of his mouth lifting the slightest bit. "I'm glad you like it."

She thought she might like him too, then felt her cheeks heat again. What was she thinking? She couldn't have feelings for this man. For a whole host of reasons, one of them being that he was her ex-boyfriend's older brother.

What was wrong with her? Now was not the time to be thinking about his lips, or the way his tongue swept over them when he sipped his soup or the way his teeth looked when they bit down on his bottom lip —

Heavens, what was wrong with her?

She pushed her plate away, a screech filling the room as she slid her chair back.

Erasmo looked up, his expression startled. "Are you okay?"

"I'm fine," she blurted. "I just need some fresh air. I'll be right back."

He nodded, a puzzled look still on his face as she turned on her heel and practically ran for the front door. She could feel his eyes on her back the whole time. She burst through the door and slammed it shut, pressing her back to it as she inhaled the cold air deep into her lungs.

"Get yourself together," she chided. "This is not the time to be thinking such things," she added.

A gust of winter air swept around her, and she shivered as the chill numbed her feverish skin. Snowflakes cascaded over her cheeks and collected in her hair like tiny crystals of ice. With a heavy exhale, she leaned her head against the door and closed her eyes, allowing her racing heart to slow.

A sudden gust of wind brought the overwhelming stench of rot and decay to her nose, and she gagged. She glanced in the direction of the smell, and her blood ran cold as a tall, gaunt figure stepped from the shadows of the trees. Its bony arms hung almost to the ground, and bits of its decaying flesh peeled from its frame with every movement.

A demon.

Kiki's heart raced as she grabbed for her machete, but when her fingers grasped at nothing but cotton pants, she remembered that she'd taken it off wither her leathers. Both of which were by the fire. Inside.

She whirled around, yanked open the inn's door, and slammed it shut.

At her sudden entrance, Erasmo jumped from his chair, sending it flying backward.

"Demons," she announced, breathless.

Erasmo was quick to respond and grabbed the nearest knife. He sliced open his palm and raced to the door to meet her.

"What are you doing?" she asked, horrified as crimson welled in the center of his palm. She rushed to the kitchen and grabbed the nearest clean towel she could find.

"Putting up boundary runes," he answered in a rush as he dipped his fingers into the blood and began drawing symbols along the doorframe.

"I thought you were protection enough," Kiki hissed, joining him by the door with the towel in hand.

"Every shift takes more of my humanity from me," he said as he brushed past her to mark the windows. "I use the shift as a last resort nowadays."

She tossed her hands in the air. "That would have been good to know earlier, don't you think?"

"Sorry, it didn't seem like relevant information at the time," he said, turning to add runes to the other side of the inn.

Shaking her head, she ran for her weapons by the fire.

A bone-chilling howl echoed through the streets, sending a shiver up Kiki's spine. She peeked through a window, her eyes widening when she saw several more demons had joined the first. Each figure was shrouded in a thick, inky black mist. Their claws clinked against the cobblestone as they shuffled from one shop to the next, entering briefly before quickly vanishing into the next.

Kiki whipped her head toward the fire and the light glowing from it.

They're going to see it.

She sprinted back into the kitchen, skidding across the wood floor, her eyes searching for the largest pot she could find. The smell of Erasmo's freshly made soup wafted up toward her, and a whine slipped from her throat at the knowledge of what she was about to do.

Running back to the fire, she poured the soup over the flames. The fire sputtered and died, smoke billowing out from the mantle.

Erasmo slid back into the main room, took one look at what she'd done, and she thought for a second he'd scold her for wasting the food, but instead, he nodded his head in approval and said, "Good call. The boundary spell will make it seem like we're not here. The fires would have been a dead giveaway. If we're lucky, they won't notice us at all and just walk past."

Erasmo might not have been upset about the food, but Kiki certainly was. With gritted teeth, she faced the front door with her machete raised and braced for an attack. Her heart hammered in her ears, and blood rushed through her body in anticipation.

She felt Erasmo's eyes on her and spared him a sidelong glance. His voice was husky as he said, "If something happens to me, I want you to take Ocaso and head to the eyrie."

Kiki rolled her eyes at him. "See these stars on my wrists?" She pulled up her sleeves a bit so he could see the rows and rows of stars tattooed onto her skin. There were so many that they disappeared under her sleeves. "One for every dead demon. If you're scared, get behind me. I'll take care of this," she said with a cocky smirk, hoping that he'd take the bait and that would be enough to get his mind off the coming horde.

"I don't need you to protect me — I was just saying — Oh, never mind. You're insufferable, woman," he said, stammering through his words like a fool.

It was enough to distract him, though, as he slowly extended his claws from his hands, and his canines elongated into fangs.

Seeing him as part beast and part human should have terrified Kiki. At the very least, it should have repulsed her. Instead, seeing him prepared for battle, his eyes full of fire, eager for blood, set her soul on fire.

She knew then and there that this man was going to be the end of her.

CHAPTER EIGHT

OVERHEARD AND OVERWHELMED

YARI

"*W*here am I?" *Yari wondered out loud as she turned in a circle, taking in the dim cabin. An empty hearth, cold to the touch, dominated one wall of the small room. Even in the muted light, she could make out the dust-covered furniture and thick cobwebs, indicating that no one had been in this secluded house in a very long time.*

"Hello?" she called out, her voice echoing through the otherwise silent house as she walked cautiously through the sitting area and towards the kitchen.

She noticed a single door off to the side, old and battered, with claw marks dug deep into the wood and smears of dried blood visible in between the grains. The door was ajar, letting in a chill wind which caused it to creak open as she approached.

She paused at the top of the stairs, her heart pounding in her chest. The stairs creaked beneath her feet, echoing in the darkness as she descended. She navigated the creaking wooden steps by feel, one hand on the splintering railing and the other held out before her. When she reached the bottom, she was met with an overwhelming sense of darkness that seemed to swallow her whole.

As she stepped into the dark cellar, a musty metallic scent filled her nostrils. Her feet slipped on something wet, and before she could catch her balance, she tumbled to the cold dirt floor, jarring her bones. Her hands were quickly soaked in something sticky and warm, and the taste of coppery iron was on her tongue.

Trembling, she lifted her hands close to her face, and her eyes widened at the sight of the deep red color that stained her skin. It was blood. And it was everywhere.

She scrambled backward, her head and shoulders colliding with something warm and solid. She slowly looked up, her mouth agape at the horrific sight before her — it was a leviathan beast with the head and chest of a bear and the lower half of a muscular man. His long, shaggy fur glimmered silver in the moonlight and the size of him alone was enough to make her heart skip a beat.

A piercing scream ripped through the air as her gaze locked with the monster. Its eyes were a deep, frigid blue, and its lips curled back in a savage snarl, revealing needle-like fangs. Its barbed claws reached forward hungrily as it prepared to snatch her up.

Yari jerked awake, her heart pounding. A pile of books clattered to the ground at her feet. She wiped the dampness from her forehead, her fingers trembling slightly.

For a moment, she stared into the library's darkness, trying to calm her racing thoughts.

It was just another nightmare; she consoled herself. She couldn't seem to get away from her nightmares. Every time she slept at night or drifted to sleep during the day, the same monster haunted her mind.

She remembered the demon that chased her through the gardens and wrapped her arms around herself. Despite Arlando sending off some of his men to check into the breach, it turned out that there had been no demon on the grounds after all.

It had all been in her mind.

She heaved a weary sigh. It was no wonder that the demon continued to haunt her sleep; she hadn't gotten a decent night's sleep since thinking she'd seen it in real life.

She set the book she was reading down and looked out through the window, the snowy landscape of the Northern Territory stretching out before her. The sun hung high in the sky, and a lone rider approached the outer gates.

She paused, book forgotten in her hand, eyes tracing the lonely figure on horseback struggling against the snowdrifts that threatened to bury him. Sunlight glinted off his armor and the flag he bore, which she couldn't make out from so far away.

She frowned in worry, for no one had ever visited this estate before, and she hadn't received any word of guests coming. She quickly set down her book and rushed toward the door, calling for Arlando to meet her in the courtyard to greet their surprise visitor.

As she descended the stairs into the main hall, Arlando was already there with the stranger, who dangled a silver rose medallion before Arlando's face.

They were speaking in hushed tones, their expressions tense. She stayed hidden around a marble column, watching as they continued their argument.

Arlando's voice was sharp as he said, "You disappoint me, Tomás. I'm starting to wonder if I should have hired another for this job."

The man, Tomás, scowled. "My men are dead. I can't control the demons in the woods any more than you can." Arlando made a noise of disbelief. "I will deliver as promised. I just need more time."

Arlando stiffened suddenly and turned, facing her direction. "Don't hide, my love. Come out. It's okay."

Yari held her breath, feeling exposed like an animal caught in an archer's sight. She tiptoed around the column, her heart hammering in her chest and her face hot with embarrassment.

Arlando reached his hand out to her, and when she reached him, he clasped it in his. He turned to the man called Tomás and said, "Allow me to introduce my betrothed. Yarixa Canahuate. Isn't she the most beautiful creature you've ever seen?" he said, his chest puffing up as he tipped her chin up and pressed a soft kiss to her lips.

Tomás lowered himself into a bow and peered up at her from his bent waist. "It's a pleasure, lady."

Yari didn't like the looks of this man. His face was covered in grime, likely from traveling, and he smelled like he hadn't bathed in weeks. Worse, she didn't like the way his gaze trailed down her body when Arlando wasn't looking.

She clutched her shawl closer to her body, hoping to cover any exposed skin.

Arlando stroked his hand down Yari's face. "Dearest, Tomás and I have some business to attend to. Why don't you go to the kitchens and have the staff prepare your lunch? I'm afraid I won't be able to join you."

She wrung her hands in front of her, casting a wary glance at Tomás. "Is something the matter?"

Arlando's warm, comforting gaze met hers, and he lightly pressed his lips to her forehead. "Nothing for you to worry your pretty head about."

He then smiled reassuringly and gently nudged her away, his hand lingering at her waist as she reluctantly walked toward the kitchen.

Tomás voice reached her ears before she turned the corner. "I see your plan is going as expected," he said, his voice rough and coarse.

"Of course, it is," Arlando said, his tone uncharacteristically cold.

She didn't understand what he was referring to and decided to put it out of her mind. For the first time in her life, she was safe. She had a warm bed to sleep in. Food to fill her belly. Warm clothes to ward off the chill. And a sweet man that wanted to provide everything for her.

She was spoiled beyond her wildest imagining. Whatever was going on, she decided that she had to trust that Arlando had it well in hand.

CHAPTER NINE

WHEN LOVE AND BLOOD DON'T MIX (BUT MAYBE THEY SHOULD)

KIKI

"Do you think they left?" Kiki asked Erasmo as the minutes ticked by into hours.

Erasmo's eyes darted to the windows, and he shook his head. "They're still out there. I can feel them," he said.

"You can feel them?" she hissed. "Yet another piece of useful information you could have shared earlier."

He narrowed his eyes at her. "I can only sense them if they're close. Now keep your pretty mouth shut before you draw their attention."

She couldn't help but feel a rush of heat course through her veins when he mentioned her pretty mouth, but she quickly dismissed the thought.

A loud bang on the inn's front door startled her, and she jumped, the floorboards creaking beneath her feet.

Erasmo huffed. "I'm going to say this now while we're both still alive, but if we die here, I want you to know that it's your fault."

She sneered at him as another bang sounded at the door. "I'll keep that in mind when I'm saving your life," she spat back.

The door shuddered and groaned under the force of the pounding; then, with a thunderous crack, it was torn from its frame. Splinters of wood flew through the air as the colossal figure of a demon emerged from the gloom, snarling and lurching forward.

Kiki didn't hesitate and ran toward it with her machete, chopping off its head in the process. It exploded in a gush of ichor and blackened flesh, but she didn't have time to wipe the gunk from her face. Another demon charged at her and threw her back. She fell into a nearby table, the wind knocked from her lungs, before sliding to the floor in an undignified heap.

Erasmo roared as he rushed forward and slashed at the demon's chest with his claws. Four more demons poured through the door. Hauling herself off the floor, Kiki rushed to the nearest one. The battle was a blur of exploding demon bodies as her machete stabbed them through the heart or removed their heads.

Suddenly, she heard a grunt of pain. She spun around, her eyes wide with horror, to see Erasmo's mouth wide open on a silent cry.

A demon twice Erasmo's size held Erasmo suspended in the air; its immense claws impaled through the center of Erasmo's body.

Without thinking, Kiki acted. White-hot rage coursed through her veins as she sprang forward and cut through the two demons scuttling toward her with swift precision.

Her blade flashed in the dim light as she jumped onto the tops of the wooden table, agilely leaping from table to table.

She propelled herself in the air with a fierce yell and drove her machete toward the demon's neck. A sickening thud echoed as the creature's head detached, and ichor splattered onto the floor while it disintegrated into a cloud of black mist.

Erasmo staggered and crumpled to the floor, knees buckling beneath him. His eyes were glassy and lost as the deep gash oozed thick streams of crimson blood onto his hands.

She let out a sharp cry as she stumbled to his side, easing him onto his back. He winced at her touch, but she worked fast, removing her own shirt and pressing it against his wound to stop the bleeding.

"You're going to be okay," she said in a rush, knowing full well that every word she said was a lie.

This was a lethal wound. He'd bleed out before she could get him back to Luna in the eyrie.

"Blood," he whispered, his eyes becoming unfocused.

"Yeah, you're bleeding, you idiot," she said, trying to make light of the situation, but her heart was cracking in two as his beautiful golden skin paled.

He shook his head. "No. I need — blood," he choked. "To heal."

"What?" she reared back, looking down at his wound. "A transfer isn't going to fix this, friend," she added, feeling more blood gush between her fingers as she applied pressure to the wound.

"I haven't fed in weeks. I'm weak. Need — " his eyes fluttered closed, and her heart leaped into her throat.

Blood. He said he needed blood, like when he put the boundary runes up to protect the inn.

Without a moment's hesitation, she grabbed the machete and cut it into her palm, creating a deep wound. Her blood pooled in the center, and she pressed it to his lips.

The crimson droplets of her blood stained his lips, and for a moment, she thought he was gone. But then her skin heated beneath the warmth of his tongue, and his throat moved as he consumed her offering.

Hope bloomed in her chest, but then Erasmo's hand shot up and clamped down around Kiki's wrist. His eyes snapped open, and his lips created a suction against her palm.

She yelped in surprise but then felt a heady feeling overcome her as heat pooled in her pussy and filled her body with tingling pleasure.

A soft moan escaped her lips as Erasmo continued to drink her blood. He suddenly let go of her hand, and she fell back, her head spinning.

Erasmo suddenly rose up; his body bent over his legs as he gasped for breath. Then, his head snapped over to her, his gaze ablaze with a fiery glow, and a menacing snarl ripped from his bloody lips.

She was still catching her breath from the adrenaline running through her veins when he moved faster than humanly possible and positioned himself in a crouch as if preparing to pounce on her.

His eyes were crazed, and Kiki scrambled back, fear coiling in her gut. "Erasmo?"

Without warning, shadows burst from his skin, and he was suddenly on top of her, his large arms pinning her wrists to the floor and his hips pressing against hers, keeping her in place.

Kiki struggled against his hold, fear spiking into a panic. "What are you doing? Get off me. You're hurting me."

But Erasmo wasn't himself. She could see that now. His eyes were full of a primal need as if a beast lurked under his skin, and that beast had decided that she would be the one to sate its hunger.

She continued to struggle, but he was much larger than her and much stronger. "Erasmo, please, if you can hear me, it's me. Kiki," she pleaded.

This couldn't be the way that she died. Drained of blood in some abandoned inn in the middle of who knew where. She still had to save Yari. She had to find her best friend and bring her home.

A growl vibrated through Erasmo's chest as he bared his elongated fangs.

"Please," she begged. "It's me. Kiki. It's Kiki!"

But he didn't hear her. The beast was in control now and had taken him to some basic instinctual need.

She begged him to hear her, even as his hold on her wrists pressed so hard into her skin that she knew she would have bruises. If she survived, that is.

The tune he'd been humming while he cooked floated in her mind, and without thinking, she began to hum it. She didn't know the words, but the melody was very simple and easy to remember.

Erasmo's face changed as she continued to hum his song. Then his eyes cleared, and he blinked rapidly as if waking from a living nightmare. His eyes darted across her face, and his pupils dilated in recognition.

"Kiki?" he asked; the desperation in his voice cleaving her heart in two.

"Yeah, it's me," she said, breathless from the full weight of him pressing down on her chest.

The pressure on her wrists let up, and he shifted his body so that he carried most of his weight. He dropped his head until his forehead pressed against hers. "I'm so sorry," he whispered. "Thank you for bringing me back."

She stared at his face so close to hers, his breath caressing her face. She was distinctly aware that he was still on top of her, his hips pressing into hers, and she felt a different kind of heat build in her lower belly at the feel of him.

Swallowing a lump in her throat, she said, "You're squishing me."

Erasmo jerked back, a blush coating his cheeks as he scrambled backward.

"Sorry," he said, eyes darting away to stare at the blackened logs of the fire.

She pushed up to her elbows, her chest still heaving for air. "Do you care to explain what the hell any of that was?"

He ran his hands through his hair; his face still turned away from her. "I told you before that each shift took more of my humanity every time."

She nodded, still not understanding how the two were related.

"Feeding is even worse. I usually don't do it unless my cousin, Mauricio, is around to bring me back."

Her throat was suddenly very dry. "How often do you have to feed?" she asked timidly.

"Every few weeks, more if I can keep the beast at bay long enough."

"The beast? As in, there is a living thing inside of you with a mind of its own," Kiki asked incredulously.

He nodded, the motion full of shame.

A few heartbeats passed, and she said, "I'm sorry."

He jerked his head up, his eyes blazing as he stared at her, his mouth open. "What are you sorry for?"

She shrugged. "I'm sorry about this whole curse thing. It's not like you asked for any of it. I mean, you can't help who your parents were. Why should you be punished for the crimes of your father?"

He mumbled his agreement and pushed to a stand. He brushed dirt from his pants, saying, "I don't know about you, but I could really use a drink right about now."

She felt her lips curl into a smirk as he reached down and offered her a hand up. "You and me both," she said.

His eyes slid down to her exposed midriff and the simple bra she wore. His pupils blew wide as his gaze slowly trailed down the line between her breasts toward her belly button. Kiki felt heat blossom in her pussy at the way his eyes slowly admired her.

"First, you need to put some clothes on," he said ruefully. "You're killing me with this," he said, motioning toward her.

Kiki huffed and put her hands on her hips. "I think what you mean to say is, 'Thank you for taking the shirt off your own back to save my life, Kiki. I really owe you.' That would be a start."

A slow grin overtook his features, and Kiki instantly regretted teasing him. This man. He was trouble, indeed.

CHAPTER TEN

SOLIDARITY IN THE MIDST OF CRISIS

SOLANA

S olana yanked open the door to her bedroom and slammed it shut with her foot. With angry fingers, she pulled her tlazons from the bandolier strapped across her chest and slammed them onto the dresser, their metallic tips ringing. With a grunt, she yanked her machete from its scabbard and dropped it onto the dresser as well.

Moments later, Bernat poked his head into the room, his eyes wary as he entered and quietly shut the door behind him.

"Sol?" he asked, his voice timid. "Do you want to talk about it?"

She let out a huff of frustration and shook her head.

Bernat slowly approached and placed his warm palms on her shoulders. "We'll try again tomorrow," he said in soothing tones.

They had gone out in search of Kiki and Bernat's brother but had come back empty-handed. Solana wasn't used to failing missions, and the sting of it made her mood sour.

"It could be too late by tomorrow. We should have kept looking a little longer," she said.

"Sun was already setting, and Mauri was right. We had to get back before dark," he said.

"When did you suddenly become so afraid of demons," she hissed and instantly regretted lashing out at him as soon as she saw the wounded look in his eyes. "I'm sorry," she quickly added, running her hands over her face. "I'm just sick of getting nowhere here. We're no closer to finding our people and somehow keep losing more."

"I'm frustrated too," Bernat said as he started to knead the tension from her shoulders.

She let out a moan as he massaged a particularly tense spot, and Bernat froze.

He leaned down and pressed his lips to her ear. "Keep that up and see what happens," he said, his voice low and husky.

A thrill ran up her spine at the promise in his words, and heat pooled in her lower belly.

"Maybe that's what I want," she whispered breathlessly.

"You're such a tease," he said, his laugh vibrating through her spine.

She moaned again as his fingers shifted to her shoulder blades, and he spun her around, pressing his hip to hers as he pinned her between him and the dresser.

Grabbing her face between his hands, he growled, "What did I say?"

She felt a smirk tug at her lips, and his eyes filled with hunger at the sight.

He crashed his lips to hers, his tongue darting into her mouth as a moan escaped her lips.

All thoughts of her failure flew from her mind as she focused solely on him. His hard muscles flexed as he ground his hips into her. The almost frenzied way he kissed her as if he'd never get another chance. It made her head swim, and she was happy to drown in that feeling.

A knock at the door had her whipping her head away.

"Go away," Bernat growled, his eyes never leaving her face.

"We need to talk," Mauri's voice filtered through the door.

"Later," Bernat called as he dipped his head to Solana's neck and gently grazed it with his teeth.

"It's about those disappearances you were telling me about," Mauri said, his tone insistent.

Solana pulled away from Bernat, ignoring his groans of protest, and ripped open the door. "What about them?" she asked, facing Mauri.

He looked between her and Bernat, his eyes not failing to catch their swollen lips or the pink marks along her neck. "Sorry, brother," he said to Bernat, realizing what he'd interrupted. "But you'll want to hear this."

Solana and Bernat followed Mauri down the stairs and into the dining hall, where a meeting had been called.

A man in an emerald tunic and boots covered in mud stood in the center of the hall. As Mauri walked forward, he slammed his fist down and hollered, "Everyone shut the hell up."

The man had strange symbols tattooed in black across his neck and along his hands. She suspected the tattoos covered his arms and chest from the looks of them as they disappeared under his collar and sleeves. "Who is this?" she asked Mauri, leaning over to whisper in his ear.

"That's Guillermo. He's a magi," Mauri explained as if that clarified anything for her.

Guillermo nodded to Mauri and turned to address the crowd. "I've just received news from across the territories. There have been reports of entire villages deserted. No trails or clues as to why."

A hand flew up, and someone asked, "Demons?"

Guillermo shook his head, "No signs of struggle either. It's like they vanished."

Solana exchanged a worried glance with Bernat. So it was happening here too. She curled her hands into fists as she listened.

"If that isn't bad enough," Guillermo continued. "The other magi have reported a disturbance in the weather patterns. There is a large storm over the northern territory, and it seems to be magically generated."

She didn't understand what any of that meant, but as she looked around the room, several people exchanged worried glances with one another.

"So what?" A boy in his late teens stood up. "So Arlando is up to his games again. What do we care?"

Mauricio stepped forward and grabbed the boy by his neck, and sat him back down. "Sit your ass down, Benji, and let the magi talk."

Guillermo nodded his appreciation to Marui. "The storm seems to be getting stronger and has started to push further south. It could be days before it hits us here in La Aguilera, but we need to prepare. Check the food stores, begin thinking about rations, start distributing winter gear, blankets, furs."

The room erupted into chaos at Guillermo's words. Shouts echoed off the walls, voices of men raised in anger, their faces contorted into expressions of confusion and rage. Fists pounded against the table, papers flew through the air, and the atmosphere was electrified with tension as everyone argued over what to do.

Mauri palmed his face and groaned. Looking at Bernat, he said, "Do something."

"Me?" Bernat said, taken aback. "What can I do?"

"You're the rightful king. If you tell them to do something, they'll do it. No questions," Mauri insisted.

Bernat's eyes darted around the room as he shifted from foot to foot. Solana noticed his distress and gently grasped his hand, her thumb lightly rubbing circles over his knuckles in a calming motion.

Bernat's gaze met hers, and he gave her a small smile, his eyes conveying his gratitude for the small gesture.

Bernat slowly spun to face the sea of people. He took a deep breath and cleared his throat, stalling as a murmur swelled within the room with warnings to be silent.

"We will approach this news strategically," Bernat announced, his deep voice booming through the hall. "Any threat to our basic resources is of the utmost importance. We will continue to search for more answers. In the meantime, send out groups to address each of the measures Guillermo mentioned and any additional efforts to aid those who will be affected."

The room was pregnant with an oppressive silence as Bernat talked. But the moment he stopped, a few people jumped up and started barking orders, taking Bernat's command to action seriously.

Guillermo approached Solana and Bernat with a grateful smile. He extended his hand, and Bernat shook it. "Hi, it's nice to meet you, cousin," Guillermo said with a grin that made his tired eyes light up.

"Likewise," Bernat said, pulling Guillermo into a hug. "This is Solana," he said, pulling her forward by her hand. "She's my Commanding Officer in the Demon Corps."

Guillermo shook her hand and gave her a warm smile.

"What is a magi?" she blurted.

Guillermo quirked his head. "Do you not have them where you come from?"

She raised a single eyebrow at him. "That's why I asked."

"Sorry, I'm an idiot sometimes. I was born gifted with magic. I can use spells and potions to create things."

"I see," Solana's mind whirred with more questions as she remembered the intruder vanishing the other night. "Are you able to vanish into thin air at all?"

Guillermo frowned at her question, his confusion making it clear that he had no idea what she was talking about. "No, that's not the type of magic I use. Blood magic is forbidden," he told her.

"But it's possible," she hedged, recalling the smear of blood on the handle to the outer courtyard.

"Technically, yes, it's possible. Why?"

"No reason. I'm new to all of this curses and magic thing."

"Of course. Well, if you're ever interested, you can come to my study. I have loads of books and scrolls on magic."

A growl vibrated from Bernat's chest, and Guillermo's face turned white at the sound.

"Or not," he said, backpedaling. "You know what, forget I mentioned it." He scurried off and disappeared into the crowd of people.

She whirled on Bernat. "What was that for?"

Bernat's pupils were blown wide, and he shook his head as if clearing it. Placing his palm to his forehead, he winced. "I'm sorry. I don't know what came over me."

Mauri watched the whole interaction with rapt attention. Clapping his hand on Bernat's shoulder, he said, "We need to talk."

Bernat stiffened. "Anything you have to say to me, you can say in front of Sol."

Mauri angled his head. "Trust me. This is something you'll want to hear about first."

"It's fine," she said. "I'm going to go check on Luna." Without waiting for his response, Solana ducked into the crowd in search of the Healer.

She found Luna tucked into a corner of the dining hall, sitting alone at a table with her eyes darting around as if she were scared.

Solana pulled a seat out for herself and dropped into it, startling Luna from whatever nightmare she was reliving in her mind.

"We'll find her," she assured the Healer.

Luna shuddered. "It should be me. I was the one Tomás wanted. Now he has Kiki — "

Her heart broke for Luna at the desperation in her voice. But she clenched her hands into fists because she knew that if she ever got the chance, she'd cut the smuggler's dick off and shove it down his throat until he choked to death.

She had been helpless to stop his violation of Luna. Luna had been a shaking leaf ever since, and Solana didn't blame her. The unwanted touch of any person was a violation of one's fundamental rights.

"I should have just gone willingly," Luna whispered. "Been stronger. Not shown how scared I was — "

The rage simmering in Solana's veins boiled over. Luna shouldn't have to feel any kind of guilt or shame for what happened. She hadn't asked for Tomás to target her. She hadn't consented to his roaming hands.

Yet here she was, feeling like she should have taken it better. Solana's stomach churned, and she thought for a second that she was going to be sick, her own haunting memories clawing for the surface.

She steadied her breathing and cleared the red mist before her eyes, knowing that what she was about to say, she had to say with perfect clarity.

Reaching across the table, she held out her hand to Luna. She left her palm there as an open invitation and would leave it there whether the Healer chose to take it or not because it was her choice. Always.

Luna's eyes stared at Solana's palm with wariness.

"I'm only going to say this once. So listen up," Solana started, taking another deep breath to calm the rage that was still boiling under the surface. "You did not ask for what happened to you. You did nothing wrong. The only person at fault here is the man who put his hands on you without your consent."

Luna's shoulders slumped, and she dropped her head to her chest. "But I could have handled the situation better. It's not like he — " she paused and swallowed the lump in her throat. "He didn't take me. He merely touched me. I could have done something different. If I had — "

Solana cut Luna off because she couldn't bear to hear the Healer talk about herself like she was at fault here.

"Stop it," Solana said, her voice hard. "Did you ask for Tomás to touch you the way he did?" Luna shook her head. "Did you want him to? At all?" Again, the Healer shook her head. "Then none of what happened is your fault. He is the one who is wrong. He is responsible for his actions, and he will be the one to pay the consequences. It doesn't matter that he wasn't allowed to take his sick fantasy to the fullest extent. He touched you against your will. That is enough to condemn him. Nothing you did encouraged his actions, deserved his actions, or consented to his actions. Do you understand me?"

Luna's eyes brimmed with tears, and Solana felt her heart crack in two.

Luna may not have been under Solana's command, but the moment she joined Kiki's group, the Healer had fallen under her responsibility, and Solana had failed her. Failed to protect her. To shield her.

Out of the corner of her eye, Solana noticed Mauricio return from his conversation with Bernat and take a seat at a nearby table. She didn't fail to notice that, despite his distance, he seemed to be raptly paying attention to her conversation with Luna. As if he had heard enough, he stood in a rush, his chair screeching as it slid back and fell with a clatter to the ground. His jaw was clenched tight, and she could see the agony on his face, plain as day.

She didn't understand his fascination with Luna, but so far, she had seen him be nothing but protective of the Healer.

Solana didn't like how his eyes seemed to always follow Luna's every move, and she questioned his motives, but he had made it his priority to shield Luna since her arrival. For that alone, Solana tolerated him.

Mauri took three long strides toward them and stood over their table, his face cast in shadow. "What did Tomás do?" he asked, his voice deathly calm, but his white knuckles told another story.

Luna ducked her head in shame and wrapped her arms around herself as if trying to make herself as small as possible. She shook her head slowly; her lips pressed tight together.

This wasn't helping. Mauricio may have meant well, but he was unintentionally driving Luna back to those moments in the woods.

Solana jumped to her feet and wrapped her fingers around his impressive bicep, and yanked him away from the table.

"You're not helping," she hissed. Looking back at Luna, to see that she'd pulled her knees to her chest and was hiding her face.

His face turned anguished as his gaze followed hers, and Solana felt a twinge of sympathy for him, but not enough to let him pester Luna.

"I'll kill him for touching one hair on her head. I'll kill him," he seethed, his nostrils flaring and his eyes burning with the need for blood.

"Then get in line," she said through gritted teeth. "Because I'm killing the bastard the first chance I get."

Mauricio took a faltering step forward, his eyes still trained on Luna, but she stepped in his path. His face twisted with agony, and he winced his eyes shut, pinching the bridge of his nose.

"What can I do for her? I — I want to help, but — " He ran his hands up his face and twisted them into the roots of his hair. "What can I do?"

"Right now, give her some space." Solana's answer seemed to take his heart and mince it into tiny pieces. So she added, "Then be there for her when she needs you."

He finally looked at her directly, and his whole face brightened with hope. She still didn't understand his protectiveness of Luna, but it was clear to her that he'd taken it upon himself to see the Healer cared for. That redeemed him in Solana's eyes, and she nodded her head before patting him on the shoulder and turning away to sit in companionable silence with Luna.

If her own trauma had taught her anything, it was this: the simple act of shared silence, the presence of another person willing to sit with you in your discomfort, brought more solidarity than mere words often had the power to do.

So she sat there. In silence. The room around them was full of sound, but their shared space was a silent bubble. She sat there and offered Luna her silence and her understanding.

Then, when Luna was ready, the Healer reached out and took Solana's hand into hers.

CHAPTER ELEVEN

VULGAR IS THE NEW ROMANTIC

LUNA

L una lay in her bed, eyes wide open and fixed on the rolling shadows of the room cast by the moonlight. The churning of thoughts in her mind was relentless, and despite her exhaustion, rest eluded her like a ghost in a dreamscape.

She shifted to her side, then to her back, then to her tummy, each position offering no respite from her racing mind. An hour later, Luna was still wide awake, wishing for the solace of sleep.

Her mind drifted to the Commander's steadfast presence next to her tonight. The way Solana's calloused hand squeezed Luna's gently, soothing her frayed nerves. Every time Luna gazed back into Solana's ice-blue eyes, it was like looking into the other woman's soul, and what Luna found there cleaved her heart in two. She knew without a doubt that Solana had been hurt before.

Luna could see the pain that lingered in the Commander's eyes when she told Luna that what happened was not her fault. That Luna hadn't asked for anything that Tomás had done to her. That it didn't matter that he hadn't gotten the chance to rape her, he'd touched Luna in her most private places when she did not want him to.

Luna could see the anger that simmered beneath Solana's skin, and she felt the need rise within herself to take revenge on whoever had caused the Commander the same torment.

A shuffling noise outside Luna's bedroom door made her heart constrict. She held her breath and clutched her blankets to her chest, eyes darting to the door. When the noise stopped, she was on her feet and flying to the door. She threw it open and leaped into the hall, but her feet got tangled by something bulky that sent her tumbling.

She felt herself falling and instinctively braced for impact. A muffled grunt and sharp "Ow!" confirmed she had landed on something solid.

The faint light illuminated Mauricio lying beneath her, softening her fall. She quickly scrambled off of him, and at his large frame laying across her threshold, a thin blanket tangled around his muscular thighs.

"Mauricio?" she hissed. "What are you doing here?"

Mauricio groaned as he clutched his lower abdomen, no doubt where she had accidentally kicked him trying to leave her room.

His face reddened as he breathed deeply through his mouth and managed a tight-lipped response.

"Keeping watch," he mumbled.

Luna's brow creased with confusion. "Why?" she asked, her voice barely above a whisper.

"I can't bear the thought of someone hurting you again," he said, his dark gaze searching hers as if pleading for understanding.

Her mouth went dry, and she forced herself to swallow to coat her throat. "You could have told me you were out here. I thought — "

She didn't know what she thought, to be honest. She didn't feel unsafe in this house. In fact, she'd never felt safer in her life. She was in a house full of cursed men who had the power to shift into leviathan bears at any moment, yet she felt perfectly at ease.

No, the demons that lived in her head, her memories, kept her awake at night. She'd been scared of what was outside her door, and all rational thought had left her mind. That was all.

She clenched her fists, and her expression was pained as she said, "Nevermind what I thought."

"I can leave," he said, moving to get up, but she stopped him with a gentle hand on his arm.

"No. It's okay," she said softly, forcing a weak smile.

She got to her feet, her legs shaking from exhaustion, and sidestepped him. Mauricio began adjusting himself to resume his post at her threshold, and Luna winced with guilt when she saw the cold hardwood floor and imagined him sleeping on it.

"Don't sleep there," she scolded firmly, her voice rising an octave higher. "I'll hate myself if you do. Come inside, at least."

"No," he said, shaking his head slowly. "I'm fine here."

She stamped her foot on the ground, her hands shaking in frustration. "Come inside or leave entirely because I won't have you sleeping out in the cold and having you catch a cough."

Mauricio's gaze dropped to the floor, and he nervously bit his bottom lip. He looked up at her, his eyes full of questions. "Are you sure?"

Luna crossed her arms over her chest and planted her feet firmly in place. "I won't be telling you again," she said sternly. "You have until the count of five to decide."

Mauricio scrambled to his feet, his towering frame casting an imposing shadow as he stood. He courteously inclined his head as he edged around her and stepped into her quarters.

He started settling into his previous position on the ground, but she rolled her eyes and sighed deeply. "Seriously, Mauricio? There is plenty of room on the bed. It's big enough for a whole Slayer squad; you won't bother me."

He shook his head vehemently. "No, I'm good. The fire is going, so it's nice and warm in here."

Luna sighed and shook her head in exasperation. "Fine. Do what you want," she muttered. Clambering back into bed, she resumed her vigil of the ceiling, frustration pulsing through her.

A few hours later, a soft whisper broke the silence. "I'm sorry," Mauricio said.

She twisted towards him and saw his back illuminated in the moonlight, still tense with wakefulness.

"What are you talking about?" she asked, her voice slightly softer than before.

He rolled onto his back, his eyes wide as he stared at the ceiling. "For the way, I treated you earlier," he started, his voice thin and hoarse, "I was trying to flirt with you — I had no idea about Tomás — you have every right to hate me. I should have never talked to you like that. I'm an idiot. A jackass and a fool. I'm so sorry. I had no right — I'm just so sorry," he shook his head vehemently as he turned away from her.

"I don't hate you, Mauricio," Luna said quietly, her voice breaking through the stillness of the night air.

Mauri sucked in a sharp breath and slowly rolled over. His eyes found hers, their gazes locking as time seemed to stand still. His lips quivered ever so slightly, mouth slightly agape in disbelief. "You don't?" he asked in a whisper.

"You flustered me, sure. But you made me think about something other than my own misery for more than a second. You made me feel something other than the self-loathing I've been drowning in. You distracted me from myself," she said, confessing all the hurt that she'd been carrying in her heart. The guilt for Kiki being taken in her place had been suffocating her ever since.

Her heart beat wildly in her chest as she confessed in a low voice, "Besides, I'd be lying if I said I didn't like it."

His breath hitched, and a fire burned in his eyes. "You did?"

"You didn't keep me in the kitchen against my will, Mauricio. I could have left at any moment. I just chose not to."

She rolled over, turning her back to him, and the tension in her shoulders eased as she recalled the way he'd caged her in with his arms. The heat of his body so close to hers. She liked it. She felt a connection to the man who hid in the shadows and didn't understand why.

It was more than just physical attraction, though; she had to admit that he was very hard not to stare at. Any woman would be hard-pressed not to find the man devastatingly handsome. But there was something else that drew her to him. Something she couldn't put her finger on...but she was willing to find out.

Before she knew it, she slipped into her first peaceful sleep in years. The knowledge that Mauricio was there on the floor, shielding her from any danger that may come, was the balm her soul needed to finally let go.

CHAPTER TWELVE

THE DIFFERENCE BETWEEN DESIRE AND DISTRACTION...THERE IS NONE

KIKI

E rasmo slid a glass of clear liquid toward Kiki, and she could smell the sharp scent of tequila from where she sat.

He didn't waste any time and chugged the contents of his glass in two huge gulps. She watched as he poured himself another glass and tossed it back before resting his forearms along the bar's edge. His hands pushed through his black hair, and Kiki noticed a streak of silver in the front before it blended into the rest.

She lifted the glass to her lips and drained it in one swallow, feeling the liquor burn as it raced down her throat and settled in her stomach. She wiped her lips with the back of her hand and looked at Erasmo. His shoulders sagged under an invisible weight, and his eyes held a deep sorrow.

"What happened to your hair?" she asked.

He lifted his chin just enough to meet her gaze, and she felt something inside her chest twist painfully.

"It's a side effect of the curse," he said, his voice a low rumble. "The more the beast takes over, the more our hair turns silver. A symbol of our losing battle." His voice cracked as he said it, and he quickly looked away.

She wanted to reach out to him, to assure him that everything was going to be okay, but she knew nothing she said could make his burden any lighter.

"How long do you have left?" she asked softly, knowing that her line of questioning could come off as rude, but she had to know.

She had to know what Turi's fate would be. It was her fault he'd come into the Cicatrix in the first place. Her fault the curse had taken hold of him.

Erasmo's voice was thick with resentment as he said, "Some of us will have many years left. Might even be lucky enough to see middle age. Others aren't as lucky." He sighed, but she heard the anger and bitterness bubbling, threatening to burst out of him like a geyser. He shook his head and clenched his jaw. "The curse affects those with the most darkness in their hearts. The silver is an outward sign of our inward depravity. Or so my twin used to tell me."

Kiki shifted in her seat and raised an eyebrow. "Where's your twin now?"

Erasmo sneered, his eyes darkening with anger. "He controls his own territory in the north. We had a falling out several years ago and don't speak anymore."

"I'm sorry," she murmured. Kiki didn't know what it was like to have any blood relatives. The closest thing she had to family was Luna and Yari. She shuddered at the thought of having a falling out so bad that the three of them stopped talking.

He shook his head and sighed. "Don't be. Arlando is a weasel. I didn't realize it at first, but he loves the power that control gives him. He was always telling me what to do and who I could talk to. Whispering lies in my ears. Making me paranoid. Keeping us isolated from the rest of the family. He's selfish and only cares about himself and what he wants."

"I can't say that I judge him too harshly. I'm much the same way. Or I've been told," Kiki said, pushing her glass toward him for a refill.

He slowly raised his eyes to meet hers, and the tension between them was palpable. His voice was low and edged with anger when he asked, "Would you sacrifice anything — anyone — just to get what you want?"

She recoiled slightly at the implication, her heart pounding in her chest. "No," she said adamantly. "Not for my own gain. But if someone was preventing me from protecting Luna and Yari, then yes, I'd do anything."

He clenched his jaw and snorted. "That's where you and Arlando differ. He looks out for himself and no one else."

"What did you fight about?"

He hung his head, avoiding her gaze. "The curse," he muttered. She didn't respond, but he continued anyway. "How to break it."

She leaped up from her stool and pressed her palms against the wooden bar top. "You mean you know how to end the curse?" Her eyes were wide, her voice desperate.

He gave a bitter laugh and shook his head. "No. But Arlando is convinced that he does." He downed another gulp of liquor. "You see these totems," he said, holding up the wooden pendant he wore around his neck. "We got them from a spirit woman. She told us of a prophecy that foretold the end of the curse. But it didn't make any sense. Not to me or to any of my cousins. Only Arlando seemed to think he understood."

"I don't understand," she said, her voice strained with frustration. "Don't you want to end the curse?"

He poured himself another drink and tossed it back before setting the glass down firmly. "There are some prices that are too high," he replied, his voice as hard as steel.

She scoffed in disbelief and shook her head. "That's ridiculous. If you've known this whole time, why haven't you done anything?

Why hasn't your brother? I'd give anything to find Yari. To know she's safe."

"What if lifting the curse meant losing everything that you love? Everything you've ever cared about. Would it be worth it then?" Erasmo asked, his voice almost a whisper.

The question hung in the air between them as Kiki mulled over Erasmo's words.

Erasmo sighed and ran a hand through his thick dark hair. "My brother believes the prophecy demands a sacrifice. One from each of the cursed princes. To end the curse, we much each kill the one person in this world that we love most."

Ice slowly crept up Kiki's spine at hearing his words. She felt as if someone had punched her in the gut and knocked the wind from her. She shook her head slowly, her mind balking at the idea.

"Turi would never agree to that," she whispered.

Erasmo's fists tightened around the edge of the bar as he looked at her with a sad, knowing expression. "Now, do you understand?"

Anger and frustration and confusion bubbled up inside Kiki's chest. She didn't like the feeling of being backed into a corner and left with no options. There was always a solution.

"No," she growled as she slammed her glass down on the bar. She yelped as a shard pierced her already injured hand and she quickly grabbed a nearby towel to wrap the wound. "There has to be another way. You said you didn't believe your brother's interpretation. There must be another way to look at it."

Erasmo exhaled deeply, and his shoulders slumped with exhaustion. She could see how the mantle of leadership weighed on him. She understood that feeling all too well. "If there is, we haven't figured it out yet."

"What about this spirit woman? Maybe we can ask her — "

Erasmo shook his head vehemently. "Absolutely not."

"Why?" she asked, desperation leaking into her voice. "I can't just let Turi become some mindless beast. We have to cure him!"

Erasmo gripped the neck of the tequila bottle so tight that his knuckles turned white. "You must really love him."

She pushed away from the bar and began to pace. "Why does everyone think that?" she asked, her tone harsher than she had intended. She softened her voice before continuing. "I didn't mean it like that. Your brother, he's a good guy. Sweet. Considerate. Kind. Caring. But, no, I don't love him like that. I care for him. Even though I try not to. I do care for him. I want the best for him. But we never should have dated. I realized that too late, and I regret it every day."

Erasmo seemed to calm at her response as he tipped back the liquor straight from the bottle.

But Kiki felt anything but calm. She grabbed the bottle from him and took five big gulps herself. Everything was going to hell. And she hated feeling helpless about it. She wanted to act. To find a solution. But it was like every way she turned, there was a thirty-foot wall waiting to stop her.

He searched her gaze and asked in a low, quiet voice, "Have you told him that? That you regret being with him?"

She hung her head, her black hair obscuring her face. "I didn't want to break his heart more than I already had," she whispered.

"And if you were with someone else?"

Her head shot up, and her eyes blazed. "There is no one else! Nor do I want there to be."

Erasmo walked from behind the bar and ran a hand over his weary face. "What do you want?" He was so close his body heat wrapped around her. Without thinking, she took a deep breath of his scent. He stepped closer. "Tell me, what does the fearless demon Slayer want?"

Without thinking, she blurted out the only thing that had been on her mind for the entire day. She wanted to escape her reality for just a moment. She didn't want to think about curses or ex-boyfriends, or best friends. She just wanted a moment of peace.

"A distraction." Heat warmed her cheeks at the admission.

Erasmo moved even closer and lifted his hand to her face, gently tracing the line of her cheek until his thumb brushed across her bottom lip. "What kind of distraction?" he whispered, his voice low and husky.

The tequila made her feel bold, so she said, "The kind that no one ever has to know about."

Erasmo's eyes flared, and he crashed his lips to hers, his hands threading into her hair as he pried her mouth open with his tongue. A moan slipped past her lips, and he yanked her from the stool, wrapped his hands around her waist, and hoisted her to sit on top of the bar. He pressed himself between her thighs, and she felt his hard cock press against her pussy.

He broke away, his chest laboring for breath and his eyes hooded as their gazes locked. "Is this what you had in mind?" he asked, breathless.

"Definitely." She pulled his mouth back to hers and ran her hands down his perfectly sculpted chest. His muscles twitched under her touch as she continued to explore his body, her hands inching further and further south. She looped her fingers into his pants and began to tug at the buttons when he pulled away again.

"Not here," he growled, his gaze flicking to the broken glass on the bartop and the sticky black demon ichor that splattered over every inch of the place.

Without warning, he gripped the back of her knees and lifted her off the bar. He slammed his lips into hers, and she could feel him moving them to another part of the inn.

Erasmo reached a closed door and kicked it open. Kiki yelped in surprise when he plopped her down onto the bed, but her protest died in her throat when he climbed on top of her, his full weight pressing between her legs, his chest flush against hers.

He pulled at the zipper of her Slayer leathers, exposing her breasts. Taking one into his mouth, he used the other hand to roll her nipple between his forefinger and thumb. She felt her back arc off the bed as he worked her body into a spiral of pleasure.

He popped his mouth off and assaulted her mouth with his tongue, his lips frenzied and his breath ragged as he claimed her mouth.

She ran her hands down his torso and yanked at the hem of his shirt, ripping it off his head and tossing it onto the ground. For a second, she marveled at his smooth skin and the smear of blood where his wound had been just hours before. "It's completely gone," she said as he leaned down and nibbled at the side of her neck.

"Your blood healed me." His hot breath ghosted across the shell of her ear, sending a shiver through her body.

She wanted more of him. The feelings he was stirring up in her body — she had never felt this way before. She didn't know sex could be so passionate. So desperate and charged with lightning. She wanted more.

She set to undo his pants again, but he gripped both of her wrists into one of his hands and hoisted them above her head, pinning them to the mattress.

"I thought pregnancy killed a Slayer's career faster than a demon," he said, his tone teasing.

She wriggled beneath him, the heat building in her pussy too much and demanding release. "Just pull out when you come."

Even to her ears, she sounded desperate, but she was too full of need to care. Pride be damned. She wanted this man. More than she had ever wanted a man before. She wanted to feel him inside her.

He kissed her lips once more and smiled. "When I fuck you, it will be completely and without restraint," he said into her ear, his words coaxing a moan from her lips.

He released her hands and yanked the zipper of her leathers until she was totally exposed. His eyes flared as he took her in, and he peeled the leather from her skin until she was completely bare before him. He spun her around until her back was pressed to his chest and dove his hand between her thighs.

"For now, you'll just have to settle for this," he said as he plunged his fingers into the wetness between her thighs and pushed into her pussy, sinking his fingers inside.

She cried out in surprise and felt him tuck his head between her neck and shoulder. He grazed her skin with his teeth as he continued to work his fingers in her pussy.

She let out a soft moan as the feel of his fingers inside her stroked a fire, kindling it until it was a raging inferno. She had never felt this way before. All the times she'd slept with Turi had been sweet and exploratory, but she had never crested over that hill before. Never felt herself climb to that peak.

"Come for me," he hummed as he wrapped his other arm under her and cupped her breast. "Let me feel it," he added, his voice hoarse.

His words were her undoing. She couldn't take the pressure filling her for a second longer. A burst of pleasure ripped through her body, so intense that she cried out Erasmo's name.

"That's a good girl," he said as she gasped for breath, the rhythm of his fingers slowing as he worked her down that exhilarating high.

He pulled his fingers from inside her and brought them to his mouth. His eyes locked on hers as he licked his fingers, a moan leaving his lips as he tasted her.

"You taste divine."

A shiver ran up her spine at his words. He licked his lips and then pressed them to her mouth. She tasted herself on his tongue, and that sent a bolt of hunger through her belly, straight to her pussy.

"Do you want more?" he asked, a smirk tugging at the corner of his mouth.

She nodded. Yes. She wanted more. She wanted all of it. But if this is all he would give her. She would take every second he was willing to offer. He grinned as she spread her legs to grant him access, and he thrust his fingers inside her once more. Giving her exactly what she asked for.

CHAPTER THIRTEEN

CRYPTIC CLUES AND CONFUSED MINDS

YARI

Yari rummaged through the numerous closets in the grand castle, finally coming across a wooden box filled with paints, brushes, and easels. She settled onto a stool and inhaled the smell of turpentine that reminded her of her childhood, sitting at her father's feet as he painted.

Tears misted her eyes at the memory, no matter how faint it was. She quickly brushed the tears away and focused on the blank canvas before her. With a deep breath, she unscrewed the cap to an emerald green paint tube and set to creating a color palette.

As she laid out her materials, her mind went blank. Though joy filled her heart at how many colors she had at her fingertips, she couldn't think of what to paint. Back at the Demon Corps base camp in Norcera, she would jump at any opportunity to draw or paint. Even when she had no supplies, she would still find a way to create, even drawing out stories in the dirt to tell Kiki and Luna.

Her heart lurched at the thought of her best friends. She missed them so much. She was heartsore knowing that she would never see them again. She could only hope that they were safe and had taken assignments along the Southern wall as the three of them had always planned to do after graduation.

Without thinking, she dipped her paintbrush into a pool of pitch-black paint and let her brush move as if of its own accord.

Yari hunched over the canvas, oblivious to the passage of time. Sweat dripped down her forehead, and the smell of paint and turpentine filled the air.

Her eyes widened in horror as she stepped back to inspect her work. The half-bear half-man demon had come to life on the canvas. The monster stared back at her, a feral growl on its lips and its talons stretching out to grab her. Yari shuffled back, feeling a chill run up her spine. Then, with a scream of frustration, she ripped the still-wet painting from its frame and threw it across the room.

A loud thud from just outside the sitting room suddenly made Yari look up. Pilar stumbled into the room, her features wild and disheveled. Her grey curly hair was an unkempt nest of tangles atop her head, and her nightgown was smeared with what appeared to be dried blood. To make matters worse, she was barefoot, her lips a shade of blue that Yari knew could only come from being outside in the cold for too long.

Pilar's eyes were wide and vacant, but then suddenly they seemed to focus on something behind Yari. The only thing that made Yari recognize her was the shiny silver necklace hung around her neck. Pilar appeared crazed, like a feral animal seeking food, yet when their eyes met, Yari could see a moment of unexpected recognition pass between them.

Yari recognized the look in Pilar's eyes. She had seen it before when Pilar was wandering around the West Wing, mumbling to herself and launching into incomprehensible rants. She'd scarred Yari half to death when she yelled at Yari before running off.

At the time, Yari didn't know who Pilar was and didn't recognize her. Now that Yari had seen Pilar at the dinner table several times, she recognized her appearance but didn't understand the state of the older woman.

Yari cautiously walked up to Pilar as the woman's thin, reed-like fingers fumbled for the locket around her neck. "Aunt Pilar? Are you alright?" she asked, her voice low and soft.

Pilar's shoulders tensed, and Yari recoiled, expecting her to whip around and yell at Yari again, but the woman didn't seem to hear Yari as she shuffled past her toward the bookshelf along the back wall.

Pilar's lips were trembling, and her voice was soft. She was desperate and on edge. "It's here. I know it is. No, don't tell me what to do. I have to find it. I have to. He'll kill her. He will. He must be stopped."

Yari felt a chill rush through her body, and she stepped back. Her heart raced as she asked, "Who must be stopped? Pilar?" She tried to touch Pilar's shoulder, but she recoiled and held up a sharp letter opener against Yari's neck.

Pilar's voice rose to a fever pitch, and her eyes filled with terror. "He must be stopped. He'll kill her!"

Yari froze. The letter opener quivered against her neck. "Who? Who is he? Who is he going to hurt?" She repeated the question, but Pilar didn't answer. The fear in Yari's belly grew as Pilar's hand trembled and the blade pressed harder against her neck, causing a trickle of warm blood to run down her chest.

"Pilar Ozetero!" a deep voice boomed from the doorway, making both Yari and Pilar jump.

Arlando strode into the room, eyes widening as he spotted the knife opener clenched in his aunt's hand and a bead of blood trickling down Yari's neck. He ripped it from her fingers, his movements quick and angry.

"What do you think you're doing?" he demanded, voice booming through the room.

Pilar merely shook in response, her muttering too quiet to decipher, and Arlando leaned forward, rage scrawled across his face.

"ANSWER ME!" he shouted.

Yari felt a chill in the air when Arlando's voice grew loud and angry with Pilar. She quickly sprang between them, her heart pounding in her chest, her eyes pleading.

"Please, don't yell at her. She's clearly unwell!" Yari begged him.

His fists clenched tight, and his face contorted with rage. But Yari held her ground and stared straight into his eyes, hoping he'd see the concern that she felt. The tension was palpable, yet she stood firm.

Finally, he exhaled a heavy sigh, and his body relaxed. "You're right," he said softly. "I'm sorry."

Pilar drifted to the far corner of the sitting room, her eyes darting around the bookcase. She yanked the nearest volume from the shelf, flipped open its cover, and gave it a vigorous shake before tossing it to the floor. She continued to rip each book from its shelf, roughly flipping through its pages before dropping them with a dull thud, creating a small pile on the marble floor.

"What's happened to her?" Yari asked, slowly inching closer to the woman. "Why is she acting like this? She wasn't like this the other night," she continued, her gaze shifting to Arlando for an answer.

Arlando ran a hand over his face as he released a pent-up breath. "That's because you met Mara, my aunt's alternate personality," he said, gently placing a hand on Pilar's shoulder. "And this," he gestured, his voice softening, "is Pilar."

Yari had heard of split personalities before. Luna once explained that most people are born with the condition, but sometimes, severe trauma could cause a person to create another personality to take over. There was always a more dominant personality; it just depended on which was strongest.

"I'm so sorry," Yari said, her voice faltering as she spoke. Her brown eyes filled with sadness, and her hands twisted the edges of her dress as if wringing out the last drops of hope.

Arlando sighed and shook his head slowly. "Pilar is the dominant personality, but only Mara is the one that is lucid. She takes care of my aunt."

Just then, a knock echoed from the door to the sitting room, and a guard stepped forward with a letter in his hand. "A raven, Lord."

Arlando ran his hands through his black hair and sighed, the tension radiating off him in waves. With a determined chin, he turned to leave and then swung back around, his dark eyes meeting Yari's. "Can you make sure she gets back to her room? I don't want her wandering around and getting hurt."

Yari nodded, her lips pressed into a firm line. "Of course."

Arlando snapped his gaze away and strode towards the door, the guard on his heels like a shadow.

Yari watched as Pilar's eyes darted from one book on the shelf to the next. She seemed desperate as if the fate of the world depended on finding it. Turning to Pilar, Yari asked her again, "What are you looking for?"

Pilar let out a deep breath, her voice wavering as she finally looked away from the bookshelf and met Yari's gaze. "It's here," she said. "I know it is. The answer."

Yari stepped forward, each movement precise and cautious. She extended her hand and asked, "I'm going to hold your hand, now. Is that okay?"

Pilar eyed Yari's outstretched hand warily before giving a slow nod.

Pilar's hands were cold and rough; her fingernails caked in dirt. When Yari looked down at Pilar's feet, she saw they were crusted with snow and bleeding from the sharp rocks they had walked over.

Yari turned to Pilar and pleaded, "Aunt Pilar, can I take you back to your room and get you cleaned up? You'll catch a cold if we don't get you warmed up."

For a moment, Pilar's eyes seemed clear, the fog that had taken over her mind seeming to have vanished. But just as quickly as that clarity emerged, it was quickly smothered. With a vacant expression, Pilar nodded her head and let Yari lead her out of the room.

Yari led pilar through the cold and damp castle corridors, their footsteps echoing in the empty hallways. When they reached Pilar's room, Yari opened the wooden door to reveal a small but opulent room. The ivory-colored walls were draped in thick curtains of red velvet, and delicate chandeliers adorned with sparkling crystals hung from the ceiling, giving the room a warm, inviting glow.

A beautiful tapestry hung over the headboard of the large bed covered in swaths of white fur blankets. Gold and silver trinkets decorated every available surface in the room, and leather-bound tomes lined the shelves of a floor-to-ceiling bookshelf. Yari stared in awe at the stark contrast of Pilar's room to the rest of the castle, almost like it were a hidden oasis.

Yari didn't linger too long before leading Arlando's aunt into the adjoining bathroom. Yari sat on the edge of the large porcelain tub and turned on the hot water. It still amazed her that the water here wasn't ice cold no matter what tap was used. When the tub was full, she helped Pilar out of her filthy nightdress and guided her into the warm water.

Pilar looked up at Yari with childlike eyes, and her heart ached for the woman. She didn't have to know what Pilar had been through to know that she'd endured something truly awful.

"Can I wash your hair?" Yari asked, moving to grab a bar of soup and a washcloth.

Pilar nodded her consent, and Yari began to gently pick out the twigs and brambles trapped in her grey tresses.

After the bath, Yari helped the fragile woman dry off and sat her in front of a vanity with a mirror so she could brush her hair. The whole time Yari cared for Pilar, she muttered incoherently.

Yari ran a soft bristle brush through Pilar's long curls when Pilar's hand snaked out and grabbed her wrist in a vice grip.

Yari snapped her eyes up to the mirror in shock as a pair of intelligent eyes clashed with hers. "I can take it from here," Pilar said, her voice strong and confident.

"A — Are — Are you Mara?" Yari stuttered.

Mara nodded and took the brush from her numb fingers. "Pilar told you to go."

Yari's brows drew together in confusion.

Mara ran the brush through her dark hair, her eyes not once leaving Yari in the mirror. "That day in the West Wing. Pilar warned you to leave."

Yari gulped the lump in her throat. "I didn't know that was her at the time. She looked — "

Mara stared at her with Pilar's features, but her entire demeanor had changed. This personality was sharp and coarse. The same woman she had met at dinner a few nights ago. "You should run while you can," she said.

"I don't understand why you keep saying that. Why would I run?"

"From him," Mara said. "From Arlando."

"Why?"

Mara's opened her mouth, but a choked sound came out instead. She tried to speak again, but her face turned red, and she gasped for air. Giving up, she said, "I. Can't. Say."

"I don't understand," Yari whispered, shaking her head.

Mara slammed the brush to the top of the vanity. "Run. That's all I can say."

She backed away from her. "But why? Arlando has been nothing but generous to me. Why do you hate him?"

Mara's eyes shot daggers at Yari. "RUN!"

Yari backed into the edge of the bed, holding her hands out to protect herself.

Mara leaped to her feet and cornered her. "RUN!"

Yari held her hands up and covered her face. "Stop, please, you're scaring me!"

"RUN!" Mara wailed again. "RUN!"

So she did. Yari ran from Pilar's room and stumbled into the room she shared with Arlando. Her skin crawled as if a thousand cockroaches ran across her arms and she shivered as she dove into the bed and covered her head with the blankets.

She stayed there, tears falling from her face. She didn't understand why everyone here was so awful. She felt bad for Pilar, but it was clear that Mara was equally lost.

Yari wished for her friends for the hundredth time. She wanted to be with Kiki and Luna. She wanted their comfort and their protection. She wanted them to hold her and tell her that everything was going to be okay. But she couldn't have those things. So her heart cleaved in two, and her tears ran like a waterfall onto her pillow.

CHAPTER FOURTEEN

SPIES GET NO GOODBYES

KIKI

The smell of eggs and bacon lured Kiki from her sleep. Bleary-eyed, she wandered out of the bedroom and into the main hall of the inn. There the sizzling sound of cooking greeted her ears, and she found Erasmo moving about the kitchen as he added fresh tomatoes and peppers to the eggs.

"Smells delicious," she said as she leaned over the counter, her mouth watering as he moved the bacon to a plate.

"Morning," he said, a satisfied smirk on his face. "Did you sleep okay?" There was a note of gloating in his voice, and if the way he was licking his lips, she knew exactly what he was actually talking about.

She felt herself blush at his innuendo, and her mind happily rushed to relive the night before. Her body hummed as it remembered his expert hands. The way he moved those hands. The feel of his mouth against her skin. The way his teeth grazed along her most sensitive parts.

"I take that look on your face to be a 'yes'," he said, a look of triumph settling over his handsome features. He tossed a towel over his shoulder and flipped the eggs in the pan. "How do you like your eggs? Soft yolk, medium hard yolk, or yolk cooked all the way through?"

Kiki had no idea what Erasmo was talking about. There was only one kind of egg in the Demon Corps, the yellow squishy kind that looked like clumps of sour milk. That's even if eggs were available.

He turned around to face her, and his eyes missed nothing. He quirked his head and said, "You don't know, do you?"

She shrugged her shoulders and took a seat at the end of the counter on a tall wooden stool. "When there isn't enough food to go around, you don't exactly have the luxury of being picky."

He nodded. "I'll make one of each. Then you decide which you like best," he said as he pulled an egg from the pan and plated it.

The outside of the egg was white, and the center was a gooey bright orange. The next egg had more white as did the last, but when she cut into each, one had a hard inside, and the other the orange liquid spilled across the plate. That was the one she liked the most.

She dipped her bacon into the running yolk and closed her eyes, savoring the taste of grease and real meat on her tongue.

She didn't notice that she had been making little sounds of pleasure until Erasmo dropped his fork and braced his hands on either side of his plate.

He leveled his brilliant blue gaze at her, his eyes half-lidded. "If you keep that up, I'm going to get jealous."

She felt a thrill rush through her spine at the look of hunger in his eyes. Feeling brave, she dipped the last of her bacon into the yolk and made a point to stare him right in the eyes as she let a soft moan leave her lips.

Erasmo's eyes flared, and he leaped from his seat and crashed into her, his arms wrapping around Kiki as he pressed his hips into hers and pinned her to the counter.

"Are you asking for more?" he growled as he dipped his lips to the shell of her ear. "Did I not satisfy you?"

She whimpered at the hard feel of him pushing against her and felt her stomach flipping over itself.

He groaned against her neck and, in one fluid motion, lifted her on top of the counter. Without hesitating, he ripped the loose-fitting sleep pants she had been wearing into ribbons and grabbed her knees, spreading her legs wide open.

"What are you — " she started to protest, but then he dropped to his knees before her pussy. Whatever she was going to say died in an instant.

"I've already had my main meal for the day," he growled as he tossed her legs over his shoulders, wrapping his arms around her legs and settling his hands over her lower belly. "It's time for dessert." He lowered his mouth to her pussy and pressed his expert tongue against her sensitive clit.

A spike of pleasure had her arching her back, but he only tightened his grip on her hips, his tongue becoming demanding and insistent. He released one hand and snaked it under her shirt, his fingers latching around her nipple as he rolled it between his fingers.

She knew this man would be the death of her. She just didn't know that she would enjoy that death so much.

She cried out his name as the pressure built at the base of her spine and threaded her hands through his soft black hair. He hummed in approval, and that was enough to send her crashing over the edge.

His tongue slowed as he coaxed her back down from that ledge, and she gasped for breath, her chest heaving for air.

He got to his feet and stood between her legs, his hands gripping her thighs. "I love hearing you say my name as you come." He lifted a hand to caress her cheek as he pressed his lips to hers.

She tasted herself on his tongue, and he moaned softly into her mouth.

His kiss became more insistent, and she gripped the waistband of his pants, wanting him inside her.

He broke away, his chest heaving. "I want you so bad," he said, and she could tell just how much he wanted to be inside her pussy.

She wrapped her legs around his waist, pulling him closer because she wanted the same thing. "Then take me," she said as she crashed her lips to his.

He moaned against her mouth and broke away, pushing her back with both hands on her shoulders. "We can't," he said, panting.

"Just pull out," she insisted, trying to bring him in closer.

"No!" He pressed his forehead to hers, and she could see just how much she was fraying at his willpower. "Not yet. Not until I can have you completely."

She sighed and unwound her legs from his waist. "Fine. Then I'm going to take a bath." She slipped off the counter and walked past the destroyed pair of pants.

Feeling bold, she gripped the hem of her shirt and pulled it over her head. Turning to face him, she tossed the fabric at him before turning on her heel and letting him get a full view of what he was missing out on.

She heard a feral growl follow after her, and she smiled to herself.

A couple of hours later, they were on the road again. Kiki sat in the front of the saddle with Erasmo seated right behind her.

Erasmo pointed out landmarks in his territory as they rode. She listened, but barely. Her mind was now abuzz with the fact that the moment they reached La Aguilera, reality would set in.

Yari was still missing. There was still a curse to break, and she had no idea how to break it. And there was still the matter of the abducted people from the Norceran base camp.

"Are you even listening to me?" Erasmo's voice broke her from her whirlwind of thoughts.

"Sorry," she mumbled. "I just have a lot on my mind."

They rode on in silence for a few more moments when she opened her mouth. "About last night," she started.

"Yes?" he said, his voice playful. "Does someone want more?" he asked as he switched the reigns into one hand and pressed the other to her lower belly, his thumb slowly moving further south.

"No," she blurted. His hand stopped. "I mean, yes, to that. But also, no. That's not what I was talking about." Kiki felt him freeze behind her, and she let out a heavy sigh. "He can't know, okay? It'll kill him."

Erasmo's voice darkened as he said, "You mean my brother." It wasn't a question.

She nodded, feeling like an asshole for saying it.

"Do you want to stop?" he asked, the crack in his voice betraying that he didn't want her to say 'yes'.

She shook her head.

"So you want to keep us a secret?"

She nodded.

"For how long?"

Kiki stayed silent, feeling like a complete jerk the longer the silence grew between them.

Erasmo pulled his horse to a stop and tilted her chin so that she looked up at him over her shoulder. His eyes bore into hers with an intensity that set her heart racing.

"This isn't just some fling," he said roughly. "You know that, right? This thing between us is something more. You feel it, don't you?"

She did. She couldn't explain it, but Erasmo made her feel alive. Like he knew what she needed and delivered without her having to ask. She closed her eyes and nodded into his hand.

"Good," he whispered as he ran his thumb across her bottom lip. "It'll be our little secret," he added, an unspoken promise behind his words.

She let him tip her head back further, and he slammed his mouth over hers. His tongue went to war with hers, and when they parted, they stared into each other's eyes, their chests heaving and bodies humming.

They continued on in silence, and Kiki found herself studying every detail around them just so she wouldn't fall asleep. She noticed a flash of black against the grey and white trees and spotted a black raven perched on a limb.

She ignored the bird at first, thinking nothing of it until an hour later, she saw the raven again. But that was silly. There had to be lots of ravens in this area. There was no way it could be the same bird.

Another hour passed, and the hairs along her back stood on end. There it was again. The raven.

Sensing her unease, Erasmo spoke up. "What's wrong?"

Kiki shook her head. Maybe she was imagining things. She was tired, and riding was taking a toll on her body. "It's probably nothing," she said softly.

"Tell me," he said, his voice gentle.

"You're going to think I'm losing my mind."

"Try me," he said, a chuckle vibrating through his chest and into her spine.

"There is a black raven up there," she motioned with her chin, "in the trees, and I swear, it's following us."

Kiki felt Erasmo shift in the saddle behind her as he looked. He shifted back and gripped the reigns tighter. "You're not losing your mind. It's a spy."

"What?" she hissed, twisting in the saddle to get a good look at his face to make sure he wasn't messing with her.

His gaze trailed along the bandolier across her chest and the obsidian tlazons tucked into their sleeves.

"How good of a shot are you?" he asked, a hint of mischief glittering in his blue eyes.

She didn't dignify his question with a response, simply leveled him with a steely gaze that said it all.

"Okay, don't kill me for asking," he chuckled. "Think you can reach it from here?" he asked, jerking his chin in the direction of the raven.

She nodded and slipped a tlazon from its sheath. Slowly, she glanced back to the raven, making sure that it wouldn't take flight as soon as she moved too quickly. Getting a good gauge on its location, she flipped the tlazon in her hand flat against her palm and quickly raised her arm, flicking her wrist and letting the throwing lance fly through the air.

The bird squawked as the tlazon arced in the air right toward it, and, at the last second, the bird jumped out of the way, a few black feathers falling to the ground in its wake. But Kiki had anticipated that the creature might attempt to flee and had aimed at a spot just above the raven's head. The raven let out a piercing squawk as her tlazon pierced through its heart, and it fell into the snow with a dull thud.

"Damn," Erasmo murmured, a note of awe in his voice. "Remind me to never doubt you again."

A rush of satisfaction filled Kiki's veins at his praise, but she forced herself to push it away. No more distractions. Shaking herself free of the unwanted emotion, she asked, "Who'd send a spy, to begin with?"

"I have a feeling I know who," he said, his tone dark. "And I think I know who hired Tomás to kidnap us." He hung his head and shook it. "My brother. My twin. Arlando."

"Why would he do that?" Kiki asked, her brows furrowed.

"Because he wants to break the curse," Erasmo whispered darkly as a red sheen clouded his eyes.

Kiki didn't press him for more information as they continued in silence for the rest of the day. Close to sunset, they crested a hill that overlooked a massive structure situated in the center of a piece of land separated from the rest.

Kiki marveled at the sight sprawled before her. This was the eyrie. La Aguilera.

CHAPTER FIFTEEN

A LITTLE ROMANTIC CHEMISTRY

LUNA

Mauricio's face lit up as he spotted Luna in the dining hall and waved her over. He had a gleam in his eye and motioned for her to follow him, saying excitedly, "Come, I have something to show you!"

Luna looked up at him and his toothy grin, feeling the corners of her mouth tugging into a matching smile. She quickly finished the last bit of her empanada and stood up, not wanting to keep him waiting.

She carried her plate to the end of the hall, where two servants leaned against the wall, ready to take the dishes into the back for cleaning.

As she approached Mauri, her heart fluttered; his deep brown eyes meeting hers.

He smiled a mischievous grin before reaching out to take her hand in his. A wave of warmth cascaded through her body as her fingertips touched his, and a blush bloomed across her cheeks.

"What's so important that I couldn't finish my breakfast," she teased.

However, Mauricio didn't catch her playful tone and dropped her hand. "I'm sorry — I didn't mean — "

He started to stumble over his words, and she laughed as she grabbed his hand and started pulling him away from the dining hall.

"I'm just playing with you. I've never eaten so much in my life," she said as she looped her arm in his. She couldn't explain her seemingly sudden comfort around him. Perhaps it was because he'd slept on her floor all night, providing her a much-needed sense of security.

She had woken this morning to find him curled on the hard wooden floor, his head resting on his arm and his knees tucked into his chest.

She had slept better than she had in a long time, and she credited his presence for feeling so well-rested. She didn't know what it was about him that made her feel safe, but she rather enjoyed his company, and for now, that was enough.

"Are you sure?" he asked, his brows knitted together with worry.

"Yes," she said, visibly relaxing as she tried to convey her lightheartedness with a wide grin.

Mauricio's gaze shifted to their entwined hands, and she felt the familiar warmth of his skin as he softly squeezed her fingers. His face softened as his eyes slowly returned to hers, and she tried to read his expression. A mix of anguish, guilt, longing, and hope radiated from him, and at that moment, she wanted nothing more than to understand why.

He pulled her forward. "Come, I have something that I know you're going to like."

She noticed the subtle shift in temperature as they descended a spiraling stone stairwell. At the end of the hall was a heavy, wooden door with a strange mechanism that glowed with enchantments.

"You said you were a Healer in the Demon Corps," Mauri said. "My cousin has just returned from a successful reconnaissance mission and brought back some incredible items. I thought you might like to meet him."

A hint of a smile crossed her face as Mauricio pushed open the door, revealing a long room filled with bubbling potions and shelves of strange artifacts. But her grin disappeared quickly as the highly acrid smell of sulfur and smoke filled the air.

She gagged, and Mauricio stepped in front of her, his tall frame blocking the smoke from her face. His face twisted in disgust as he tucked his chin into his elbow to protect himself from the fumes while his voice reverberated through the smoky room.

"Guille! What the hell are you cooking down here? It smells like ass."

A raspy cough and slow dragging footsteps echoed through the laboratory, culminating in Guillermo, the magi, appearing before them. He wore a strange black mask that completely covered his face and was adorned with vents around the nostrils and mouth, and clear windows over his eyes. He gave a start of surprise at the sight of them, ushering them out of the lab and into the fresh air of the hallway.

Guille tugged off the mask, revealing his tired face, and asked, "What are you doing here? Is there something wrong?"

Mauricio peered over Guille's shoulder as he inspected a pile of metal scraps, glass tubes, and other assorted contraptions that had been cobbled together on the lab table. "What monstrosity are you working on now?" he asked, eyeing the smoke wafting from the lab with mild suspicion.

Guille smiled, his fingers twitching with anticipation. "I'm close to a breakthrough. I just need to make a few more tweaks," he said.

Luna drifted closer, her nostrils flaring as she registered the smell of burnt sulfur and the metallic taint of charred metal. Curiosity got the better of her as she opened her mouth to speak. "A breakthrough to what?" she asked, her nose crinkling in distaste. The pungent scent in the air smelled like failure to her.

Guille turned to face Luna, and his eyes darted over her delicate features, taking in her hazel brown eyes, full lips, and high cheekbones. He opened his mouth to answer her question but suddenly seemed tongue-tied.

A deep, menacing growl reverberated through Mauricio's chest like thunder, and Guille quickly shook his head as if clearing it.

"Erm, sorry," Guille stammered, flushing. "I'm not used to seeing women in the manor — except for those that come to service the men — "

Mauricio quickly jabbed an elbow into Guille's stomach, earning himself a reproachful glance from his cousin.

"What are you working on?" Luna asked, deciding to ignore the fact that he mistook her for a sex worker. She could forgive him for that misjudgment, but only this once. Besides, her curiosity was still piqued.

Guille shifted his weight and pointed in the direction behind him without turning around. "Oh, that? I'm trying to infuse objects with magical abilities, sort of like the totems used by the Ozero males to control their shifts."

Mauri scrunched up his nose and coughed, a hand covering his mouth as he looked towards the room Guille was referring to. "Why does it smell like something died in there?" he asked.

"Well, there was a little explosion when the spell and the object came into contact, but that's better than what's been happening!" Guille's eyes were bright, and he looked hopeful.

"If an explosion is an improvement, I'd hate to see the failures," Luna said with a playful smile.

Guille stared at her, open-mouthed once more, and a blush flooded his cheeks.

Marui kicked him in the chin, which made him snap out of it.

"Ouch," Guille cried as he bent down to nurse his leg. He shot Mauri a glare, his nostrils flaring. "What are you doing down here besides beating me up?" he asked, his heated gaze still on his cousin.

Mauri motioned toward Luna. "She's a magicked Healer, and I thought she'd like to take a look around your lab. Maybe help you with some of the healing that you do."

Guille turned his eyes to Luna and grinned. "Are you really a magicked Healer? We haven't had a Healer since the shift took our uncle permanently."

Before Luna could express her condolences for their loss, Guille grabbed her hand and pulled her into his lab.

She heard Mauricio make another feral sound, but this time Guille didn't pay him any attention.

Guille's smile was infectious as he pulled Luna into his lab and started to jabber on. "We don't need a Healer most of the time since the Ozero males can heal on their own, but sometimes, there are injuries that need help or those of us who aren't part of the direct line get injured, then we need a real Healer." He motioned to a work desk with an array of poultices and glass bottles of tinctures. "I've been keeping everything stocked up and fresh, so you can do what you want with it. Rearrange it, reorganize it, dump it all out, and start from scratch if you want. It won't bother me."

She was speechless as she looked at the multitude of herbs, oils, tinctures, cleansing agents, and bandages that Guille offered. "I don't know what to say," she plucked a glass jar from the table and examined the contents. "Is this what I think it is?"

Guille examined the glass. "Yes, those are human teeth."

"What possible use could you have for them," she asked, somewhat appalled but also curious.

"They act as a good mixing agent for the more viscous ointments," he responded matter of factly. "Don't worry; they're ethically sourced. Anytime someone loses a tooth, they bring it here."

Luna supposed if that was the case, then she could accept it. Even if the sight of so many made a shiver travel down her spine.

She grabbed another bottle and recognized the contents as oil of lavender. "A bottle this size would be worth a fortune where I come from," she said, gently setting it back down.

"What do you use for pain relief?" Guille asked, his eyes bright and curious.

"Usually nothing," she murmured, her eyes appraising the bottles and their contents. "Maybe some tequila if we can spare it." Guille's face twisted as he made a noise expressing his horror. "We're not well supplied in the north. Or anywhere, for that matter. Meals consist of more broth than meat or rice most days, so it's no surprise we lacked in supplies."

Mauricio made a choked sound next to her, and she looked at him with raised brows, but he quickly cleared his throat and moved off to another part of the lab. She frowned after him, watching the way his hands curled into fists at his sides.

"We don't have a shortage of supplies here, so if you need anything, just let me know, and I'll get it for you," Guille offered.

She felt a smile tug at the corner of her lips as a feeling of gratitude spread through her chest and made her stomach fill with butterflies. Shortages and lack of supplies, and going without had been her entire life. The people she could heal with the right tools — it took her breath away.

She turned to Mauricio, who lurked in the shadows, and said with a smile, "Thank you for bringing me here. I can't begin to tell you how much this means to me."

His eyes grew wide at her thanks, and he rubbed the back of his neck as he turned his gaze away. "Anything you want, *chiqui*. All you have to do is ask."

She felt herself blush at his words and quickly looked away and busied herself with rearranging the glass jars. "Maybe I can see you later?" she said, trying to hide the hopeful note in her voice but failing miserably.

"Without a doubt," he murmured before he slipped out of the lab.

She followed him with her eyes and felt a shiver run up her spine as she watched his muscular form leave and go up the stairs.

"So," Guille's voice forced her to tear her gaze away. "What do you want to work on first?"

A wild thought popped into her head at his question, and she couldn't help but blurt out, "What do you do here for contraceptives?"

Guille's eyes widened, and a blush ran across the bridge of his nose. "I cook up a brew and give it to the interested party," he said, his face turning redder by the second. "I can make one for you right away if you need it," he added, turning his face away to hide his embarrassment.

Realizing he thought she was asking for herself, she quickly said, "Oh, no, not for me. I haven't — I mean — I don't — What I meant is I've noticed a lot of the Ozero men seem to have really high sexual drives. I was just wondering what protections you have in place for the women who help them satisfy those urges. I've been propositioned at least a dozen times already," she added with a laugh, but it quickly died on her lips at the look of pure embarrassment on Guille's face. "Maybe we can work on infusing an object with a contraceptive brew or spell so that you don't have to cook one up every time one is needed."

He rubbed the back of his neck and said, "Right, of course. I didn't mean to imply — I just thought — you and Mauri — "

"I'm not with him," she blurted and winced at the defensiveness she could hear in her own voice. "I mean — he's handsome, so very kind — and he has the body of a warrior — " She snapped her mouth closed at the realization that now she was the one rambling. A blush blossomed across her cheeks, and she turned her face away so Guille couldn't see.

"How about we just get started?" Guille offered, clearly equally embarrassed by their line of conversation.

"Yes," she said, turning back to face the work table, "Let's do that."

CHAPTER SIXTEEN

SECRETS, LIES, AND MATE BONDS

ERASMO

E rasmo's grip on the reigns tightened as they cantered down the winding road leading to La Aguilera. The closer they got to the looming black gates, the tighter the knot of dread in his stomach became.

Without thinking, he grabbed Kiki's waist and pressed her against his chest, dipping his nose to take in the smell of her hair, her skin, her very essence. His grip tightened as he tried desperately to memorize her scent. He knew that the second they passed through the gates, she'd leap off his horse and go running into his younger brother's arms. Leaving Erasmo behind.

He told himself that she would embrace her other friends too, that they must all have been worried about her, but it wasn't enough to dampen the feelings of jealousy ripping through his gut.

Guards along the ramparts sounded the alarms, alerting the rest of the eyrie that Erasmo had returned.

The sound of metal scraping and grinding against the stone walls filled the air as the gates opened. The ancient mechanisms creaked and groaned as they passed through and were greeted in the main courtyard by a growing crowd.

Mauricio stood in front of everyone; his arms were crossed over his chest, and a look of disapproval on his face. Standing on either side of him were two men that Erasmo didn't know but immediately recognized by the invisible threads connecting them.

One of the men was larger than even Mauri, his chest wide and his arms thick with muscle. Despite his threatening size, his eyes were welcoming, and he smiled at Erasmo. Erasmo guessed that this was his eldest brother, Bernat, and a gentle tug within his chest confirmed that.

The other man standing with Mauricio was smaller in frame and height. His curly black hair fell to his ears, and his eyes were warm as they fell on Kiki. A pang of jealousy coursed through Erasmo's veins at how much affection he could see Turi had for her. After a moment, his younger brother flicked his gaze to Erasmo and smiled shyly. Turi.

Erasmo slowed his horse as they approached Mauricio. With a gentle tug of the reins, Erasmo brought Ocaso to a stop and leaped off to the ground. He turned to Kiki and held out his arms for her, his eyes twinkling with anticipation. She hesitated for a second before taking his hands and allowing him to help her dismount with a light thud.

As her feet touched the ground, Kiki groaned and rubbed her legs and back. "I'm never riding a horse again," she whined.

Turi rushed forward, his eyes bright with admiration as he reached up and caressed her cheek.

Even from where he stood, Erasmo could see the obvious tenderness in Turi's touch. The way his eyes trailed over Kiki's features as if committing them to memory.

Erasmo's jaw tightened with a warning growl that he refused to release. Though she was his mate, he knew he could never claim ownership over her. Not that he'd ever want to. So he swallowed his rage and clenched his fists at his side, the beast within him thrashing violently in his chest.

Mauri stepped closer, his gaze flicking between Kiki and Turi before he muttered softly to Erasmo, "We need to talk."

Erasmo exhaled heavily and nodded, rubbing his face with his hands. "No kidding."

Bernat stepped forward, his face etched with emotion. "Erasmo?" he choked out. His eyes brimmed with emotion as he opened his arms and embraced Erasmo. He pressed Erasmo to his chest in a tight hug and let out a satisfied sigh. "Look how you've grown," he said, marveling at his younger brother's stature and taking in his appearance. "It's good to see you again, little brother. Though you're not so little anymore."

Erasmo hadn't considered how he'd feel about being reunited with his eldest brother. For so long, he'd pushed away the memory of Bernat, thinking that he'd never see his older brother again and the grief that accompanied those thoughts.

But now, as he was confronted with Bernat standing before him, he couldn't control the wave of emotion that washed over him. The pure relief he felt at seeing Bernat alive and healthy was a strong one — overwhelming even.

Erasmo returned his brother's embrace, feeling like a part of his soul had returned to him.

Before he could get choked up about it, he pulled away and turned to Turi, who had his hands on either side of Kiki's face and was peppering her with questions.

"Are you okay? What happened? How did you get away?" Turi asked Kiki, his eyes roaming over her body as if searching for any injuries.

Erasmo did his best to ignore the primal urge to rip her out of Turi's arms. The beast beneath his skin thrashed against the bars of Erasmo's ribs, begging to be released. It was enough to make Erasmo feel like he was teetering on a razor's edge.

Mauri noticed Erasmo's white knuckles and tapped Turi's shoulder, motioning towards Erasmo.

Turi's eyes widened in surprise as he recognized Erasmo, and a delighted grin spread across his face. "Erasmo! I can't believe it's really you!" He quickly stepped forward and embraced Erasmo in a tight hug.

Erasmo allowed himself to bask in the joy of finally reuniting with his little brother, forgetting, for a moment, that Turi had just put his hands all over Kiki. At this moment, he was just little Arturito.

Yet, the wave of nostalgia quickly faded as a wave of dread washed over him — the implications of their reunion boding ill for the prophecy that loomed above them all.

A sharp, shrill voice cut through the air like a whip, and Erasmo whipped around to see a woman with a body as slender as a birch and hair a deep, fiery red. She was marching down the stairs, a scowl on her face, her frosted blue eyes locked on his mate.

Erasmo felt a deep, guttural growl coming from somewhere within, and he stepped in front of her, blocking her path.

She stopped abruptly and glared at him; her fists clenched at her sides. "Excuse you!" she snapped and made an attempt to dodge him, but he refused to move.

Crossing his arms over his chest, he said in a coarse tone, "I take it you're Solana."

She stepped back, the clicking of her boots the only sound in the tense silence. With deliberate movements, she swept her gaze across him, and he felt himself shrinking under the weight of her appraisal. His shoulders tensed, and he could feel her disapproval.

"So you've heard about me," she said, her voice deadpan. "Good for you. Now, if you'll excuse me, I'd like to have choice words with my subordinate."

Kiki stepped from behind him and wiggled her fingers at Solana in a mocking wave. "Hello to you too, Commander."

Solana cut her gaze to Kiki, her almost white eyes narrowing before she took a deep breath and let it out slowly. The expression on her face softened in a show of relief before she quickly masked it. "You have some explaining to do, Slayer," she said, her voice a dangerous purr, as she pointed her finger at Kiki.

Kiki rolled her eyes as she said in a monotone, "Yeah, yeah. Get in line."

Solana's brows creased into a frown, her hands clenching at her sides.

Before the situation could escalate, Erasmo stepped between the two women. "How about we take this inside?" He looked around at Mauri and his two brothers. "All of us."

"So that's how I ran into Erasmo and how we got here," Kiki said as she finished recounting her story.

Everyone shifted their gaze to Erasmo expectantly. He scanned the table, his eyes not failing to catch the way Marui's eyes lingered on the slender woman with dark ringlets sitting beside Kiki. Her hands were clasped over Kiki's, and she seemed to be close to tears. Erasmo figured this had to be Kiki's best friend, Luna.

Luna broke the silence, her voice quivering as she sobbed, "I'm so sorry!"

Kiki pulled her friend closer and softly murmured something in her ear.

Turi's face contorted in disbelief. His mouth hung open, and his dark eyes were wider than usual. He leaned forward and said, in a voice thick with dread, "So you're saying the only way to break this curse is to kill whoever we love most?" He gave a slight shake of his head; his face twisted in disgust. "That's ridiculous. I won't do it. Not in a million years," he said, his gaze slipping to where Kiki sat, but she was too busy consoling Luna to notice his stare.

But Erasmo certainly noticed, and a wave of red-hot jealousy swept over him. His hands curled into fists, and if it weren't for Mauri clapping his hand on Erasmo's shoulder, pinching the muscle hard, there was no telling what could have come next.

Mauri grabbed a bottle of rum and set it firmly in front of Erasmo, his eyes boring into him as though to say, 'calm the fuck down'.

Erasmo knew that his cousin was right. But that didn't stop the beast within from snarling and thrashing against his ribcage.

As if sensing that Erasmo might lose this battle, Mauri poured a glass full of the amber liquid and shoved it into Erasmo's hand.

Without hesitating, Erasmo leaned back in his chair and tipped back the rum, relishing in the way it burned down his throat, clearing his head of his spiraling thoughts before setting it back down on the table with a thud.

"Don't get all worked up, little brother," Erasmo said, putting emphasis on the word "little" and feeling like a jerk at the way Turi immediately shrank into himself. "I don't believe in Arlando's interpretation of the prophecy, and neither does any of the others who live in the eyrie. No one is sacrificing anyone."

Turi looked away, his mouth a thin line as his hands twisted together in his lap.

Solana shifted in her seat, and she leaned her elbows on the table, steepling her fingers as she said, "What does this prophecy say anyway?"

Mauri answered, his voice taking on a sing-song quality as he said, "For love was sacrificed at the start, so too shall love be sacrificed at the end."

Erasmo spoke up as Solana's face twisted in confusion. "My mother sacrificed her life to put the curse on my father, not knowing that she had also cursed all the males of his bloodline. Alrando believes that the sacrifice must match our mother's death in order to break the curse."

Turi's brows furrowed. "But how does that make any sense? The whole reason our mother cursed our father is that she felt betrayed by him, right? He raised an army of demons, and she wanted to punish him. Why would another betrayal be the key to breaking the curse?"

Erasmo shrugged. If he knew the answer to that, then none of them would be here having this conversation right now. "Arlando believes that the sons must pay for the sins of the father. He thinks there is a symmetry to it." He pushed out his glass for Mauri to fill and drained it before he continued. "But it's horseshit. So, I'll say it again, no one is sacrificing anyone."

Solana turned to whisper in Bernat's ear, and Luna and Kiki began talking with Turi. Seeing that everyone was distracted, Erasmo kicked Mauri's shin and jerked his chin toward the door.

With Mauri on his heels, Erasmo slipped away from the table and walked through the crowded dining hall, making his way to the inner courtyard. He stepped outside, and a cool breeze whispered across his skin. He rolled his shoulders in an attempt to ease the tension that had built there. The door snicked shut behind him, and he turned to face Mauri, opening his lips to speak —

But Mauri rushed forward and grabbed Erasmo's shirt in his hands. "I found her," he said, his irises blood red. "She's here. I found her."

"What the fuck, man? Get off me," Erasmo growled, shoving Mauri away with a look of shock and a hint of annoyance. He'd invited Mauri out here in the first place, yet, it was clear that whatever was going on with his cousin, that tiny detail mattered very little.

Mauri's hands trembled as he ran them through his hair, and Erasmo could see his eyes darting around the courtyard. His jaw clenched and unclenched, and he paced back and forth as if he were searching for a way out. "I didn't think I'd ever meet her. But she's here. And she's perfect — "

Erasmo reached out and firmly grasped Mauri's shoulders. "I'm only going to tell you this once. Calm down and explain what's going on, slowly and clearly."

"My mate," Mauri gasped, his chest heaving. "Luna. She's the one."

Erasmo released his grip and stepped back, stunned into silence.

Mauri began to pace frantically, his fingers twitching as if he were trying to keep a hold of his sanity. He abruptly spun to face Erasmo, his finger inches from his face. "I swear, if anyone lays a hand on her perfect head, so much as disturbs a strand of that luscious hair, I will rip their throats out with my bare hands."

The intensity of his gaze showed that he was ready to make good on his promise. Not that Erasmo would ever doubt Mauri. Everyone knew Mauri was just a tad unhinged.

Erasmo swatted Marui's hand out of his face. "Calm down, psycho. No one is going to hurt her."

Mauri shook his head. "I can't get her out of my head, man. She's all I think about. I'm all frustrated and shit. I can't even go through the day without yanking myself off in some corner. It's fucked up. All I want is her."

Erasmo understood his cousin's frustrations only too well. He felt the same way about Kiki. The image of her perfect backside, as she walked away from him earlier today, sent a rush through his blood and straight to his cock.

"How do I tell her, man?" Mauri asked, resuming his pacing. "How do I say that she's my mate and all I want to do is fuck her into next year?"

Erasmo leaned against a railing and crossed his arms over his chest. With a chuckle, he said, "Well, I wouldn't start with that if I were you."

Mauri groaned in frustration and pulled at his hair with his hands. "What do I do?"

Erasmo shook his head. "Hell, if I know, brother." He had the same problem on his hands. He was about to say so, but the door to the house opened, and a shock of red hair peeked out.

Solana strolled through and closed the door behind her. Her eyes trained on Erasmo, and she said, "Can I have a word with you?"

Erasmo jerked his chin at Mauri, a silent request for him to leave. With a growl, Mauri stormed off back into the house. Through the window, Erasmo saw Mauri take the straightest route back to their table, where Luna still sat with Kiki.

Solana followed his gaze and shook her head. "Should I be worried about him?"

Erasmo shook his head. "No. Mauri is many things, but he wouldn't do anything to hurt your friend."

Solana sighed and faced him. "I thought you should know that one of your magi returned the other day with some disturbing news."

Solana proceeded to fill him in on the disappearances and the storm brewing in the north. He felt his jaw tense at hearing about a storm of magic in the north. Arlando was most certainly up to something. There was no denying that now.

"There's one more thing," she said, looking over his shoulder and out into the maze of hedges. "Bernat and I caught someone sneaking around out here the other night. They sent off a raven, and when we tried to apprehend them, they ran and got away. Vanished, actually. There was a smear of blood on the handle of that door when I came out here. I asked that magi of yours — "

"Blood magic," he finished for her. He felt his face drain of color.

She nodded, her lips pressed into a tight line. "Whatever you plan to do about it, I want in." She crossed her arms over her chest. "Bernat means a lot to me. And I don't take kindly to treachery."

Erasmo couldn't keep the grin from his face. "Are you and him together?"

A blush crept across her nose. "Yes," she said in clipped tones. As if the act of admitting such a simple thing somehow made her weaker.

Erasmo felt a bubble of laughter building in his chest. The Commander and his mate were more alike than Kiki wanted to admit, that was for sure.

"Good," he replied. "Bernat needs someone like you. Someone strong."

She scoffed. "I don't take kindly to flattery."

He chuckled, his respect for her growing. "I'm not blowing smoke up your ass. I can tell you're a leader. The moment you walk into a room, people pay attention. I don't have to know you very well to see those things."

She chewed her bottom lip and nodded, which he guessed was the closest thing to a 'thanks' that he'd ever get from her.

Suddenly, her eyes darted over his shoulder, and she grabbed him and shoved him down. "Get down," she hissed. "Someone is here. Look, over there," she whispered.

He followed her line of sight and saw a figure in a dark emerald cloak slipping through the shadows on the other side of the courtyard.

Whoever it was, didn't seem to see Erasmo and Solana, the chest-height hedge shielding them from sight.

"They're back," Solana hissed. "I'm going after them."

Erasmo grabbed her arm as she darted forward. "Wait."

She yanked her arm from his grip and bared her teeth in a feral snarl.

"Just hold on a second," he said, holding his hands up in a gesture of peace. "You just said you're with my brother. Imagine what he'll do to me if something happened to you on my watch."

"I can take care of myself," Solana hissed.

"I have no doubt. But let me go first. You can cover my back. How does that sound?"

Solana's nostrils flared, but she nodded in agreement. With Solana hot on his heels, they dodged through the gardens, hiding behind hedges until they got closer to the figure in the cloak.

A familiar voice pricked Erasmo's ears, and he knew exactly who was sneaking around. He motioned for Solana to stay put and stood to his full height as he barked out his cousin's name.

"Aurelia!"

His cousin practically leaped out of her boots as she spun around to face him. A jet of black flew from her hands, and a raven cawed indignantly as it soared through the air and away from the manor. He narrowed his eyes as he stared Aurelia down.

"Raz!" she exclaimed, forcing a smile onto her face as she rushed forward and wrapped her arms around him. "I'm so glad you're back! So much has been happening. Did you meet the people I brought with me?"

"Drop the act, Aurelia. You want to tell me what you were doing sneaking around out here when there was a perfectly good party going on inside? It's not like you to pass up a game of cards and a stiff drink."

She shrugged. "It's a bad habit, Raz, don't encourage me," she said with a playful grin. But her smile didn't meet her eyes.

"What's with the raven?"

"Oh, that? You know, just sending my mom a letter. I miss her."

"Really?" he asked. "I didn't know you and Aunt Pilar were on speaking terms these days."

She scuffed her toe in the dirt. "Who told you that lie," she chuckled. "Mom and I made up."

He found that incredibly hard to believe. Aurelia didn't seem to care and continued to prattle on.

"Have you seen your older brother yet? And that redhead around him all the time? Whoa, the looks those two give each other — " she trailed off and laughed. "If I still placed bets, I'd say that Bernat found his mate."

Erasmo stiffened, not liking the turn this conversation had suddenly taken. He risked a glance behind him, knowing full well that Solana was hiding in the bushes. He had to steer the conversation away from mate bonds.

"Stop talking out of your ass and tell me what you're really doing out here."

Aurelia tossed her hands in the air. "You're no fun, Raz. Aren't you the least bit curious? I mean, look at you. How old are you these days? Twenty-six? Twenty-seven?"

"Twenty-four," he said curtly.

"Right! That's what I said. Don't you think it's time you found your mate? I mean, we could finally end the curse. The only one left is you because it's pretty clear that Kiki is Turi's mate — "

A growl ripped from his throat, and before he knew what he was doing, he grabbed his cousin by the throat and pushed her against the ten-foot tall hedge.

"Shut your mouth. You have no idea what you're talking about!" he snarled.

Aurelia's confused face quickly changed to one of understanding. She gasped, her mouth in the shape of an 'O'. "You mean — Kiki — she's *your* mate?"

Erasmo released her from his grasp and stormed off a few paces before coming back and pointing his finger in her face. "Not one word to her. Or I swear — "

The bushes rustled, and he whipped around to see Kiki standing there her mouth open. Solana was standing beside her, wearing an equally shocked expression.

"Kiki — " he sputtered. "I can explain."

If looks could kill, he would be a dead man.

Kiki spared him one last seething glare before turning on her heel and storming off. Solana's gaze darted between him and Aurelia, disgust twisting her features before she ran to catch up to Kiki.

Erasmo hung his head in his hands, knowing full well that the truth was bound to come out. He had just hoped that it would have been under better circumstances.

He rubbed the back of his neck as he returned to the manor. He had a sneaking suspicion that he was about to have his ass handed to him. And if it was Kiki doing the ass-kicking, then he'd endure it with a smile and a 'thank you' at the end of it all. Because he was a lovelorn fool, and she was his entire world.

CHAPTER SEVENTEEN

BREAKING THE BOND

KIKI

L una's hands shook as she enclosed Kiki's in her own, as if she was scared that if she let go, Kiki would vanish in an instant.

Tears glistened in Luna's eyes as her voice trembled. "I'm so, so sorry for all the hurtful things I said last time."

Kiki withdrew her hands from Luna's grasp slowly before bringing her palms up to either side of her friend's face. She settled her gaze on Luna's eyes, hoping that the next words that came from her mouth hit home and clear any doubt Luna may harbor.

Kiki pressed her forehead to Luna's as she said, "No, I'm the one who is sorry. I overlooked the changes in you. It's not that I didn't notice how different you've been since we crossed the Cicatrix. I blatantly pushed my concerns to the side because I was single-minded in my pursuit to rescue Yari. But that was wrong of me. I'm so very sorry. Truly. If I had been there for you, like I should have, then you probably wouldn't have let Aurelia into your heart. She wouldn't have had the power to hurt you."

Tears slipped from Luna's eyes and carved a path down her delicate features. She dropped her chin to her chest as if she was weighed down with shame. "I was a fool. I'm not like you or Solana. I'm weak."

Kiki's grip on Luna's arms loosened, and her eyes softened with understanding as she spoke. She reached up and caressed Luna's cheek with her thumb. "No," she said. "You were hopeful. You were kind. Trusting. Compassionate. All of that makes you Luna. Don't apologize for being exactly who you are, and don't change just because one person fails to appreciate you."

Luna's lips tugged into a sad smile, and her eyes glistened with tears. Kiki wrapped her arms around Luna and drew her into a comforting hug.

"I missed you," Luna said into her shoulder.

"Me too," Kiki said, her voice muffled by Luna's hair. She pulled back slightly and looked into Luna's eyes. "I promise we'll find Yari, and everything will go back to the way it was."

Luna exhaled heavily, her shoulders drooping in hesitation. "I don't think I want that," she murmured.

Kiki's eyebrows lifted in surprise, her mouth slightly agape.

Luna hesitantly continued, her voice barely above a whisper. "I mean, I want to help break the curse, but I like it here. The air is always filled with the aroma of freshly baked goods. The people here are warm, and they treat us like family. I feel safe."

Kiki stared at her friend, her mouth still open in disbelief. "Luna, we're in more danger than we've ever been. We're in the very core of the monster's lair. How can you say any of that?"

Luna avoided Kiki's gaze as she mumbled her apology. "Never mind. It's stupid anyway."

Kiki let out a sigh and rubbed her forehead, regret filling her eyes. "I'm sorry. I've done it again. I'm not actually listening to you, and I'm sorry. I still don't get why you want to stay, but I'm ready to listen and understand."

Luna offered a timid smile, and her voice was barely above a whisper when she said, "Maybe I'll finally tell you about what I saw during the crossing."

Kiki embraced Luna again and said, "Whenever you're ready."

Luna clung tightly in return, and Kiki basked in the comforting warmth of her only family in the world. She vowed to do better for Luna.

Out of the corner of her eye, she noticed Erasmo and Mauricio slip away and duck outside. She looked out the window, following them as they stepped into the courtyard.

Mauricio paced and waved his hands around, looking like a madman.

Erasmo leaned against a railing, his arms crossed over his muscular chest and his feet crossed at the ankles. Dark circles plagued his eyes, and his broad shoulders dropped, showing his exhaustion.

Her mouth went dry at the sight of him, and she felt a ring of heat coil in her belly. Memories of his mouth on her skin came flooding forth, and she had to force them back before Luna noticed and started asking her questions.

A few moments later, Kiki saw Solana join the two men before Mauricio stormed back inside, his eyes darting toward Luna as he pushed his way through the throng of people in the hall to get to her.

Luna's eyes followed his path, and Kiki didn't miss the blush that bloomed across her friend's cheeks.

When he reached the table, Mauricio spoke to Luna, his eyes on her alone. "Can I get you anything? Are you hungry?"

Kiki's stomach rumbled at the mention of food, and she spoke up, "Actually, I'm famished. I'll take whatever is being offered."

Mauricio didn't so much as spare Kiki a glance. His gaze was still trained on her friend. "What about you, Luna?"

"I'm a little hungry," she said shyly. "But only if everyone else is eating. I don't want to have more than my share."

Mauricio snorted and rolled his eyes as a wicked smile spread across his face, revealing his perfect white teeth. "You can have whatever you want, *chiqui*," he said, the corners of his eyes crinkling in a playful grin. He then pushed through the crowd, leaving Kiki and Luna staring in his wake.

Kiki turned to her friend with a questioning look, her eyebrows knitted together in confusion. Luna's face was hidden behind her hand, and her cheeks flushed pink.

"What's going on there?" Kiki asked.

"I don't know," Luna said softly, turning away. "I can't explain it. I just... it feels nice with him. I like the way he is always watching out for me. It makes me feel special."

Kiki couldn't judge. She felt similar toward Erasmo. Speaking of —

"Hey, there are more supplies here, right?" Kiki blurted, her mind returning to the previous night when Erasmo had her squirming beneath him. The thought sent a rush of heat through Kiki's veins, the delicious memories flashing through her mind.

Luna nodded, her brows raised in curiosity.

Kiki wrung her hands together and stared at them, afraid that if she met Luna's gaze, her friend would see right through her.

"Can you make me one of those contraceptive brews? You know, sort of like what you made me that one time my cycle was late, and we thought Turi got me pregnant, but it was just late, so we sold it for extra meat in our soup? Except that I need this one to be preventative."

Luna pursed her lips together as if to suppress a laugh. "How could I forget? You were freaking out, and I had to trade a lot of valuable supplies to get the ingredients."

Kiki bit her bottom lip before asking, "Do you think you can find them more easily here? Leadership here don't seem to be struggling to feed and care for these people."

Luna's narrowed her eyes at Kiki. "Are you planning on getting back together with Turi?"

"Absolutely not," Kiki said, her eyes trained on the window where she could still see Erasmo and Solana talking.

Suddenly, Solana dragged Erasmo to a crouch, and she quirked her head as they scampered off into the hedges.

"Then what do you need it for?" Luna asked, catching her line of sight and frowning when she saw nothing through the windows. "Kiki?"

But Kiki barely heard her. "What are those two up to?" she murmured softly.

It didn't bother her that Solana and Erasmo raced off somewhere together. It was the look on their faces that had her curiosity piqued.

Deciding that she had to find out for herself, she stood in a rush. "Be right back," she said to Luna before darting through the crowd and racing outside.

She followed the deep impressions in the soil, each footstep a testament to Erasmo's lack of training in this particular skill set.

Meanwhile, Kiki found no trace of the Commander's footsteps, another testament to Solana's superior training. Even Kiki had to give credit when it was due.

As Kiki rounded a corner, she collided with a body crouched low to the ground.

"Ouch," Solana hissed. Without hesitation, Solana grabbed Kiki and yanked her down so that they were both kneeling. She pressed her finger to her lips, urging Kiki to stay quiet.

"What's going on?" Kiki whispered, earning her a glare of death from Solana's ice-blue eyes.

Kiki resisted the urge to groan and rebel against Solana's orders. Fine. She'd follow along. This time.

A pair of voices drifted toward them, and Kiki willed her hammering heart to slow so she could hear better.

Kiki immediately recognized the high pitch of Aurelia's voice and balled her hands into fists. There was a list a mile long full of the things she would like to do to the smuggler.

The first of which was to deliver a solid punch to Aurelia's face.

"Don't you think it's time you found your mate?" Aurelia said to Erasmo. "I mean, we could finally end the curse. The only one left is you because it's pretty clear that Kiki is Turi's mate — "

Suddenly, a growl ripped through the air, and the sounds of a struggle reached her ears. "Shut your mouth," Erasmo snarled. "You have no idea what you're talking about!"

What was all this nonsense about mates? What was that? And why was Aurelia saying that she was Turi's mate?

Aurelia made a choked sound, and she guessed that Erasmo was holding her by the throat. Kiki grinned. Good. The lying little thief deserved it.

The sounds of Aurelia struggling paused as she managed to choke out, "You mean — Kiki — she's your mate?"

There was that word again. Surely Aurelia was just making things up. There was no way Erasmo would entertain her for much longer.

But then ice slid down Kiki's back when she heard him say, "Not one word to her. Or I swear — "

Kiki sprang to her feet, her eyes blazing with indignation as she realized that Erasmo knew exactly what Aurelia was going on about. He knew, and he'd kept it from Kiki.

Erasmo whipped around toward the sound of snapping branches and dropped Aurelia to the ground when his gaze snagged on Kiki.

His face turned crimson, and he was already sputtering with an excuse dripping from his mouth, "Kiki, I can explain."

But she couldn't get past the look of guilt written all over his face. He knew what Aurelia was talking about. He knew, and he hadn't bothered to tell her beforehand.

She didn't know what made her madder, that he had kept something from her or that Aurelia had, once again, figured something out before her.

Kiki's face contorted with anger as she whipped her head around and bolted back toward the party.

She pushed her way inside, her body trembling with rage. She clenched her fists tightly, the need to punch something becoming overwhelming.

Just then, she saw Mauricio leaving the kitchen with three plates loaded with food, balancing precariously in his hands. He had a tortilla clamped between his lips as he worked through it.

Ordinarily, the sight would have made Kiki laugh. But right now, she was a hurricane of fury.

She stopped in front of him, hands on her hips as she blurted. "What is a mate?"

Mauricio choked and spat the tortilla on the floor. "What did you say?" he croaked.

Kiki crossed her arms over her chest; her lips pursed in a thin line of annoyance. "You heard me."

Mauricio glanced nervously around the room before jerking his chin toward the kitchen. He scurried in, quickly laying the plates down on the counter before turning back to face her.

She watched him the whole time, her foot tapping impatiently on the floor.

He ran a hand through his hair. "Look. I can explain," he started, his hands held before him as if he'd been caught doing something he shouldn't. Kiki didn't stop tapping her foot, watching with satisfaction as her impatience made him nervous.

Mauri chewed at the inside of his cheek before adding, "It's not like I asked for it. I didn't even think I'd find her. I knew she was out there, sure, I could feel it as much as any of my brothers, but she was so far away. And then, bam, there she was, and it was like everything else became meaningless compared to her."

Kiki's brows furrowed. The man wasn't making any sense. She heard the words he was stringing together, but they didn't make any sense.

Seeing the look on her face and mistaking it for anger, Mauricio stumbled. "Nobody asks for this. The mate bond comes with the curse. It's why Arlando thinks the way he does. The mate bond is sacred. Treasured. It's more than just profound love for your mate.

It's the equal matching of two complete souls, not because one is lacking without the other, but because together is just better. Trust me; I didn't expect the mate bond to click into place when I met Luna. I don't deserve her. I know that — "

He continued to prattle on. But Kiki's ears had stopped hearing him the moment Luna's name had slipped from his mouth.

Luna? As in her Luna? She was bonded to this man? Or whatever it was called. Mate.

Kiki's head started to feel light as Aurelia's accusation just moments ago returned to mind. *"You mean — Kiki — she's your mate?"* Those were her exact words to Erasmo.

The kitchen door flew open, and Erasmo burst in, looking wild-eyed and out of breath. His gaze landed on Kiki, and his eyes seemed to grow even wider.

Mauricio was unperturbed and continued on as if Erasmo had not just appeared. "The mate bond is like a marriage. Only it's more — "

Erasmo's chest heaved as his eyes darted between them. "Mauri!"

Mauricio froze and flinched. "I'm sorry! She called me out, and I panicked!"

Erasmo's lips pressed into a thin line, and he raked his hands through his thick, black hair in frustration as he exhaled loudly.

"Does Luna know?" Kiki asked Mauri, ignoring Erasmo as he paced behind them.

"Do I know what?" Luna's voice echoed through the kitchen.

Mauri's mouth fell open upon seeing her standing at the entrance to the kitchen.

Luna, for her part, looked completely confused. Her gaze fell to the food on the counter, and she said to Mauricio, "I was wondering what was taking you so long. Then I realized you were probably carrying three plates and needed some help." Her words drifted off as she looked between the three of them standing in the kitchen. "What's going on? Did I miss something?"

Kiki crossed her arms over her chest and looked daggers at Erasmo. "I don't know, *Erasmo*," she said, placing extra emphasis on his name. "Is there something you'd care to explain?"

His shoulders sagged, and she could see how anguished he was, but she didn't really care at the moment. She was feeling all kinds of rage to feel sorry for him.

"Anything you'd like to shed light on?" she pressed. "A particular part of your curse that you failed to mention?"

Erasmo sank into a nearby stool and leaned forward on the counter, his face buried in his hands.

Anger blossomed in Kiki's chest at his behavior. "Oh, no, you don't," she snarled as she walked right over to him and pulled his hands from his face. "You're going to look me in the eyes when you tell me this. You owe me that."

His face was twisted with agony, but he didn't drop his gaze from hers. "I've always been able to feel you. That's what the mate bond is, a supernatural connection that binds two people together. Through the bond, I've felt your every triumph and every failure. But I had never felt your pain before like I did the day you learned your friend had been abducted. That pain drew me to find you. That's what I was doing in the woods. I was looking for Aurelia so she could help me cross the border. But then you crossed yourself, and I could feel you more clearly than ever. But then Tomás captured me, and then he had you — And everything has been one thing after another ever since."

Kiki pressed her lips tighter together, her jaw clenching so tightly she thought she might break a tooth. Letting out a frustrated breath, she said, "So this whole time. You knew."

He nodded, his eyes trained on his hands. "I didn't know how to tell you. I'd just met you. I wanted to give you a chance to — "

"To what?" Kiki growled, pushing her face close to his. She wanted him to see her wrath. "Let the spell work on me? To fill me with emotions that weren't real and never were, to begin with?"

"No," he said, his words a whisper. "That's not how the bond works." Kiki scoffed and paced the length of the kitchen. "No, I wanted to give you a chance to fall in love with me. On your own. Without the pressure of knowing that we're destined to be together."

"Destined?" she sneered.

Luna pulled her to a stop and looked at her with sadness. "Kiki, maybe you can just let him explain. Like we talked about?" Luna asked, her tone pleading. It sent a pang of guilt through Kiki's gut, but she was mad as hell. Old habits die hard.

"Okay, I'll let him talk while this one over here stops cowering in the corner and tells you what he needs to," she said, pointing at Mauricio, who had retreated into the shadows of the kitchen.

Luna quirked her head. "What are you talking about, Kiki?"

"I'm talking about the fact that you are his mate, or he is yours, or whatever. That these assholes knew this whole time and didn't say a word."

Luna's mouth fell open, her eyes darting toward the corner in search of Mauricio. He let out a choked sound, and she immediately rushed over to him.

But instead of screaming at him, she wrapped her arms around him. And the man started to sob.

Kiki could hear Luna whispering sweet soothing words to him, and she felt like she was going to be sick.

She rounded on Erasmo. Her anger the only thing she knew. "Get rid of it."

"What?" Erasmo stood up, his stool crashing to the floor.

"I don't want it. Get rid of it. The bond or whatever it's called."

He opened his mouth to speak, but she cut him off, the rage boiling inside of her making her she feel like she was going to explode.

"No. Unless the next words out of your mouth are 'yes' and 'ma'am,' I don't want to hear it." Kiki stormed from the kitchen, ignoring Erasmo's voice calling after her.

This wasn't what Kiki wanted. She deserved a chance to choose. Now she knew that all the feelings she thought she had for Erasmo weren't real. That truth made her so angry that she needed to get her frustrations out. She ran through the house, not knowing where she was going but determined to find someplace where she could destroy something.

Anything.

CHAPTER EIGHTEEN

MIDNIGHT BONDING

LUNA

Kiki stormed out of the kitchen, leaving Erasmo staring after her with a pained expression on his face.

"Give her space," Luna counseled before he could run after her. "She needs time to cool off before you try talking to her. Trust me."

Erasmo's shoulders sagged, and he leaned against the counter, crossing his ankles. Meanwhile, Mauricio still clung to her like a baby, his arms wrapped around her like steel bands. His sobs had quieted, but his shoulders still shook.

"Marui?" she asked, trying to pull back enough to see him face-to-face. "Are you okay now? Can we talk?"

Mauri nodded and reluctantly unwound himself from around her. His face was twisted in agony, and he couldn't meet her in the eyes. "I'm sorry," he said in a choked sob.

"For what?" she asked.

He jerked his head up, and his mouth fell open. "For this. For the mate bond. For not telling you — "

Luna drew closer and put her hand on his shoulder. Perhaps she should have been upset. At least, that was one response. One that Kiki certainly had no problem devolving into. But her? Luna was oddly calm about the whole thing. What she'd seen as she crossed the Cicatrix came to mind, and she shuddered. she still hadn't given that bit of fear the attention it needed, and she certainly wasn't about to do so right now.

But if she'd learned anything since her crossing, it was this: there was a whole lot more in the world that she didn't know nor understand. That she'd lived a very sheltered existence. That she lacked care and attention, both of which she'd given to others freely because of her innate magic as a Healer. But no one else had really bothered to do the same. Kiki and Yari were the only exceptions to that, but even Kiki tended to be blind to what she needed. Kiki had a bad habit of giving to others what she needed herself, not really looking at a person and seeing what they actually needed.

Luna loved Kiki dearly, yet, she'd always felt like something was missing. Then she came here. To La Aguilera. To Mauri. And suddenly, she felt like she'd come home. She couldn't explain it, and maybe this mate bond was the reason. But, regardless of why; she was happy. And that happiness was not something she was willing to let go of. Spell or not. Curse be damned.

"For the first time in my life, I am happy. I am safe. And cared for. Protected. I don't care the reasons why," she said, making sure to hold his gaze the entire time. "I have always been the one to care for others. Always giving of myself and receiving little to nothing back. The moment I met you, you've paid attention to every little detail about me. You've ensured that I have everything I need and then some. I've felt a connection to you the second I laid eyes on you. Now I know why." She heaved a breath, and Marui seemed to hold his as if waiting for her to punch him in the gut. "For whatever reason, you and I have this bond, and I'm willing to accept that."

Mauri released the breath he was holding and swept her into a bone-crushing hug. He tucked his face into the crook of her neck and whispered, "Thank you," over and over.

Erasmo cleared his throat, and Luna parted from Mauri, not having noticed that the other man still lingered in the kitchen. "I'm happy for you," he said to them both before ducking his head and leaving the kitchen entirely.

With his cousin gone, Mauri pulled her close and placed his palm against her cheek. "There is so much I want to tell you. I don't know where to begin."

Luna smiled. "Let's start at the beginning. Where were you born?"

They spent the next several hours talking, and as she learned more about the man that fate, destiny, or whatever you wanted to call it, had decided was meant for her, she felt completely at peace. She didn't know that she'd been looking for this kind of connection until it quite literally fell into her lap.

They moved into one of the sitting rooms and continued to talk, their legs tangled on the sofa as they discussed their pasts, the people they'd lost, and their hopes for the future. As the hour drew late and the sun had long set, she reached her arms into the air and yawned.

"Tired, *chiqui*?" Mauri asked as he tucked a strand of hair behind her ear. She nodded and started to get up from the sofa. He stood up and shuffled from foot to foot. "Would it be okay if I took up my spot on the floor again tonight?"

She shook her head, and his face fell. She grabbed his hands in hers and lifted them to her lips. She pressed a kiss to his knuckles, noting the old scars he had from the many faces he'd bashed in — his words, not hers. "We're mates, are we not?" she asked, feeling a blush rush across her cheeks. He nodded, his lips slightly parted as his gaze traced every feature along her face. "Do mates usually sleep on the floor, or do they share a bed?"

His pupils grew wide, and the temperature in the room heated as he continued to stare at her. "Are you asking me to share your bed?"

A shiver ran down her spine, and, feeling emboldened by the look of hunger in his eyes, she whispered, "I may be asking for a little more than just that."

Without hesitation, Mauri slammed his lips against hers, taking her breath away. He threaded his hands through her hair, and she felt a gasp of surprise slip past her lips as he wound his arm around her waist and pulled her flush against his hard, muscled body. A growl vibrated in his chest, and his tongue battled with hers as she opened her mouth to him.

He pulled his lips away and pressed his forehead to hers. His chest moved up and down as he heaved for breath. "Tell me what you want, *chiqui*. Anything at all, and it's yours."

"Right now, all I want is you."

That was enough. Mauri swept her off her feet and carried her out of the sitting room and into the main foyer of the manor. They passed by a cluster of men drinking outside on the porch, and at the sight of them, the men let out hoots and hollers, to which Mauri responded with a feral growl, his teeth bared and his canines lengthening. That only served to encourage the men who jeered at him and offered suggestions for how to pleasure her. Their words sent heat through her body, and she realized that she wanted all of those things.

Mauri whipped past them and rushed up the stairs with her still in his arms. When he reached her door, he kicked it open, and crossed the threshold, slamming the door shut again with his foot. She heard a roar of laughter trickle up the stairs from the drinking men and laughed as well.

Mauri didn't give her a chance to say anything about the men making fun of him. He smashed his lips to hers and corralled her towards the bed. "I want you so bad," he said between kisses. "I want to taste you on my lips. I want to make you feel so good, *chiqui*."

She felt heat rush through her body at his words, and she tilted her head to the side to give him better access to her neck. He nipped at the tender flesh, sending a bolt of pleasure spiraling through her pussy. His hands roamed across her body and landed on the buttons of her shirt. Her hands flew to his, her eyes wide as she realized what they were about to do. She blushed and felt a sudden rush of shame wash over her.

Mauri dipped his head to meet her eyes. "What's wrong, *chiqui*?" When she didn't respond right away, he drew his hands away from her shirt and placed his hands on either side of her face. "We're moving too fast, aren't we? I'm sorry, I didn't mean — I let myself get caught up in the moment — we don't have to do anything — "

She shook her head. "No, it's not that. It's — " She took a deep breath. "I know how this is going to sound, and I feel silly for saying it. But — " She looked into his eyes and saw nothing but adoration. It was enough to help make what she was about to say next that much easier. "I've never had sex before," she confessed. "I've never really been close to anyone other than Kiki and Yari, and I love them, but not like that. I dated a few guys, but I never wanted to sleep with them."

"Luna, we don't have to do anything at all. I'm just happy to breathe the same air as you."

She smiled at the earnestness in his voice and shook her head. "No, I'm not saying that, though. I do want to. With you. I just — I don't know what to do."

A look of longing filled his eyes, and he pressed a tender kiss to her forehead. "Do you want me to show you?" he asked, his voice husky.

She nodded. "Yes, please."

Mauri slowly kissed her, easing her back until her knees hit the edge of the bed. He gently lowered her down and lay alongside her, pressing featherlight kisses to her neck and trailing them down her collarbone until he reached the top button of her shirt. With agonizing slow movements, he undid each button, one by one, pressing a kiss to the newly bared skin beneath. A shiver raced across her skin and settled between her legs. Her breathing came in ragged pants as he continued to undress her, his lips and tongue caressing her skin all the while.

Once her clothes were undone, he helped her shrug out of them until she was left in nothing but her underwear. He stared at her, his mouth parted as if in awe, and he exhaled a deep breath. "You're so beautiful," he whispered as he leaned his head down and dusted kisses along the tops of her breasts.

"I want to see you," she said, placing her hands on either side of his face. He nodded and sat up so she could pull the shirt over his head. His chest was perfectly defined, and his abs were chiseled as if from granite. But along his skin were the scars of over a dozen claw marks, cuts, bites, and stab wounds. Her fingers instantly reached out and touched a wound that ran right above his heart. "What happened here?"

He placed his hand over hers as he said, "There are a lot of things that you don't know about me, *chiqui*. I've done some bad things. Things that would make you look at me differently if you knew."

She shook her head. "You're not the only one with secrets, Mauri. But I don't want any secrets between us. I want to know you. All of you."

He nodded his head. "I'm Erasmo's enforcer. His interrogator. His assassin. I've killed more people than I can count. These scars, they're all just part of the job."

She inhaled sharply at his confession. "Why do you do those things?"

His eyes grew dark. "Because I wouldn't have it any other way. Anyone who threatens the people I love is a dead man walking. Simple as that."

She nodded, understanding that need to protect people. She'd been doing it her whole life. She'd taken lives, too — but that was something she wasn't ready to talk about. Not yet.

"Do you hate me for it?" he asked, his brows furrowed and his face twisted with worry.

She shook her head. "No. I know what it's like to do things that others wouldn't understand."

He nodded and pressed his lips to hers. "I understand. I'll never judge you."

She melted into his embrace and rested her face on his chest. "I know. I'm just not ready to talk about it." He hummed his understanding and pulled her tighter into his chest so that she was lying alongside him, and his arms were wrapped around her in a protective embrace.

He kissed the top of her head and said, "You should get some sleep." She nodded in agreement, letting the heat of his body envelop her and lull her into a deep and peaceful slumber.

CHAPTER NINETEEN

INTELLIGENCE IS NOT FOR PRYING, OR YOU'LL END UP CRYING

YARI

Yari's breath hitched as she stepped into the snow-covered clearing, her frightened gaze sweeping over the surrounding trees.

The dead limbs had long since lost all their leaves, and the crisp air carried the sickly sweet scent of decay. Sunlight filtered through the tangled branches, curling and warping the light like shards of glass.

Her boots crunched against broken twigs and frozen earth with each step that brought her closer to the abandoned cabin in the woods. The obsidian handle of the machete was cold and unforgiving in her palm, reassuring her with its weight and steadiness as she ventured deeper toward the source of all her nightmares.

The weight of the weapon in her hands felt like a distant memory. She had been an Attendant in the Demon Corps, though she'd never been much of a threat, to begin with. But now Kiki wasn't here to protect her, and Yari was determined to fight off the monster that haunted her dreams. Every instinct told her this was a battle she had to win, and she couldn't stop until it was over.

Her heart thumped wildly in her chest as she approached the door to the cellar, a place she had visited countless times in her dreams but never managed to escape.

Taking a deep breath and steeling herself for what lay beyond, Yari swallowed down her fear and opened the door.

She tiptoed down the stairs, each footstep careful and precise. Her heart raced while fear churned in her stomach. She wanted to turn around and run but knew she had to face her demons if she ever wanted to be free from the dread that haunted her days and stole away her peace of mind at night.

She stepped off the final stair and slowly turned, her eyes darting to the corners of the dark cellar. She saw nothing but shifting shadows.

She raised her machete in front of her body, prepared to strike should the monster jump out at her.

But nothing did. She waited. And waited. And the suspense sent her heart beating double time. She sucked in a breath to calm her nerves when she heard a creak behind her.

She whirled around — to come face to face with air.

Perhaps she'd gotten lucky, and the monster was gone.

Lowering her machete, she turned to go back the way she'd come when a hairy arm jostled her and sent her plunging backward. She cried out in shock, slipping down the slick cellar wall until she landed in a head on the cold dirt floor. Her machete tumbled from her grasp and spun into a dark corner along with any courage she'd mustered.

"Yarixa," a deep gravelly voice called out.

As the monster stepped forward, its massive silhouette blocked out the meager light from the cellar's entrance. Its black maw opened to reveal two rows of razor-sharp teeth, glinting menacingly in the darkness.

The ground vibrated beneath her hands as the demon stalked closer, her name a growl on its lips.

She quickly patted the ground, searching for her machete. But her hands came back empty.

"Looking for this?" the demon laughed as it dangled her machete in front of her face, gleefully throwing it across the room with a flick of its wrist. "You can't escape me, Yarixa. I am your destiny."

Yari's body shook as fear tightened its grip on her heart. Her breath shuddered in shallow pants, and a single strangled scream escaped from her lips.

Y ari jolted awake and sat upright, clutching the blankets to her neck. Her chest moved up in down in ragged gasps. Fear still wrapped its claws around her throat, and a choked sob escaped her lips.

Her eyes flicked across the room, searching for the source of her fears. But she was safe. The demon couldn't chase her into her waking hours, despite the fact that it plagued her thoughts.

Rivulets of moonlight poured through the window and pooled around the edges of the plush mattress, bathing the room in an ethereal blue light.

She ran a hand over her tired eyes and patted the space beside her, seeking comfort in Arlando's warmth. But when her hand touched the cool sheets instead, she let out a disappointed sigh.

He had been gone more and more lately. The disputes at his border kept him occupied, leaving Yari to eat and sleep alone.

Though she tried not to be selfish with him, she couldn't help but miss those early days when she was his sole focus.

She pushed the heavy fur blankets from her feet and swung her legs over the bed. The floor was cold against her bare feet, and a shiver ran down her spine. She grabbed a fur blanket and wrapped it around her shoulders before going to the door and peeking out into the hall beyond.

Candles flickered in the hall as a cold wind swept through the castle. The walls seemed to howl as the wind whipped through passageways. She pulled the blanket tighter around her shoulders and ventured out. As she walked down the stairs to the main hall, she heard hushed whispering.

She slowed her steps until her feet practically hovered over the granite tile. The closer she got to the voices, she recognized Arlando's voice and a distinctly feminine voice.

Her heart leaped into her throat at the possibility that he was having a late-night rendezvous with a lover. Her cheeks heated with shame as a deep seeded fear sprouted and blossomed within.

She should have known a man like him would grow weary of her. She couldn't say she blamed him, even if her heart felt like it was being ripped from her chest.

"Calm down?" the woman's voice screeched. "You promised me she'd be taken care of. You promised that if I did everything you asked, you'd watch over her. Yet, now, you're telling me that my mother is gone? Vanished? Into thin air. You expect me to believe that?"

Yarixa quirked her head to the side at the stranger's words. She wondered what they could be talking about.

She didn't have to wait long because Arlando said, "Pilar was here a few days ago. She had another one of her episodes, and the next thing I knew, she was gone. I kept my word to you. I protected her. Provided for her. Cared for her. I can't control if she decides to take off without telling anyone. You know how she gets."

A different kind of shame overcame Yari. She had made a mistake. Arlando wasn't talking to a lover. He was talking to his Aunt Pilar's daughter, which would make this strange woman his cousin.

Yari wrapped her arms around her body tighter as embarrassment crawled up her spine. She had been a fool to think Arlando would toss her aside so easily. Hadn't he proved his love for her over and over? Hadn't he ensured her every need was taken care of? Yet, here she was, pouncing on the first seed of doubt that crossed her path.

She had heard enough and turned to go back up the stairs, guilt for eavesdropping worming through her gut, when she heard Arlando say, "Everything is falling into place and is going exactly as planned. The prophecy will be fulfilled, and the curse will be broken."

She frowned as her mind swarmed. She couldn't begin to understand what Arlando was talking about. Curses and prophecies were the stuff of novels, not real life. She paused on the stairs hoping to hear more, when she heard footsteps approaching.

Arlando's voice wound up the staircase, and Yari froze in place. "Now, if that's all, Aurelia, I'm going back to bed. We can discuss matters further in the morning."

Yari picked up her nightdress and dashed up the stairs, careful to keep her steps light and not make a sound. She rushed into the bedroom and closed the door with care before jumping back into bed.

A few moments later, Arlando slipped into the room, closing the door quietly behind him. She listened as he removed his jacket and the rustle of his pants as he removed those too. The bed dipped as he got under the covers and slinked closer to her. She kept her eyes shut as he pulled her into his arms, settling her firmly in his embrace.

"Yari?" he murmured. She kept her eyes closed and tried to keep her breathing slow and deep. She couldn't bear it if he knew she had been eavesdropping again.

He'd treated her with nothing but devotion, and she was repaying him with spying. Her gut churned with guilt.

He caressed the side of her face with his fingers and pressed a featherlight kiss to her temple. "I know you're awake, *mi amor*," he whispered into her ear.

She cringed as she turned to face him. "I'm sorry," she said, feeling even more shameful that he'd caught her and didn't even seem upset by it.

"Why do you sneak around the castle, my love? Don't you feel safe here?"

She shrugged. "I feel safe when I'm with you. I didn't mean to eavesdrop again. I had a nightmare, and you weren't here."

"So you came looking for me." She nodded, sheepish. He smiled and pressed his lips to hers. "I'm sorry I wasn't here. I would have much rather been with you, believe me."

"Who was that? The woman you were talking to?"

"That was my cousin, Aurelia. She's Pilar's daughter. She's been working for me as a spy on my brother. But she thinks Erasmo suspects her, so she came back."

"Why are you and your brother at odds?" she asked, running her fingers through the soft fur blanket. "You never really said before."

He closed his eyes and sighed deeply. "No. I didn't, did I? It pains me to talk about him. We used to be very close. We're twins, after all. But there was one thing we couldn't stop fighting over, and that was what was best for our kingdom. As the eldest, I felt responsible for our people. But my brother, as much as I love him, he's selfish."

Yari didn't know what to say to that besides a dumbfounded, "Oh."

Arlando nodded, his arms tightening around her as if he needed her comfort as much as she needed his. "We decided it was best if we stayed away from each other. But I never stopped caring for him. He's my blood. We shared our mother's womb. That kind of bond is deeper than anything in this world."

Yari's brows knit together as she turned her head to see Arlando more clearly. "Why spy on him then?"

Arlando's face shifted, and his features turned hard before softening. It was such a momentary shift that Yari was convinced that she'd imagined it entirely. "Because I worry what he's up to," Arlando said, his voice dropping so low that it sent goosebumps erupting along her arms.

"But what could he be doing to make you suspicious of him?" Yari asked, her voice wavering. If Arlando was afraid of his own brother, surely that meant he wasn't a good man.

Arlando's lips tugged into a playful grin. "Why so many questions tonight, *querida*?" He brushed the hair from her face and tucked it behind her ear. "Don't you trust me?"

"Of course!" she said, bolting to a seat. She didn't want him to think that she wasn't grateful to him for everything he'd done for her.

"Then trust that I have my reasons for spying on my brother. And trust that I will protect what I love most with every fiber of my being," he said as he pulled her back into his arms.

She rested her cheek on his chest. "I do trust you," she muttered. "I just wish — " The words were on the tip of her tongue. That she wished she understood why he did what he did. She wished she knew where he took off to every day, leaving her to wander the castle alone. She wished she knew why she was forbidden from the West Wing. "Nevermind, it's silly."

"Tell me," he said, and for a second, she thought it sounded like an order, but she shook that thought from her mind.

"Sometimes I wish I knew what you were doing all day. Where do you go when I'm not with you?"

He ran his hand down her hair. "My day-to-day duties are quite boring, my love. I wouldn't want to bore you."

"But I am bored," she whined. "You said you have important things to do. I want to help you with those things. I want to carry the burden with you."

He chewed his bottom lip in thought. "Very well, I'll show you if you really want to know."

She nodded. "I do. Very much."

"Then it's settled. But for now, sleep. For the days ahead will be long."

She rolled over so that his chest was pressed against her back, and eventually, she felt his breathing slow into a gentle rhythm.

Despite his assurances, she couldn't get his words out of her head. His brother was a selfish man. A dangerous one. Those thoughts plagued her as sleep finally dragged her into the black depths, and she found herself in that cellar in the woods, the blue-eyed demon hounding her until morning.

CHAPTER TWENTY

A LOVERS DUEL

KIKI

S weat dripped down Kiki's brow as she swung her blunted practice sword at a wooden training dummy. She ignored the chips of wood that flew in the air as her strikes became more forceful.

She tried to clear her head. She didn't want to think about the curse. Or Erasmo. Or the mate bond. Even though she didn't want to think about those things, her mind kept returning to them.

She hated feeling like she wasn't being given a choice. It's like that had been her whole life. Two bad choices to pick from; pick one and be grateful.

She growled as she swung the sword in an arc and hit one of the wooden arms so hard that the wood split, and a piece of the arm dangled off like a broken tree limb.

"There you are," a familiar voice echoed through the training yard.

"Go away, Erasmo," she said, gritting her teeth as she hacked at another protruding limb of the wooden dummy.

"Can we talk?"

She rounded on him, bringing her sword up and stopping it just shy of his throat. He swallowed hard, his gaze following the tip of her blade up to her eyes.

"I have nothing to say to you," she sneered.

"How about we make a deal?" he said, holding his hands up. "It's obvious that you're imagining me in place of that dummy there. How about you spar with me? If you win, I'll drop the issue. If I win, you'll stop throwing a tantrum long enough to hear what I have to say."

She considered his offer with care. If she won, he'd leave her alone. She felt a pang of regret in her chest at the thought and quickly pushed that weakness away.

This was what she wanted. So why did she suddenly feel so unsure?

Not willing to dive into her reasons, Kiki withdrew her blade from Erasmo's neck and held out her hand. "Deal."

Erasmo gripped her hand in a firm shake, and Kiki did her best to ignore the explosion erupting in her chest at such simple and innocent contact.

Erasmo moved off to grab a blunted practice sword and assumed a defensive position. "First move is yours," he said, motioning her forward.

She smirked. "Your funeral."

She charged at him, her jabs and slashes flying faster than the eye could see. She had him on his back foot, every block and parry coming in the nick of time. Despite being smaller than him by at least a foot, she moved with agility and precision, making up for what she lacked in brute strength alone.

She wasn't called the Sicario for nothing.

Erasmo seemed to grow bolder as they sparred, his attacks becoming more precise as if he were learning her weak spots.

Or was he simply trying to end this fight as quickly as possible? His breathing came out in ragged pants, and she realized he was growing weary.

Kiki couldn't help but admire his form. He moved with grace and pure power. His perfectly muscled body was quite literally made for being a warrior.

If Kiki weren't so mad at him, she might have actually enjoyed watching him.

But the fact of the matter was this: she was furious. Furious at herself for how much she wanted him. For the feelings he stirred inside her. That she had allowed one more person inside the fortress of her heart.

One more person with the power to destroy her if they ever left her.

Like her mother.

Fear and anger fueled every strike as she continued to drive harder against Erasmo. She backed him against the wall and, in one fluid motion, struck the back of his sword hand, forcing his hand to open and drop his sword.

For a brief moment, she felt victorious at disarming him. He was an even match for her, and she hadn't been challenged by another quite like him in a long time.

But then she saw the devastated look in his azure eyes, the way his brows furrowed and his lips parted as if to cry out.

She hated herself at that moment. Because he didn't deserve her anger, it wasn't like he had chosen this fate for himself any more than she had.

And if she were being honest with herself, she had never felt the way she did for him for anyone else in her life.

Before she knew what was happening, Erasmo knocked her sword to the side and grabbed her wrist, wrenching her around so that her back was flush to his chest, and pressed her own sword across her neck.

"A deal is a deal," he panted, his breath ghosting across the shell of her ear, sending goosebumps racing along her skin.

Kiki heaved for breath as a feeling of relief washed over her. She cursed her traitorous heart for creating the opening that led to her defeat. But she wasn't truly upset that Erasmo had won.

His arms tightened around her like steel bands as he continued to hold her against himself. With his other hand, he yanked the sword from her grasp and tossed it out of reach. He then whipped her around so that she was pinned against the wall and was caged in by his arms on either side of her.

His chest moved up and down as he still caught his breath. His azure eyes bore into her, and she saw twin flames of desire pooling within.

Here was this devastatingly handsome man who had seen her sharpest edges and had not flinched. His soul called to hers like a moth to a flame. She'd happily burn in his flame if it meant he'd never stop looking at her like he was now.

His eyes dropped to her mouth, and before she could stop him, he slammed his lips to hers.

A whimper slipped past her lips at the heat that rushed through her veins at his touch. He wrapped a hand around the back of her neck, pinning her in place, and curled his other hand into her scalp, gently tugging at the roots of her hair.

She didn't know who opened their mouth first. Their tongues danced as he consumed her every breath. She was happy to give it to him.

Her head felt hazy, and she lost herself to the feel of him. She wound her arms around his neck and pushed up onto her tiptoes.

He moaned against her lips and released his hands from her neck and hair to wrap them around the back of her legs. He hoisted her up, wrapping her legs around his waist as he pushed his hips into her harder, using the wall as support.

She felt his hard cock between her legs, and she wanted more. All the anger she had felt was forgotten, and the heat swirling in her pussy demanded to be released.

"Fuck me," she said against his lips.

He pulled back, his pupils blown wide as he drank in every detail of her face. "With pleasure," he growled before crushing his lips to hers. His fingers expertly unzipped her leathers, and he rolled them off her shoulders until she was exposed up to her waist.

He broke away, and his eyes grazed along her breasts, a smirk tugging at his lips as he said, "I love your breasts." He lowered his head and popped one of her nipples into his mouth. She tossed her head back, eyes to the sky as a rush of pleasure ran through her body. She threaded her hand into his hair, keeping one on his shoulder for balance.

He moved to the other nipple, giving it as much attention as he did the first. She felt the pressure build until it pushed her over the crest, and she felt a wave of pleasure wash over her.

He released her nipple with a pop and smiled down at her, his eyes full of gloating as he drank in her expression. "Did you just come?"

"Shut up and kiss me," she growled, pulling his face to hers as she crashed her lips to his.

This felt so right. Mate bond be damned. She'd choose this man a hundred times over. Destiny or not.

He unhooked her legs from his waist and rolled her leathers down her legs until she stood completely bare before him.

"I'm never going to tire of this," he breathed as he dropped to his knees before her. Lifting one leg over his shoulder and gripping her other behind her knee, he buried his face into her pussy.

He licked at her sensitive clit, and her legs quivered as a bolt of lightning sped through her veins. He guided her back with gentle swipes of his tongue.

When he pulled away, he looked up at her and said, "You just love it when I'm on my knees for you, don't you?"

Breathless, she quipped, "If only you had learned your place sooner."

Erasmo growled at that, a look of mischief in his eyes as she moved her leg from his shoulder and pulled his face to meet hers.

She tasted herself on his lips, and her hands were frenzied as she pulled at the buttons of his pants. Breaking away, he yanked his shirt from his shoulders and undid his pants, pushing them over the chiseled 'v' of his hips, allowing his glorious dick to spring free.

She inhaled sharply at the sight, and her mouth watered. He watched her with a raptor's gaze as he gripped the backs of her legs once more and lifted her into the air.

Using the wall to support her back, he pulled back enough to guide his cock along the entrance of her pussy. Her breath hitched as his tip pushed into her pussy. He tossed his head back as he pushed an inch further, slowly letting her adjust to him. It was delicious torture as he slowly sank himself inside her inch by inch.

When he was fully sheathed inside her, his head collapsed into the crook of her neck, his breathing heavy and labored. "Do you know how much I've wanted this?"

"I've wanted you too," she said as he pulled back and filled her once more. She moaned as she tossed her head back.

"Do you like that?" he asked, lifting his head to watch her.

"Don't stop." She wrapped her hand around his neck.

He chuckled and pressed his lips to her ear, sending a shiver down her spine. "I'm going to make you come so hard."

"Then do it already," she challenged, meeting his gaze head-on as she curled her nails into his shoulders.

He responded to her taunt by moving his hips in a steady languid rhythm, torturously slow and just enough to bring her to the edge but not enough to send her over that cliff.

"Tell me what you want," he teased.

She moaned again, the feelings in her body rushing through so fast as she tried to grind her hips against him to get more pressure where she needed it.

"Say it," he said, the rhythm of his hips becoming faster, meeting her pace. "I want to hear you say it."

"I want to come," she said in a whisper, her breath catching in her throat.

"I didn't hear you."

"I want to come all over you!" she shouted, the pressure building in her spine, her vision blurring as stars filled her eyes.

"Yes, baby," he said as he moved faster, the friction building until a tidal wave of pleasure swept through her body.

Erasmo pumped his hips three more times before his body stiffened, and he threw his head back and let out a thunderous roar.

She felt his cock grow as he pumped his warm cum inside her, which sent her cresting over the precipice again. When he was spent, he dropped his head to the crook between her shoulder and neck, his chest heaving as he caught his breath.

She gasped, her chest rising and falling erratically. "Damn, if I knew that was what I've been missing out on, I would have jumped on top of you that first night."

He lifted his head, and his eyes were bright as he smiled at her. He leaned down and pressed a tender kiss to her lips. His body still joined with hers as he slowly worshiped her lips.

When he pulled back, he said, "I'm sorry I didn't say anything before. I didn't want you to feel burdened by me. By the bond." He lowered his head. "I still don't. If you don't want this — "

She stopped him before he could finish by crushing her mouth to his. "I do." He lifted his head, and his eyes misted over. "I do want this. I want you."

"Are you saying you'll accept the bond?" he asked, chest rising and falling rapidly. "Because if you do, you'll make me the happiest man alive."

She nodded, feeling a smile tug at the corner of her lips at how his entire face lit up.

He inhaled sharply as if he was honestly surprised by her response. As if she'd go anywhere after he fucked her to the moon and back.

He slammed his lips to hers, a growl vibrating in the base of his chest as she felt him harden once more.

She reared back. "Are you — can you go again?" she asked, not bothering to hide the surprise in her voice.

He grinned devilishly. "You haven't seen anything yet, baby."

CHAPTER TWENTY-ONE

SEALED WITH A KISS

SOLANA

S olana's fingers drummed restlessly against her biceps, her eyes fixed on nothing as she replayed Aurelia's words over and over in her head. Mates? What did that even mean?

She could feel the weight of the unknown pressing down on her shoulders, making it hard to breathe. But Solana was nothing if not determined, and she knew that she needed answers. She would find out what this whole mate business meant, and she knew exactly who she had to confront to get those answers.

She entered the manor house just in time to witness Kiki storming out of the kitchen. Erasmo stood rooted to the spot, a pained expression on his face that made the air heavy with his emotions.

She couldn't say that she felt particularly sorry for him. She didn't know the man well enough to care much to begin with.

The only person she had her sights set on was Bernat.

She found Bernat in the dining hall, his cousin Yasir laughing at his side.

She slipped through the crowd of people clustered in the dining hall and stopped before Bernat's table. His eyes followed her every move, and the heat in his stare sent her stomach flipping over itself.

Falling for this man was dangerous and put her entire career in the Demon Corps at stake, but there was a part of her that didn't care. She loved him. Simple as that.

"What do you know about something called 'the mate bond'?" she asked, setting her hands on her hips as she looked between the two men.

Yasir choked on his beer and spat it out in a spray. "What did you say?" he gasped, his chest heaving.

Bernat averted his gaze and stared into the mug between his hands.

"You heard me," she said in clipped tones. "Though I take it from your silence, Bernat, that you know exactly what I'm talking about."

Bernat hung his head and raised his gaze to meet hers. "Mauri told me a few days ago."

She let silence fill the space between them. Yasir moved to leave, and she pointed at him, her gaze still trained solely on Bernat.

"Sit down," she ordered Yasir, her voice harsh, the Commander within rearing her head. "Both of you. Explain. Now."

Bernat shifted in his seat. "I'm sorry, Sol. I was trying to figure out a way to tell you."

"Tell me what? You still haven't bothered to fill me in," she snapped.

Bernat exhaled through his nose and sighed. "The mate bond came with the curse when my mother put a spell on my father. It's suspected to be a way to ensure the curse lives on, punishing the Ozero bloodline for eternity. I didn't tell you because you don't pick your mate. The bond is pure magic. It doesn't answer to what a person wants or doesn't want." He took a deep breath. "I don't know for sure if you and I are bonded in that way. I was afraid to find out."

Solana felt like a bucket of cold water was poured over her head. She had allowed Bernat into her heart, let him see the most secret parts of her soul, and for what? To now learn that they may not even work out? That destiny or fate or whatever he wanted to call it had preemptively decided for him?

Her stomach churned with nausea, and she took a faltering step back. She hadn't realized she had started to shake her head until Bernat was inches away from her, both his hands on either side of her face.

"I don't care about the bond," he said, his voice husky. "You are the only woman I want. The only woman I've ever wanted. No curse is going to change that."

Yasir made a grunting noise that sounded very much like derision, and they both turned to scowl at him.

He shrugged and said, "You don't get a choice in the matter, brother. Once the bond takes hold, that's it. I've seen one too many hearts broken because the bond pointed in another direction. It's no one's fault. It just is what it is."

Bernat's lips drew back in a feral snarl. "Shut it, Yaz. You're not helping."

Yasir downed the rest of his beer and stood up, brushing his pants off as he stepped forward. "You really want my help?" he asked, a devilish grin on his face.

Bernat eyed his cousin warily. "Whatever you have in mind, I hate it already," he said darkly.

Yasir grinned. "Good. You're going to hate it more in a second if you really are bonded." He pointed back to the table. "Go over there for me." Bernat did as requested, his shoulders tense. Yasir turned back to Solana and asked quietly so that Bernat couldn't hear. "May I kiss you?"

She reared back. "Excuse me?"

Yasir tossed Bernat a look, making sure he couldn't hear. "It's the only way to know for sure. If he tries to kill me, then you're bonded."

She spared Bernat a glance over Yasir's shoulders. He threaded his fingers through his midnight black hair and started pacing back and forth like a predator caging in its prey.

She didn't like the idea of Yasir kissing her. Her heart belonged to Bernat. But if what he was saying was true — if this bond had the power to forever take Bernat away from her, she would rather know now than later. Better to suffer the sting of disappointment and heartbreak now, before things got too complicated.

Her shoulders slumped as she nodded her permission.

Yasir didn't hesitate. He quickly pulled her into his arms and planted his lips against hers. She pressed her hands against his chest, pushing him slightly away, but stopped, knowing this was the test. She had to play her part as much as Yasir.

For his part, Yasir didn't seem to be enjoying his role too much either. His arms were rigid around her, and she could feel the hesitancy on his lips.

But she had to know for sure. She had to know if she and Bernat were bonded.

Though everything inside of her railed against the idea, she forced herself to press closer to Yasir and wound her arms around his neck. Though it killed her to do it, she opened her mouth and let his tongue explore her mouth, all the while imagining that it was Bernat's lips instead. She held onto that fantasy to keep her dinner from coming up.

Suddenly, a roar filled the dining hall, and before she knew what was happening, Yasir was ripped from her arms, and his body was flung across the room. His large frame fell on top of a wooden table, and the legs gave way, the sound of splintered wood cracking through the air.

Staggering back, her chest heaving for breath, she watched in awe and horror as black shadows swirled around Bernat's body.

Bernat assumed a territorial stance in front of her, his arms wide as if he dared anyone to approach.

She heard a laugh from where Yasir had landed, and he leaped to his feet as if he hadn't just been thrown across the room. He shook his hair free of wood splinters and dusted his shirt off, a grin splitting his face.

Bernat charged Yasir, a feral growl ripping past his lips, and Yasir threw back his head and laughed. He welcomed Bernat's advance with open arms, letting his cousin tackle him to the ground and land a few punches before a group of men swarmed them and pulled them apart.

Black shadows erupted from Bernat's shoulders, sending the men holding him sprawling onto the ground with looks of shock on their faces. Bernat let out a furious roar as a breezeless wind swept through the room.

"She's mine!" he roared, rushing Yasir again.

"Hold him!" Yasir ordered his cousins, and a group swarmed Bernat. It took ten men to bring Bernat down to the ground, where he continued to rant and rave.

Yasir leaned over his cousin with a shit-eating grin. "You passed the test, brother. She's your mate."

Bernat instantly went still at his words, and his eyes frantically searched the crowd for Solana.

His azure eyes met hers, and something inside of her locked into place. Mate. This was her mate. The man who'd always had her back. Who supported her rise in rank every step of the way. The man who had started out as a friend but had become so much more.

Bernat began struggling against the men holding him again, and Yasir ordered them to release him.

Bernat scrambled to his feet and rushed toward her. He crushed her in his arms and pulled back enough to slam his lips to hers. Her body responded with a rush of heat cascading through her chest.

The crowd that had gathered around them began jeering and cajoling, patting Bernat on the back as they passed and went back to their own business.

"Get a room!" Yasir joked, which earned him a feral growl from Bernat.

Yasir chuckled, completely unfazed and unconcerned, before turning away to join the rest of his family.

Bernat pulled her out of the dining hall and, the second they were out of sight, pressed her against the wall.

His stare was intense, his eyes dark with lust.

He nipped at her earlobe as he groped her ass, then shoved his hand between her legs and found her wetness.

"You're so fucking wet, Sol. You're ready for me," he said in a throaty rasp.

She nodded, her tongue suddenly useless. She moaned as he slipped his finger inside her and began to pump the digit in and out of her.

The sight of Bernat touching her, the feel of his skin against hers, the smell of him... she was drunk on him.

"I want to fuck you hard and fast in your room. I want to fuck you until you scream so that everyone can hear you," he said, his voice hungry and dark.

He moved his hand up to her breast and teased her nipple through her battle leathers, pulling it softly and then giving it a sharp flick.

"What do you say?" he asked, his lips brushing her ear.

All she could do was nod. She placed her hand on his chest and led him back to the room they'd been sharing.

Taking his hand, she shut the door behind him and locked it before turning around to face him. Her breathing hitched, and her heart pounded as she stared into his darkened eyes.

"Undress," he commanded.

"Bernat," she whispered, her voice barely audible.

"No objections, Sol. I'm going to fuck you, and you're going to love every second of it."

It wasn't a question. It was a fact.

Solana couldn't help but enjoy the fact that he was taking the commanding role here. She was usually the one to give the orders, and something about trusting him entirely put her at ease.

Keeping her eyes trained on him the whole time, she slowly began to pull the zipper down on her leathers.

"We're doing this my way. I control you, Sol. All of you. I control every single inch of your body, and it belongs to me," he said, his voice dark and ominous as he slowly circled around her.

A tendril of excitement wound its way through her pussy at his words.

"Do you understand?"

Her body was on fire. All she wanted was to feel his hard dick filling her. To submit completely to him.

"Yes," she answered breathlessly.

He smiled wickedly and turned her around to face the wall, then pressed her against it and freed his cock. She whimpered at the feel of the tip of his dick brushing against her pussy.

"You are so fucking wet," he said as he pulled her hair and tugged her head back. "You want this? You want my cock inside you?"

"Yes!" she screamed. His demanding words turned her on, and she could feel her pussy dripping with desire. She'd never seen this side of him before, and the longer he let it out, the wetter she became.

He slid inside her in one smooth stroke, and she cried out from the pleasure of it. He was so big, so hard... she thought she might pass out from the sheer size of him.

Bernat stilled for a second, giving her time to adjust to the feel of his cock inside her, then began to pump into her hard and fast.

The first stroke hit her so deep and hard she screamed. The second stroke had her soaring over the cliff, her vision exploding with stars. He increased his pace, driving himself into her over and over again.

His movements were frantic, and his hands on her hips were punishing. She loved every second of it, craving more.

"Fuck, you feel so good, so wet for me. Squeeze my cock, Sol. Squeeze me," he growled.

His words made her pussy pulse with need. She squeezed her inner muscles as tightly as she could around him, and he groaned deeply.

His hand left her hips and wandered down to her pussy, then began to tease her swollen clit.

"Fuck...you're going to make me come," he said, his voice rough and raspy.

"Come inside me," she gasped. "I want to feel you."

"I want to fuck you until you can't walk, Sol," he said as he continued to pump into her.

Her pussy clenched around him as waves of pleasure began to crash over her. He continued to work her clit until she was a whimpering mess.

"Come for me, Sol."

Her entire body began to shake, and she felt herself orgasm so hard that she thought she might die now and go to heaven.

She screamed his name, and her knees buckled, but Bernat held her tight to him. He panted against her shoulder, his body close to hers, his breathing hot and hard against her neck.

The orgasm was so beautiful, so powerful, she felt her entire body clenching and unclenching as a tear escaped from her eye.

It was the most intense orgasm she had ever had, and something blossomed open inside of her. Instinctually, she knew what it was. The bond that linked Bernat and her as mates.

It had slid into place, forever tying them to one another.

She felt her chest expand, and a feeling of pure joy cascaded through her. She was full of happiness, and a sense of contentment washed over her.

Bernat released her and pulled himself from inside her, his breathing heavy. "What was that?" he panted.

"I think it was the bond," she murmured, feeling her knees weaken from their passionate and soul-consuming sex.

She felt a magnetic pull, the connection that'd been missing, finally take hold.

Bursting with emotion, she turned and wrapped her arms around Bernat and gave him a hard squeeze.

He looked down into her eyes and stroked her back. "*Mi reina*," he whispered. "*Mi cielo, mi sol, mi vida.* I love you."

She stood in his arms, feeling safe and secure, and for the first time in her life, she felt safe enough to utter those three words. "I love you, too," she whispered, then gave him a gentle peck on the lips.

Bernat grinned, his eyes full of love and adoration as he swept her into his arms and gently laid her on the bed. He turned to the water basin and drenched a cloth before coming back to her and cleaning her up.

His touch was gentle, and his eyes drank in every inch of her as if he would never get enough.

Once he finished cleaning her, he climbed into the bed and wrapped her in his embrace.

She gazed at the winter storm brewing outside and took a deep breath, savoring this moment, cherishing it, imprinting it into her very soul.

She finally felt like she had come home.

CHAPTER TWENTY-TWO

WHAT A YAWN

YARIXA

Y ari followed Arlando as he carried out his various duties, and she noticed the care with which he completed even the simplest of tasks.

He read through the mountain of paperwork piled on his desk with precision, taking care to make a note of which farmers were asking for aid and making sure to send them relief immediately.

She joined him as he walked to the stables to check in on the servants who cared for the horses, striking up a conversation with each stable hand. She noticed how he knew each of his servants' names and remembered small details about them.

He was a natural leader in every way, his very presence putting his staff at ease.

He seemed to take a certain amount of pride in his work, even in the most tedious of tasks. Watching him, Yari couldn't help but admire him; he was strong and capable, navigating the world with consummate ease. Obviously, what he was doing was important to him, and she realized how wrong she had been to question him.

The day dragged on, and yet still, Arlando was diligent and committed. Yari followed him around, marveling at his strength and resolve. He seemed to take pleasure in his work, regardless of how dull it was.

He spoke to everyone he came in contact with, seemingly teeming with energy, never once letting on that he was tired.

Suddenly, what had once seemed like an unendingly dull day was illuminated with a new light. The mundane tasks that he was doing suddenly took on a significance and a beauty of their own. Yari felt a deep respect for Arlando and a newfound understanding of the importance of his labor. As the day waned and the sun began to set, she watched him with newfound admiration, feeling grateful for his presence in her life.

Finally, after the day had fully passed, they sat down for dinner in the great hall.

"Was the day everything you'd hoped it would be," Arlando teased.

Yari hid her smile behind her napkin. "Not exactly," she admitted. "Though I can tell you care about your kingdom very much. I admire your dedication," she said.

Arlando beamed at her, a smile so full of light that any thoughts of his involvement in unseemly things faded from her mind.

Suddenly, Aurelia burst through the front door letting a howling wind and snow flurries burst through the hall.

"Where is she, you bastard?" Aurelia screeched. "I know you have her," she continued to rave.

Yari looked over to Arlando and exchanged a surprised glance with him.

He simply smiled reassuringly at his cousin, his face full of peace even in this chaotic moment. "Dearest Aurelia, I've already sent patrols to look for Aunt Pilar. I promise you, we'll get her back home safely."

Aurelia shook her head violently. "You're lying. It's your fault she's gone. I know it. You did something to her. You're planning something. I can see it. You're surrounded by it," she said, motioning to the air around Arlando.

Still calm, Arlando rested his hands in his lap and spoke to his cousin in an even tone. "I'd never do anything to hurt your mother. She's the closest thing I have to a mother myself. If you're seeing anything, it's the worry I have for her."

Aurelia stared at the air around him, and her brows furrowed in concentration as she assessed him. After long seconds of her scrutiny, her brows turned up, and her mouth formed the shape of an 'o' in surprise.

"I'm sorry," she said finally, stepping back. "I guess I'm not right in the head anymore. This Sight is messing with me. I don't know what's real anymore."

Arlando rose from his seat and drew close to his cousin so he could place a hand on her shoulder, his eyes full of concern. "It's alright, dear cousin. Soon all of our troubles will be over."

Aurelia simply nodded and stalked off, her slender frame disappearing down a dark hall.

Yari picked at the food on her plate, the entire scene still playing in her mind.

"What's the matter, *querida*?" Arlando asked after too many seconds had passed and been filled with silence.

She moved a grain of rice from one side of the plate to the other. "What did she mean by her 'sight' troubling her?"

Arlando nodded. "A few years ago, my cousin sought out help from a witch. She asked for a solution to our dying crops. In return, the witch granted her the Sight to read the auras around people."

"How did that help with the crops?" Yari asked.

Arlando shrugged. "It didn't. Aurelia's eyes turned silver, and she stopped seeing the way you and I do. She's never been the same."

"That's awful. I'm so sorry."

Arlando smiled sadly as he got up from the table and looked out at the snowy landscape outside the window. "It's been difficult for her, and I've tried to support her and help her navigate her ability. It's what makes her such a great spy." He paused, his eyes unfocused as if lost in thought. "There may be a way to help her," he added. "I'm just not sure if the sacrifice is worth it."

Yari rose from her seat. "Whatever it is, I'm sure it's worth it if it helps her," she said, moving to join Arlando at the window.

"You think?" he asked as he wound his arm around her waist and pulled her close.

"She's your family. You have to help her. I know that I'd do anything for Kiki and Luna. Not that I was ever much help. But if it were in my ability to do something, I would have done it."

Arlando nodded. "You have the sweetest heart, *mi amor*," he whispered and pressed a kiss to the top of her head. "Like usual, you're right. The outcome is worth whatever the cost."

She nodded and rested her head on his chest. There was little she could do for anyone, but if she could ease Arlando's worries in some way, she was happy to do it.

CHAPTER TWENTY-THREE

BROTHERLY LOVE

ERASMO

T he morning sun spilled through the window and painted Erasmo's bedroom in a warm golden hue. He opened his eyes to find Kiki, her dark hair splayed across his arm, snuggled against him, her chest rising and falling peacefully with each breath she took.

He smiled at the sight of his mate, but it quickly faded away as the realization of what he had done hit him.

His mate. His everything. His life.

Seeing her fast asleep in his embrace, his arms instinctively tightened around her, but he quickly softened them when she shifted slightly against him. He wanted to hold onto this moment forever. If he could freeze time, he would do it.

As he watched her sleep, her face was free of worry and stress. If it wasn't for the scars that lined her body, he would have never guessed that this beautiful woman had spent her whole life fighting for her life.

His mind drifted to the night before and the events that led Kiki and him here. Part of him is grateful that the truth was finally out. He couldn't bear to simply be her plaything for much longer.

Not that he was complaining about the pieces of her that she'd given to him before. It was just that having those tiny shards had quickly become not enough. He wanted all of her. Completely. Forever.

That was the mate bond talking, but it was also what he wanted deep down. He'd both hoped for and dreaded this moment his whole life.

Finding his mate may have filled the void in his dark and tattered heart, but it only put her in more danger.

Prophecy or not, Ozero was in shambles, and now that he had found her, there was a selfish part of him that didn't care if Ozero crumbled. So long as he had her. So long as she was safe.

Perhaps that had always been the source of strife between him and his twin. Where Erasmo would rather let the world burn than see harm come to someone he loved, Arlando thought it was noble to sacrifice what he loved most to save the world.

Erasmo scoffed at the idea. He'd rather slowly descend into madness than harm a hair on Kiki's head.

He felt her stir in his arms, and as she rolled to face him, the blanket fell off her shoulder. He cautiously moved his arm and draped the furs back around her, making sure that every inch of her was tucked in tight.

They'd been up all night, their clothes were strewn about the bedroom floor, and their skin was slick with perspiration. He had intended to go get her a contraceptive brew earlier in the evening, but it had slipped his mind. Now, as he lay there beside her dozing off, warning bells clanged through his head at the reality of their unprotected encounters.

The last thing anyone needed was a mischievous bear cub wreaking havoc throughout the manor. But now that he thought about it, the thought didn't horrify him in the way he expected.

Instead, visions of seeing Kiki's belly swelling with his child made his cock stir with desire.

He quickly pushed that thought away. As much as he liked the idea of binding Kiki to him in every possible way, he knew her stance on pregnancy. It was something she wasn't ready for, and he respected that.

Gently, he eased himself out of her embrace, the sheets rustling with each careful movement until he had quietly slipped away.

He swung his feet over the edge of the bed and tiptoed toward his clothes strewn all over the room. He shrugged on his navy blue shirt and linen pants before swiping his boots off the floor and creeping out of the room.

He slowly closed the door, careful not to make a sound, and then stuffed his feet into his boots before descending the stairs.

Guille's lab was at the bottom of the steps, just beyond the living room. His cousin always had some of the contraceptive brews on hand. With so many males in the house, all struggling with the curse in their own way, all with raging sex drives, having a healthy stock was a necessity.

Reaching the lowest level of the manor house, he pushed open the intricately carved door of Guille's lab, revealing his cousin bent over a mortar and pestle. Alchemical vials of all shapes and sizes lined the shelves of the lab, with several open and wafting vapors along the table.

Guille looked at Erasmo expectantly, one eyebrow raised in question. "I take it things turned out well."

He felt a grin tug at his lips and nodded. "Perhaps a little too well, if you catch my meaning."

Guille frowned and moved from behind the table, crossing his arms in front of him. "Did you take any kind of protective measures?" He leveled Erasmo with an intense, judgmental stare.

Erasmo leaned against the doorway and rolled his eyes. "Why do you think I'm here?"

Guille shook his head and let out a long-suffering sigh. "I swear, it's a wonder that we don't have whole litters running around this place."

He reached under his work table and pulled out a large glass bottle filled with a dark liquid. He uncorked it with a pop and poured a measure into a thumb-sized glass vial.

He handed the tumbler to Erasmo with a stern look on his face. "Have her take it immediately."

Erasmo nodded, taking the bottle from him before turning to leave, but Guille held onto his hand. His eyes were fixed, unblinking, and intense as he asked, "Have you put any thought into preventative measures?"

Erasmo felt a surge of heat rise in his chest and tugged his hand away. "I'm not planning on having a kid if that's what you're so worried about," he replied curtly.

Guille nodded his head and looked towards the adjoining room. "Good," he said in a low voice, "then maybe you'll be interested in something Luna and I have been working on." He cleared his throat and shouted for Luna to come.

The sound of clattering glass bottles filled the air, and Erasmo watched as Luna emerged from the room. Her white apron was smudged with lavender liquid, her blue dress covered in honey-colored stains, and she had a knowing look on her face. She smiled when she saw him, her eyes twinkling in anticipation.

"Good morning Erasmo," she said in a warm tone, "Is Kiki still sleeping?"

He averted his eyes, his face growing warm as he realized that she had listened to the entire conversation with his cousin. He gave a slight nod.

Luna set a small, circular pendant the size of a gold coin on the wooden table between them, tied to a soft leather string. Its object was an intricate carving of a star, surrounded by runes etched into the pale silver.

"This is a contraceptive charm," Luna explained. "It can't stop pregnancy after the fact, so Kiki still needs to take that brew. From now on, she'll need to wear this around her neck to prevent any future unwanted pregnancies. Should that change, all she has to do is take it off."

He wound his fingers around the string and lifted the pendant, so it hung in front of him. The stone had been molded into a star-shaped design, much like the many stars that lined Kiki's wrists. One for each demon she had slain.

He furrowed his brow and crossed his arms, his mouth curled in an expression of doubt. "You're sure this will work?"

Luna met his gaze with a steady look of assurance. "Yes," she said confidently. "It'll do the job."

The door crashed open, and Turi stormed into the lab, the look in his eyes like lightning and trained on Erasmo alone. A jagged vein throbbed in his neck as he stepped forward. He opened his mouth to speak, but all that came out was a feral growl.

"Did you sleep with her?" he finally asked, his voice like broken glass.

Erasmo felt himself pale at the accusation.

Turi's eyes went black with rage, and the air itself seemed to still. His face was a snarl as he lifted his fists and hurled himself forward, charging at Erasmo with an animalistic roar.

Erasmo raised his arms, preparing to block his brother's charge. He measured his brother's movements, and at the last moment, he shifted his weight to the left and gracefully stepped aside.

Turi's hands closed around empty air as he barreled past. He huffed with frustration as he turned his sights back on Erasmo. "Answer the question!" he yelled before charging again.

Erasmo slammed his body into Turi, locking onto his arm in a firm grip. He whipped him around, using his momentum to send Turi careening onto the stone floor. There was a loud crack as Turi's body connected with the ground, and the sound of stone splitting reverberated through the small laboratory.

Turi scrambled to his feet, eyes blazing and fists clenched. He charged at Erasmo in menacing strides, but Guille intervened with lightning speed. He hooked one arm around Turi's waist and yanked him back, then grabbed the back of his shirt with a fist.

Guille glowered down at Turi, breathing heavily as he shouted, "What is wrong with you? Erasmo hasn't done anything wrong."

"He slept with her," Turi snarled, his eyes wild.

Luna stepped forward, her head held high and her tone firm. "I think that's enough," she said, laying a hand on Guille's arm. "Let's give them some privacy."

Guille turned to Erasmo for direction, and Erasmo gestured towards the door with his head, indicating that his cousin was free to leave. Guille took a step back from Turi before he and Luna departed from the laboratory.

Turi's muscles bulged beneath his shirt, and he gritted his teeth as he charged at Erasmo. His deep growl echoed off the walls, and with each word, he threw a punch at Erasmo's face. "I love her," he snarled.

Erasmo deflected the punches with his forearms and countered with a swift jab to Turi's stomach.

"How could you do this to me?" Turi gasped as he clutched at his stomach. "She's mine."

Erasmo felt a rage like never before. Turi had no right to be angry with him. Kiki wasn't something to be claimed by another man. She was Erasmo's mate, and for that alone, she was precious.

He was too enraged at that moment to see the pain in his brother's eyes. Logically, he knew that his little brother had harbored feelings for Kiki. But the beast within was beyond mere logic. The beast didn't care that Turi's heart was breaking.

Black shadows swirled around Erasmo's shoulders, their tendrils reaching outward like tentacles. The beast roared for a fight. Aching to be let loose.

A fight between blood and bone.

Turi shifted his weight as if to attack again when he suddenly lurched past him, his shoulder hitting Erasmo's as he rushed out of the room.

Erasmo hung his head and heaved a breath. He couldn't let things stay like this between them. Turi was his brother. His responsibility. He owed him an explanation about the mate bond.

"Turi," he called after him. "Wait, brother!" He raced after Turi and caught up to him as he ascended the stairs to the upper levels of the house.

"You're no brother of mine," Turi spat. "A real brother wouldn't do what you did. Aurelia was right about you. You're a selfish, mindless beast who takes what he wants whenever he wants it."

Rage bled before Erasmo's vision, and he leaped over the stairs separating them, and grabbed his brother's arm in a vice grip. "How dare you suggest that I took anything from Kiki. She would sooner castrate any man who tried. I will not have you thinking that I took something that wasn't willingly given to me. I won't have it."

Turi glowered at Erasmo, his lip curling in a snarl. Then it softened as a saccharine grin split his face. "You weren't her first," he said softly.

White hot anger sparked in Erasmo's chest as jealousy coiled in his stomach, aching to spring free and lash out like a viper. But he knew he had no right to those feelings, no matter how much the beast within rammed against his ribcage, frenzied and begging for release. Erasmo forced his anger down and smoothed his features so that his face betrayed no emotion.

He forced a scoff and curled his lip in a snarl. "So?"

"It was me. I was her first," Turi spat. "Me."

Erasmo's shoulders filled with tension at the reminder, but he refused to let his little brother see that his barb had sunk deep. Erasmo shook his head and let out a weary sigh. "Is that supposed to upset me or something?" he asked, quirking his brow. "I don't care that I'm not her first. Because I will be her last. That's a promise, little brother. She's my mate."

Turi's face fell as understanding dawned on him. "No," he whispered. "No," he repeated, shaking his head. "You can't be. It was supposed to be me. I'm supposed to be her mate."

A wave of sympathy rolled through Erasmo at seeing his brother so upset. He reached out to place a comforting hand on Turi's shoulder.

"Get your filthy hands off me," Turi snarled, shrugging him off. "You disgust me. You're not worthy of her," he growled, balling his fists at his sides.

Erasmo hung his head, knowing that this conversation wasn't going anywhere. "She's not yours," he said solemnly. "She belongs to no one but herself, brother."

Turi snarled and charged at him again. Erasmo caught the full force of his body as they tumbled to the floor.

"That's enough," Luna said, stepping into the hallway, her hand on her hip. "I know you're upset, Turi, but you need to stop acting like a child."

Turi jumped to his feet, sparing a glare full of daggers for Erasmo before he turned and headed back upstairs.

Luna sighed as she turned the full weight of her glare on Erasmo. "Give him some space," she said softly. "But not too much. You need to make things right between you two."

She was right. He had to make things right. For now, he had to tell Kiki that Turi knew about them. He winced at the thought. She wasn't going to be pleased one bit.

He nodded at Luna and left her in the hallway. Ignoring the heavy feeling in his chest, he ascended the stairs and walked through the door to the room he and Kiki shared.

CHAPTER TWENTY-FOUR

SECRETS ALWAYS COME BACK TO BITE

KIKI

W hen Kiki heard the door snick shut, she opened her eyes to find Erasmo standing near the entrance of the room. His stance was tired and defeated, and his eyebrows were drawn together with worry.

"What's wrong?" she asked, scrambling for the sheets and pulling them up to cover her bare skin as she sat up. Years in the Demon Corps had trained her instincts to be ready for a fight at any hour. Now was no different.

Erasmo heaved a deep sigh, his blue eyes filled with worry as he refused to meet her gaze. "Turi knows," he said softly with a sad shake of his head.

The knowledge that Turi had learned the truth about her relationship with Erasmo made the air whoosh from her lungs. Her heart sank into her stomach, the weight of reality pressing in on her from all sides. She knew Turi would find out eventually, but she had hoped to tell him herself.

Turi would always be her first boyfriend. Her first kiss. Her first sexual experience. It felt like years ago since that day in the armory when she had entertained the idea of getting back together with him. So much had happened since then. So much had changed.

She had changed.

"How?" she asked, the words tasting like chalk in her mouth.

Erasmo steeled himself before he gingerly approached the bed and sat down, his body angled toward her. His eyes were filled with sadness and something else — regret? She could feel the air between them grow thick with the tension of unspoken words.

He finally spoke in a low voice, "I went to my cousin's lab for the contraceptive brew. I'm guessing Turi was listening at the door."

She bit her lip and glanced down at her hands as she wrung the sheet between her fingers. She slowly nodded her head, wishing she could shrink away from the moment in embarrassment even though she knew she had done nothing wrong.

She and Turi had once been something. But that time had long since passed. She knew that, and she knew that he knew it too. Any lingering affection was what anyone might expect between lifelong friends.

Still, she couldn't help but feel rotten for letting it come to this. If only she'd told him sooner.

The room was eerily quiet as she and Erasmo sat there, the air heavy with an unspoken tension that seemed to stretch on for an eternity.

She fidgeted in bed, her gaze darting around the room as she tried to find something to say.

Finally, Erasmo uttered a soft plea into the silence: "Please say something."

She inhaled sharply, steeling her nerves as she rose from the bed. "I have to talk to him. Explain what this is," she said, motioning with her hand between the two of them. "I owe him that."

She pulled on her tight-fitting leathers, zipping the material until it molded to every curve of her body. She grabbed her bandolier off a nearby chair and tucked the few remaining tlazons into their sheaths.

She glanced at her reflection in the mirror, nodding once with determination.

Erasmo joined her at the mirror, their gazes locking on the reflective surface. "I'll never get tired of seeing you like this," he whispered as he trailed his fingers along her neck and down the length of her arm.

For a few moments, time seemed to stand still, his tender gaze holding her in this sacred space for just a little while.

"I'm sorry," he said, his deep voice rumbling from his chest through her spine. "I know you didn't want anyone to know about us. You made that clear. I should have been more careful," he said with a deep exhale as he stepped away and made room for her to leave.

Kiki stopped him with a hand on his arm and placed her hand against his cheek, forcing him to meet her gaze.

Doubt and fear swirled within Erasmo's piercing gaze, and Kiki wanted nothing more than to ease his worries. "I'm not sorry for what's growing between us," she confessed, hardly believing that she was baring herself so completely. "Even though I didn't know about the mate bond, I knew there was something deeper between us. The least I could have done was be honest with myself."

Erasmo let out a relieved sigh as he pressed his forehead against hers. "I'll come with you to talk to him."

She shook her head and stepped away. "No, this is something I should have done earlier. Alone." She gave him a gentle kiss, the black stubble growing along his jaw tickling her lips, before she marched out the door, her boots clacking against the wooden floor.

Kiki walked down the hallway, feeling the heaviness of her legs as each step brought her closer to Turi's room. Her mind was spinning as she anticipated what may come from their conversation.

She paused in front of his door, attempting to regain a sense of calm with a few deep breaths before finally pushing it open and stepping inside.

But the room was a disaster. Clothes were strewn across the floor, and furniture had been upended. Pillows were tossed to the side, and the bed sheets had been ripped off in shreds. A few drawers hung open; their contents spilled haphazardly on the mattress.

"Turi?" she called out, feeling a stab of worry in her chest.

"He's not here," a voice said from behind her.

She spun around to find Mauri leaning against the doorway. There was a smear of blood along his jaw and the beginnings of black bruises forming along his left eye. He picked at something under his fingernails before looking up at her.

"Said he couldn't stay here. Took off with a horse and a bag."

"Where'd he go? It's not like he knows this land," she protested.

Mauri shrugged. "Don't know and honestly don't care. The little brat sucker punched me when I asked what he was up to."

She staggered back a step. "He punched you? That doesn't sound like Turi at all," she said, shaking her head. "You must have done something to piss him off."

"Think what you like, sister. But the curse messes with a man. Eats at his soul until there is nothing left but the hollow remains of what used to be. The Turi you used to know is gone."

A disbelieving laugh escaped her lips. "That's ridiculous," she snapped, even though she knew that Mauri was not entirely wrong.

Ever since they had crossed through the Cicatrix, she had noticed Turi retreating further and further into himself. She had thought that reuniting with his family would help him shake off whatever was plaguing him. How could she have been so wrong?

Guilt washed over her in waves. Yet another friend she had failed.

Mauri scoffed as he pushed off the doorway to leave. "Think what you like. He's gone. You shouldn't bother. The chances of finding him now are slim. The best advice I can give you is to give him space. He'll come back when he's ready."

She bit her lip as she clenched her fists, unwilling to give up on Turi.

A knock at the door drew her gaze. Standing behind Mauri was Erasmo, a concerned look on his face. "What's going on here?" he asked, pushing past his cousin to look at the state of Turi's room.

"Your baby brother high-tailed it out of here. Punched me before I could find out where," Mauri said, massaging his jaw.

Erasmo glared at Mauri. "Stop milking it. You're already healing."

Mauri dropped his hand and made a face at his cousin.

"It's not like Turi to go around punching people," Kiki spoke up.

Erasmo's shoulder's stiffened. "I didn't tell you something earlier. About Turi." She stared at Erasmo with a look that could kill. "He attacked me in the lab. When he found out about us, it was like he wasn't himself. The curse has taken a stronger hold on him than I had thought possible in someone who hasn't been under its influence for very long."

Her jaw dropped at this new revelation. "And you're just now telling me this?"

Erasmo's face was creased with worry, and his hands were clenched tightly at his sides. "The aggression doesn't usually start until we're in that awkward transition between boy and man," he said solemnly. "I thought he'd have more time. Years, at least." He looked away, regret filling his eyes.

She ran her hands through her chin-length hair. "We have to go after him," she said, determination filling her voice. She turned to Mauri. "Which direction did he go?"

"The crybaby went north." He exchanged a meaningful look with Erasmo that nearly sent Kiki's blood boiling. The two of them seemed to have this silent way of communicating, and she couldn't shake the feeling that she was being left out of the loop.

Before she could call them out on hiding something, Erasmo went deathly still. "Where's Aurelia?"

Mauri shook his head. "Haven't seen her since last night."

Erasmo started to pace through the disheveled room.

Kiki pulled him to a stop. "What aren't you telling me?" she hissed.

Erasmo looked her in the eyes, and she could see the storm raging there. He inhaled deeply before speaking, "I think my brother is behind all the weird shit that's been going on lately. The storm Guille reported. Tomás' attempt to kidnap Bernat and Turi with his bandits."

He turned, and the anger that had been seeping through his clenched jaw was released in a loud, angry roar. His arm swung back like a piston, and his fist crashed into the wall with stunning force, leaving a jagged hole in its wake. Pieces of wood cascaded to the ground, settling in a dusty pile around his feet.

"That's why I was in Tomás' camp all tied up when we met. He'd been ordered to capture me. He had my brother's crest on him."

This whole time Erasmo had pieces to this mess of a puzzle, and he hadn't said a word to Kiki. Anger rippled through her body at the audacity to keep her in the dark.

"Unbelievable," she muttered, taking a step towards the door, but Erasmo's hand shot out and grabbed her arm.

Before he could react, she had already unsheathed a tlazon from her bandolier, its razor-sharp blade held close to his throat.

Her eyes were flashing with anger and tears as she said, "Don't. I don't want to see you right now."

He winced as if something inside had broken; his once warm blue eyes were now hardened with a pain-filled glint.

"Kiki," he whispered softly, like the weight of the world was resting on his shoulders.

She stood firm, refusing to be triggered by his sorrowful expression.

"Don't 'Kiki' me. I'm pissed. You knew all of this and never told me."

Mauri began inching out of the room, his eyes darting between Kiki and Erasmo. "I'm going to be going now," he said with an apologetic look at his cousin.

"Good idea," she said to him, not taking her eyes off Erasmo. "It's about to get messy in here."

M auri scurried out of the room, leaving Kiki and Erasmo staring at each other, the temperature in the room rising as the tension simmered between them.

She took a step back, but he closed the distance between them quickly, snaking an arm around her waist and drawing her tight against him. His voice was low and soft as he said, "I just wanted to keep you safe. To protect you."

His tongue invaded her mouth, tangling with hers in a furious dance. Her traitorous body melted against him as she returned his kiss with fervor. She nipped at his bottom lip, eliciting a groan from him, spurring him to wholly consume her mouth as if he were a man dying of thirst and she was a glass of water.

Good sense made her pull away from him, his chest heaving for air. "I'm a Slayer," she said, pushing her hands against his muscled chest. "I don't need protection."

"I'm sorry," he whispered as he held her tighter in his arms, his face twisted with worry. "It won't happen again. I promise." His blue eyes searched hers as if he could somehow see his whole future within. Whatever he saw made him bold as he smashed his lips to hers again.

Fire snaked its way through her body at the urgency of his kiss. At the way his body molded to hers as if he had been made just for her.

She ripped away from his embrace, her breathing erratic. "You can't just kiss me and expect everything to be better. I'm still mad at you."

A sly smile tugged at his lips, and his blue eyes seemed to dance with mischief. He leaned close, his voice a deep rumble as he said, "Then let me make it up to you."

Her heart raced, and a wave of heat flooded through her body at the thought of what he might do.

He cupped her neck in his strong hands, the warmth of his skin radiating through her. He brushed his lips against hers tenderly, ever so gently exploring and tasting until she yielded to the sensation, her body melting into his embrace.

His lips were soft and full as he gently bit down on her lower lip. She opened for him, and their tongues intertwined in a gentle rhythm. He felt strong in her arms, and the heat from his body soaked through her leathers, driving her crazy with desire. His tunic was tucked loosely around his waist, and she ran her hands along the contours of his abdomen, feeling the warmth of his skin beneath.

His eyes were dark and wild, his muscles rippling as he effortlessly scooped her up and carried her to the bed. She felt the warmth of his breath on her face, and a low growl escaped from his throat as he moved closer. His lips possessed hers, gentle yet demanding. She could feel an intensity in their kiss that set her heart racing.

"If you're going to make it up to me, you're going to have to do a lot more than kiss me," she said when they pulled apart to catch their breath.

"Yes, ma'am," Erasmo responded with an irresistible grin that sent her heart soaring.

His eyes lit up full of desire, and his lips pressed hungrily against hers in a forceful kiss. She responded with equal eagerness, their mouths twining together with fervor. He pulled away, leaving a trail of light kisses along her jawline.

Her curves beckoned to him as her fingers found their way into his black locks. "Make this worth my while," she breathed, her voice a low hum.

He cupped her breasts and massaged them gently, sending shockwaves of pleasure through her body. She moaned in response, her body undulating against his. He pulled the zipper of her leathers away from her navel and exposed her from the waist up. He then took her nipple in between his teeth, lightly grazing it as he did so. Her body trembled at the sensation.

"You're so good at that," she breathed, her chest rising to meet his thumb as it circled around her other nipple. His thumb flicked over the erect tip before he pulled it into his mouth and tugged gently. She moaned louder this time, "Yes," she groaned. "Don't stop," she ordered and dug her fingers into his hair, bringing him in closer.

His fingertips glided along her stomach, slowly inching their way down toward her hips. One by one, he undid the buckles of her leathers and, with a gentle tug, removed them from her body, exposing her golden skin.

She tugged at his shirt, the desire to touch his bare flesh overpowering her every sense. She ran her hands over his torso, feeling his muscles tense and flex beneath her palms.

She tenderly caressed his lip with her tongue, and he responded in kind by parting his lips. She then swept her fingers through the hair at the back of his neck and brought their bodies closer together.

She ended the passionate kiss, leaving his lips plump and red. She moved downwards, lavishing his neck with tender kisses and little nips. His fingers gripped her hips as he followed her movements. Her tongue slowly caressed his body from top to bottom, sending shivers up his spine.

Gently, she pulled his pants down past his waist and dropped them onto the ground. She felt her cheeks flush as she beheld his rigid cock. The man was blessed, she had to give him that.

He delicately kissed her neck and shoulders, stopping every so often to give her collarbone a gentle nibble. His every touch sent an electrifying surge deep within her. Her hands roamed his powerful back and delicious round ass as she urged him on with a gentle pressure of her thighs.

"Hurry up," she hissed.

"Bossy," he said with a smirk before kissing his way down to her navel. "I like it," he grinned against her skin.

His hands cupped around her ass, squeezing and kneading the flesh before pulling her towards him and nudging her legs open.

She clung to him, her legs locked around his waist, as he entered her. A quiet sound of pleasure escaped her lips.

"Oh saints," she exclaimed as he slid inside her with a powerful thrust. His eyes burned with twin flames as he moved inside her, each thrust massaging her depths, stirring her body toward climax.

"Kiki," he uttered. His gaze blazing, he increased his rhythm, sounds of pleasure slipping past his lips as she met his thrusts with each swivel of her hips.

She trembled beneath his stare and clung onto him fiercely, digging her nails into his back.

He increased his pace, pumping into her faster and harder with each thrust, hitting her clit over and over again. Their breathing fell in sync as they moved together, their rhythm becoming more and more frantic.

She clung to him as the trembling began, and he slid his hand between them to tease her sensitive clit. His finger found that spot and started a rhythm that drove her crazy.

"Oh Erasmo, I'm going to come," she moaned, urging him on with her hips, her nails digging deeper into his shoulders. The sensations taking over her were overwhelming. She clenched her teeth, stifling a scream as she flew over the edge.

Her body quivered with delight as he quickened his tempo, and her pleasure grew. She felt him shudder as he climaxed and filled her with his cum.

Their lips found each other, and he kissed her with tenderness and reverence.

"I'm sorry," he said, pulling back and looking into her eyes. "I promise never to keep something like that from you again."

She smiled at him, running her fingers through his hair. "I know you won't." She believed him as his lips found hers again, and all was forgiven. "We still need to find Turi," she added.

Erasmo grunted his agreement. "I suspect he's gone to my twin," he said, shifting on top of her to lean on his elbow. He ran his fingers along the side of her face. "For now, though, I have business to attend to," he added with a smirk.

He was still inside her, and she felt him lengthen and harden once more. A grin tugged at her lips as her pussy filled with heat. "I don't suppose that business has anything to do with me," she said, and she shifted as if making a move to leave.

Erasmo growled and grabbed her wrists, pulling them over her head and pressing them into the bed. "Oh, it has everything to do with you," he said huskily.

CHAPTER TWENTY-FIVE

TRAIPSING IN FOREIGN TERRITORY

KIKI

K iki felt a chill race down her back as soon as she stepped out of the stable. She quickly proceeded to tighten the straps of her horse's saddle, her hands trembling from the cold. Above, oppressive grey clouds were rolling in, blocking out the sun and casting an eerie pallor over everything. A deep rumble echoed through the sky, and Kiki knew that it wouldn't be long until the rain began pouring.

"This is a horrible decision," Mauri complained as he threw his saddlebags onto his black stallion. "We're going to get soaked if we leave now. Why can't we wait until the weather clears?"

Kiki opened her mouth to snap at him, but Erasmo beat her to it. "We can't wait to go after Turi. If we're caught in the storm, then that means he is too. We don't know what supplies he took with him, if any. We don't know if he has a map or a compass. All we know is he took off yesterday and hasn't returned. Which means he's still traveling or he's lost."

"Or he's been eaten by a demon," Mauri mumbled under his breath.

Luna stepped around Mauri's majestic horse and jabbed her elbow into Mauri's side. She shook her head and gave him a stern look.

A look of apology flashed across Mauri's face as his mate silently chided him, but it quickly faded when his eyes darted to Kiki. He gave her a sarcastic smile and turned to help Luna into the saddle on his horse.

Kiki rolled her eyes at Mauri's territorial display.

"Ignore him. He's an ass on his good days and a nightmare on his bad ones," Erasmo said as he sidled next to her.

"I don't care if he's a demon, so long as he doesn't hurt Luna."

Erasmo scoffed. "Luna is his mate. He'd sooner cut off his dick and eat it before seeing any harm come to her." He nudged her playfully. "If it's any consolation, I feel the same way about you."

"Well, don't do that," she said, turning to face him as she pressed her body to his, shielding anyone who may be looking from what she was doing with her hand. "I'd hate for you to lose the one thing I like about you."

"Wicked little minx," he murmured as he wrapped a strand of her hair around his finger and gently tugged before pressing a tender kiss to her lips. "You know, I had hoped we'd ride together. I'm going to miss feeling your perfect ass rubbing against my cock for hours on end."

She playfully pushed Erasmo away. "I can't fight well if I'm restricted in a saddle with you. This way, I can jump off on my own if needed."

"I know," Erasmo said, his tone suddenly serious. "Should we run into any demons, I know you can handle yourself."

A familiar flash of red caught her eye, and she whirled around to see Solana descending the steps leading away from the manor house. She wore her battle leathers and was outfitted with a shining new machete and rows upon rows of tlazons tucked away into the twin bandoliers she wore crossed over her chest. She wore her customary tight bun and carried a large black bag in her arms.

Bernat trailed behind her, also wearing his Slayer gear and sporting new glimmering weapons as well.

Bernat waved at them as they drew closer and called out, "You didn't really think I'd let you take off without me, did you, brother?" A playful smile tugged at his lips.

When Bernat reached them, Erasmo reached out his hand, and they clasped forearms before giving each other a brief hug.

Bernat nodded toward the house. "Don't worry. I asked Yasir to look after things while we're gone."

Kiki looked over at Solana, and her eyes couldn't help but soak in the beauty of the fresh weapons she bore. "Where'd you get them?" she asked, pointing to the obsidian tlazons.

Solana dropped the bag to the ground with a loud metallic clatter. "I commissioned some weapons to replenish our stock when we first got here. They were only recently finished," she said, motioning to the bag.

Kiki dove for the bag and grabbed a handful of tlazons with greedy fingers.

"They're perfect," she breathed as she admired their pointed tips.

She grabbed enough to replenish her own bandolier and nearly squealed when she caught sight of the brand-new machete at the bottom of the bag.

She looked up at Solana in awe, and a wave of gratitude washed over her. Solana gave her a tight-lipped smile, but her eyes shone with more emotion than she was letting on.

A loud rumble of thunder shook the air, drowning out any further conversation.

Mauri audibly groaned and glowered at Kiki before clicking at his horse to get moving.

The rest of the group quickly gathered their supplies and mounted their horses. Their small army was finally ready for whatever danger awaited them. Everyone was silent as they left the safety of the eyrie and started their mission to find Turi.

They rode for over an hour in a somber silence, each of them lost in their own thoughts. They moved at a steady pace, careful not to push themselves too hard since they still had a long way ahead of them.

The forest came alive around them as if it were warning them to turn back; branches whipped at their faces, and the trunks of trees seemed to be closing in on them, yet they pressed forward despite these warning signs.

As they crossed over into the northern territory, Kiki felt a chill settle in her bones that set her on edge; her senses sharpening as she took in every little detail of this strange new environment. The air felt thick, almost suffocatingly so.

As if their collective anticipation had summoned it, twilight slowly descended around them, giving way to nightfall. The evening sky was painted in hues of reds and oranges, casting a beautiful glow over everything around them.

Mauri led them to an old abandoned cabin on the edge of a lush meadow, where he motioned for everyone to make camp while he went scouting with Luna by his side.

Erasmo came around with firewood, and Bernat began unloading supplies while Solana set up camp. She laid out a large blanket and several bedrolls before opening her bag to start preparing dinner.

Kiki helped Erasmo collect firewood and set up a fire pit. Once they had everything they needed, she went over to join Bernat and Solana, who was busy preparing food.

Her stomach grumbled as she approached the two of them, causing Bernat to chuckle. "You better feet that bear inside you," he joked as he passed her a bowl with rice and shredded meat.

She thanked him before digging in hungrily, feeling the warmth of the food spread throughout her body. She hardly even noticed when Mauri and Luna finally returned from scouting until a loud whistle pierced the night air.

Mauri and Luna walked into camp, both looking exhausted and grim as they approached. Kiki could sense that something was wrong, but before anyone could ask, Mauri held up a hand for silence.

He took a deep breath before sharing what he had seen. "We spotted a group of outlaws about two miles from our location."

She spoke up. "So? That's not too close. We can avoid them without a problem."

Mauri gave her an annoyed look before continuing. "They're led by Tomás," he said, sparing Erasmo a pointed glance.

Erasmo stiffened next to her, and she saw a vein bulging in his neck.

Mauri addressed Erasmo and Bernat alone, completely ignoring Kiki and Solana. "What do you want to do? We can take him out now or wait around for him to stab us in the back when we're not looking."

Erasmo chewed his bottom lip, his brows drawn as he considered their options.

She scoffed, unbelieving that he was even considering changing course.

Frustration made her speak up. "Out of the question. We're not out here for revenge. Believe me, I despise the man as much as anyone else, but we can't afford a distraction. We should stay focused and remain on mission."

Erasmo looked to Bernat, who, in turn, looked to Solana.

The Commander clasped her hands in front of her and stared into the fire, the flames dancing in her blue eyes.

After a long moment, she said, "I agree with Kiki. The mission takes priority. If we find Turi and run into Tomás again, we can deal with that problem when it arises."

Kiki's mouth fell open. She couldn't believe that Solana had agreed with her.

Solana rolled her eyes. "Don't look at me like that," she snapped.

Kiki held her hands up in a gesture of peace and exchanged a grin with Erasmo.

Erasmo cleared his throat and looked around the campfire. "I know we've all had our own run-in with Tomás, but I feel like it should be said the kind of man he is. Tomás is driven by greed and ambition. He'll do whatever it takes to get what he wants, no matter who gets hurt in the process. He's fearless, ruthless, and has no qualms about killing anyone who stands in his way."

Kiki snorted. "Yet you did business with him anyway."

Erasmo cut his gaze to her. "I purchased weapons from him. It's a little different."

"Whatever you say," she quipped.

Mauri clapped his hands together and stood, stretching his long limbs. "Well, I think we all know what needs to be done then, don't we? We'll focus on the mission and finish it as quickly as possible so that we can deal with Tomás."

"In the meantime," Bernat says, "we should try to get some rest."

Everyone nodded in agreement, and Erasmo offered to set up wards around camp. He pulled out a knife from his belt and sliced his palm open. "Come watch how I do this, Bernat. You should know how to set protection barriers too."

Together the brothers walked around the camp, setting up wards for the night. Erasmo softly chanted incantations as he moved from one spot to another, calling upon the pure spirits to protect them during their sleep.

He drew runes in the dirt with a slender stick, spilling drops of his blood along the lines as he went.

As Erasmo worked his way around the camp, Kiki could feel her own energy begin to shift. She could sense that some kind of deep magic was at work here —

It reminded her of her mother, and that thought sent a chill up her spine. Kiki didn't like thinking of her mother and hated the fact that those old memories were clawing their way to the surface.

Distantly, she wondered if her mother was still alive. It was a question she'd been careful to avoid. It was a possibility she wasn't ready to confront just yet.

When she crossed into the Cicatrix, she hadn't expected to find a whole civilization of people living within the darkness. But here they were. She flicked her gaze over the campsite, taking in the way Solana and Bernat talked quietly to one another, their bodies turned toward each other like they were merely extensions of one another.

When Erasmo was finished, he settled next to her and curled up alongside her under their woolen blanket. The heavy warmth of his body surrounded her, dashing away any lingering thoughts she had of her mother. The soft whispers of the others in camp helped her drift off to sleep.

The night passed uneventfully, and morning came too quickly. They packed up their supplies and were soon on their way again, setting a steady pace through the woods until midday when they noticed the faint outline of a shimmering wall reaching up into the clouds.

Kiki could feel the wall's energy all the way from here. But no one else seemed to notice it, or, at the very least, they weren't letting on that they could feel the evil radiating from the glimmering wall.

"Do you feel that?" she asked Solana.

The Commander's eyes narrowed as she looked at the white cloud of smoke rising along the horizon. "Yes," she whispered. "It's like... some kind of barrier."

Erasmo looked out at the horizon, and his brow furrowed in concentration as he scanned the tree line ahead of them. He pointed off into the distance, where a faint shimmering light could be seen cascading through the trees.

"That's Arlando's territory," he said aloud. "And that barrier must be the spell Guille talked about."

The closer they got to the boundary surrounding Arlando's land, the more the air around them shifted and swirled.

As they neared the edge of the wall, magic rippled through the air like a thick fog. Powerful energy seemed to undulate from the ground as they drew ever closer.

The trees near the edge of the wall twisted and contorted in strange unnatural ways, their bark gnarled and their leaves glowing with faint hues of pink and blue.

When they finally encountered the edge of the wall, they all gathered around and stared out into the thick mist. They could see the faint outline of trees in the distance, but it was difficult to make out much else.

"I'll go first," Erasmo said.

A burst of fear spiked through Kiki's chest, and she grabbed his arm to stop him. "No. We'll go together," she said, looking him in the eyes, so he understood that she wouldn't back down on this.

He nodded, and together they took a step forward. The air felt dense and heavy as she moved. Snow crunched beneath her boots, and frost invaded her eyes and mouth as she inhaled. She coughed against the stinging in her lungs. Looking down, she realized that she couldn't see the ground beneath her anymore.

A powerful force slammed into her, knocking her to her knees. She could feel the energy of the barrier sapping away her strength as it pulled at her soul. Her body felt heavy and weak, drained from the intense magical power surrounding them.

Erasmo stood a few feet away, and his arms extended in a protective gesture, his body taking the brunt of the attack. His eyes were wide, and his face was wild as the shield sucked at his own life force.

He reached out towards her, and she took his hand, feeling a surge of warmth shoot through her that strengthened her enough to stand up again. The further they moved from the edge of the barrier, the weaker the magic became until it faded away entirely.

Erasmo bent over, and she plopped down onto the ground, feeling weakened and exhausted.

"Are you two okay?" Mauri asked from the other side of the barrier.

"The shield is spelled to weaken. It's okay to cross. Just brace yourselves," Kiki called back, turning her attention to Erasmo.

"I'll be fine," he gasped, waving her worries away. "I just need a minute."

The others exchanged glances with one another, and in pairs, everyone crossed over into Arlando's territory.

Once across, they were all breathing hard from exhaustion.

Mauri spoke first. "I never liked Arlando, but I really hate him now," he huffed, pointing to the barrier. "What the hell was that?" he asked.

Erasmo shrugged. "I don't know, but whatever it was, it can't be good."

CHAPTER TWENTY-SIX

RIGHT IN THE EGO

KIKI

K iki pulled the hood of her fur cloak closer to her face, hugging it tightly. She attempted to draw comfort from the softness of the fur, but it did little to protect her from the bitter chill of icy air.

She inched her horse closer to Erasmo, trying not to be too obvious about seeking his warmth, though the idea was tempting. All she wanted was to drape herself over him and allow his body heat to seep into her bones.

She made a note to herself. When the opportunity presents itself, always share the damn horse.

Heavy grey clouds hung in the sky, sucking any warmth the sun may have otherwise offered. The trees lining the path were barren of leaves, their canopies withered and browned from the cold winter air.

As midday approached, the group stopped and pulled their packs off. Once the horses were cared for, Bernat unwrapped a bundle of dried meat and distributed it to everyone in the group.

Kiki leaped at the opportunity to wrap her arms around Erasmo's waist and bask in the warmth radiating from his body.

She noticed that even Solana sidled closer to Bernat, though Kiki knew the Commander would never admit aloud that she was uncomfortable in this cold.

Mauri opened his cloak, and Luna dove inside like a fox retreating into its burrow. His cloak covered her from her head to just above her calves, and Kiki resisted the urge to laugh at the way Mauri's face softened as Luna settled in. As if sensing her stare, Mauri caught her gaze and spared her a snarl.

Erasmo bristled and bared his teeth, his canines elongating.

Kiki elbowed him in the ribs. "Stop it. You're both acting like children."

Erasmo leaned against the tree but didn't take his eyes off his cousin.

"We should set up camp for the night," Mauri said after their staring contest went on for another few minutes. "Warm up a little and get some rest. Then head out in the morning."

"No," Erasmo said, his voice carrying a certain finality to it. He surveyed their surroundings, squinting against the glare of the white snow. "Arlando's castle isn't far from here. We keep going."

A growl escaped Mauri's throat, and from inside his cloak, they all heard Luna's squeak of alarm. "I'm not dragging her through this shit for a minute longer. If you, me, and Bernat are cold, imagine how Kiki and Sol feel?"

Erasmo's eyes darted to Kiki, and she huffed in annoyance.

"Kiki is right here and can speak for herself," she said with her hands on her hips.

Solana edged closer. "How far is the castle?"

"Another hour or two at most," Erasmo answered.

Solana locked her gaze with Bernat's, and Kiki noticed the subtle shift in the air. They both seemed to understand something without having to say it aloud. Solana finally broke their silent exchange with a curt nod and said, "Then I agree we should keep moving. The sooner we are out of this wind and snow, the better."

Mauri huffed, his eyes narrowing in frustration.

Erasmo answered the challenge by striding quickly towards him, the sound of his boots crunching in the snow. When he stopped in front of Mauri, the tension between them made it seem like no one else existed. "We're continuing, and that's final." Erasmo's voice was cold and stern.

Mauri and Erasmo stared at each other until, finally, Mauri's gaze fell to the ground. "Fine, but I call dibs on punching that bastard in the face," he said with fierce determination.

"Deal," Erasmo said as he let out a throaty chuckle.

As they continued riding into the teeth of the storm, the wind picked up speed, buffeting them with increasing intensity.

"Now, does anyone think we should have stopped for the night?" Mauri called into the wind.

Next to her, Erasmo tightened his hands into fists before releasing them. "I think I like him better when he's a bear," he murmured.

Kiki hid her smile behind her hand. "Why? Because he's silent for once?"

A smile tugged at the edge of his lips. "Exactly."

"I heard that!" Mauri called from behind them, and they continued to laugh silently.

Suddenly, a black blur raced from the treeline and crashed into Kiki and Erasmo. Kiki's horse reared up, tossing her to the ground. She rolled to avoid the horse's hooves. Nearby, Erasmo was doing everything he could to calm his horse, but Ocaso reared back, ripping the reigns from Erasmo's hands, and bolted.

Before Kiki could even process what was happening, she heard Solana let loose a terrifying battle cry as she positioned herself in front of Kiki to protect her from an oncoming demon.

Sulfur and ash assaulted Kiki's nose as the demon stalked back and forth. It looked like a giant bat with leathery wings, a long snout, and pointed teeth dripping with blood. The demon let loose a high-pitched keen, the sound making Kiki's skin crawl and the hair on her neck stand on end.

The demon roared angrily at Solana for interrupting its meal. She quickly leaped out of the way as the demon thrashed its tail, trying to wrap it around her ankles.

In one swift movement, she cut through the creature's neck with her obsidian machete, and thick black ichor drenched the snow. Then, the demon disintegrated into a cloud of smoke.

Kiki didn't have time to thank Solana for saving her hide when the cackling laughter of more demons echoed through the trees.

Kiki scrambled to her feet and pulled her bear claws from her belt, settling them over her knuckles. Nearby, Erasmo's claws pierced his flesh and extended past his knuckles, mirroring Kiki's weapons.

Next to them, Mauri let out a deafening roar, and his body exploded into black smoke before he emerged as a goliath black bear with silver markings along his nape and back.

Luna screamed at the sight and began to backpedal, but Mauri made a sad sound and lowered his head so that she could see into his eyes. Whatever Luna saw there calmed her, and she pushed her fingers into his fur, her eyes wide in awe.

Solana still wielded her machete, and next to her, Bernat brandished a machete in each hand.

The dark mass of creatures ran out of the trees with a horrifying cry, their claws and talons gripping into the snow. The snow swirled around them as the storm clouded the sky, and an odor of sulfur lingered in the air.

Erasmo stepped forward and growled, "Let's get this done."

With that, they all rushed forward; claws bared and ready to strike at the demons. They each moved fluidly like a single organism, everyone working in tandem to bring down the demons that stood in their way.

Mauri corralled Luna far away from the fighting before charging forward, his bear form razing through any demon that got too close for comfort.

Erasmo fought with impressive strength and skill, his claws tearing through the demons like paper. Kiki plunged her obsidian claws through the chest of a demon, and it exploded in a spray of black ichor before disintegrating into smoke.

They fought for what felt like an eternity, relying on one another to have their backs.

As a demon lunged for Kiki, she swiped her bear claws across its neck, but she missed, and a searing pain flared along her side.

The demon's arms were long and spindly, longer than any human, giving it a clear advantage over her. She spun out of reach, tucking her claws away, and unsheathed her machete.

She rushed to the demon and sliced through its arm as she plunged her machete into the center of its chest.

Black ichor oozed down the demon's torso and spilled over onto Kiki's obsidian blade.

"You demons need to step up your game. This is getting too easy," Kiki sneered as the demon misted into smoke.

A giddy feeling overcame her, and her head felt hazy. She ran a hand over her weary eyes and noticed crimson staining her palms.

Brows furrowed, Kiki glanced down and touched her stomach, noting the sticky red ink flowing from her body.

That's odd. Kiki didn't remember getting injured. This blood had to belong to someone else.

But her knees buckled beneath her weight, and she slumped to the ground, using her machete as a brace to keep herself upright.

Her name howled on the wind, and she vaguely recognized Erasmo's strained voice.

She had to tell him that someone was hurt. She just —

Needed a minute —

To catch —

Her breath —

Just —

A —

Second —

Erasmo kicked up tufts of snow as he skidded to a halt at her side. "Kiki!" he gasped, as he tenderly pulled her into his lap, his face etched with agony and fear. His free hand trembled as he caressed the side of her face, and his eyes danced across her features. "Hold on, okay, just be strong for a little bit longer."

"What's wrong?" she asked as her mouth filled with a sharp metallic tang. "I'm fine. The blood isn't mine," she said, wincing as piercing pain tore across her stomach.

"Oh, Kiki," Erasmo murmured, his eyes darting to her stomach with a flash of anguish before returning his gaze to her. His throat bobbed as he swallowed hard and said, "Don't you dare leave me."

"Wasn't planning on it," Kiki whispered, her lids growing heavier by the second.

A choked sound escaped Erasmo's throat, and he pressed his lips to her forehead. "I'll haunt you forever if you do," he whispered against her skin.

"Not if I haunt you first," she said, trying to force a smile. The realization finally dawned on her that the blood pooling beneath her body was indeed her own. She didn't have the strength to berate herself for getting injured. It was taking every ounce of her strength to draw in her next breath.

Black shadows swirled around Erasmo's shoulders as he continued to cradle her. "I'm going to hold you to that promise," he said with a forced laugh.

She liked the sound of that. In fact, she liked the feeling of closing her eyes too. She was so tired.

"Kiki?" Erasmo's voice raised an octave. "No, no, no! You have to stay awake! Open your eyes!"

But Kiki's eyes were heavier than boulders, and she couldn't muster the strength to open them — even if it meant one last look at Erasmo's handsome face.

"Kiki? Fuck, no! Come back to me! KIKI!!"

CHAPTER TWENTY-SEVEN

BLOOD TRAILS NEVER FAIL

YARI

Y ari was so focused on her book when Arlando hurriedly
entered the library.

"I need to go, Yari!" He exclaimed. "A fire razed a nearby village
to the ground. The people need my help! I'm taking a group of
guards with me. But I need to leave right away."

Yari sprung to her feet, her book forgotten on the table as the
urgency of the situation dawned on her. "I'll come with you! I can
help — "

Arlando let out a sigh of frustration. "No. You're staying here."

Yari opened her mouth to protest. "I want to help, please — "

Arlando rounded on her; his eyes glazed over with ice. "Don't
make me tell you again," he growled.

Yari recoiled at the sudden shift in Arlando's demeanor. She had
never seen him like this before, and it sent shivers down her spine.
It had to be the stress of knowing people were in danger, and here
he was, wasting his time on her. Feeling guilty, she hung her head
and retreated to her chair.

As Arlando left the library, Yari couldn't shake the feeling that something was off. She tried to focus on her book but constantly glanced toward the door. She knew he wouldn't be back for hours, but she couldn't shake the deep sense of unease that unfurled in her stomach.

Hours went by, and after reading the same page three times and still not comprehending what was happening in the story, she set the book down.

Suddenly, Yari heard a loud banging on the castle's main doors that made her jump out of her skin. Her heart pounding in her chest, she cautiously approached the window and peered outside.

She could make out the sole figure of a man tightly bundled in furs as he hunched, waiting for entrance.

She considered not opening the doors downstairs, but she quickly brushed that thought away, immediately feeling drowned in guilt. Here she was, warm and safe from the storm outside, while there was a helpless man out there. For all she knew, it could be a messenger from Arlando. He could have urgent news about her prince.

That was enough reason to send her rushing through the castle and frantically throwing open the doors.

But it was not a harried townsperson standing at the threshold. It was that man she had seen talking with Arlando before. The one with the wandering eyes and the smile that sent her hair standing on end.

She took a startled step back and held the door open just a crack. The man looked her up and down from head to toe, and she felt as if bugs were crawling all over her skin. She pulled her poncho tighter around herself as if doing so could hide her from his hungry gaze.

"Hello, miss," the man said. "Is the master of the house home?"

She didn't want this man to know she was here alone. She didn't like the way his eyes kept undressing her. So she lied. "Yes, but he's busy at the moment and can't be disturbed. You'll have to come back tomorrow."

"Don't you remember me, love? The name's Tomás," he said, holding out his hand for her to shake.

She eyed his hand as if it were a snake and stepped back again, closing the door an inch as she did.

The man smiled, but his eyes were hollow. "I must speak with him now," he insisted and stepped forward, his shoulder pushing against the door, wrenching it from her fingers and forcing her to backpedal into the main hall.

She scrambled away from him and stood in front of the stairs leading to Arlando's study. "No," she said firmly, planting her feet on the stairs. Even though he wasn't there, she felt she had to make herself look convincing.

Tomás took a step closer, anger spreading across his face. "Do you really expect me to believe that he's here?" His voice was low and menacing, and something dark and dangerous filled his eyes.

But she didn't move an inch. She clenched her fists and raised her chin defiantly, not about to be intimidated by this strange man who had no place here in Arlando's castle. "I told you, he's busy and will be very upset if he's disturbed."

A slow grin spread across Tomás' face, and he took a retreating step back, looking around and glancing up the stairs behind her. "Arlando!" he called. "Arlando! I have your little plaything."

A chill ran up her spine as the echo of Tomás's words swirled through the empty castle. He gave her a knowing smile, the kind of smile a wolf might give its prey before pouncing.

Fear rooted her to the spot, but only for a split second before she shot up the stairs. Panic-stricken, she glanced over her shoulder. Too late. His relentless grasp held her firm as he dragged her around and into his arms.

She screamed and kicked at him, hoping one of the servants would intervene.

His breath was hot on her neck as he leaned in close to her ear. "Not so fast, little one," he hissed. "You're coming with me."

He bunched his hands into her waist-length hair and dragged her out of the castle toward a waiting horse.

She fought and screamed, but he just laughed at her efforts.

He drew a dagger from his belt, and she shrank back at the sight of the glinting steel. Taking her hand in his, he opened up a cut on her palm.

She cried out in shock as crimson blood pooled in her hand. Tomás let a small puddle form in her palms before wrapping his hand around hers to create a fist. Droplets of blood trickled from her hand, splattering the white snow beneath their feet.

"That'll do it," he muttered before grabbing her and tossing her onto the back of the horse so that she was lying across its back on her stomach. He jumped up and kicked the horse in the ribs to get it to go.

The horse neighed in protest, and she silently wished the horse would buck them both off in retaliation. At least she might be able to get away. But the horse complied, and soon they made a mad dash through the frosted woods.

Her heart pounded as her fear increased. She was sure Tomás would do something horrible to her when they reached their destination. She held her palm to her chest as much as she could while still maintaining balance.

Then, an idea occurred to her. She dug her nails into her palm and let the blood flow again. When enough had pooled, she held out her hand and let the drops fall onto the snow. If Arlando saw them, he would know where to find her.

After what seemed like an eternity, they arrived at a cabin on the outskirts of the woods.

He jumped off the horse and roughly pulled her to the ground. She tried to run for it, but he grabbed her hair and yanked her back.

Fresh tears spilled from her eyes as the searing pain in her head increased.

"I don't like to chase, love," Tomás said as he pushed her toward the cabin.

As they neared the rundown home, she realized with increasing clarity that she had seen this cabin before.

Night after night.

It was the cabin from her nightmares.

She started to struggle again, but it was no use. Tomás pushed her through the door and locked it behind them with a heavy metal padlock.

The cabin was small, just like in her nightmares. Cobwebs filled every corner. Thick planks of wood boarded up the windows, so no one could see inside or hear her screams for help.

Tomás held his finger up to his lips as if warning her not to make any noise, then took out a pocket watch to check the time.

He pursed his lips before tucking them back into his pocket.

She wouldn't let this man hurt her. She had to survive this. Whatever his plans were, she must buy herself time. Time to escape. Time for Arlando to realize she was missing. Time. She needed more of it.

"What are you going to do with me?" she asked, steeling her voice so as not to betray the fear running wild inside her.

Tomás scoffed as he turned toward the kitchen. She heard the tickling of glass, and a few moments later, he returned with a bottle of amber liquid. He threw himself onto one of the sofas and kicked his feet onto the small table before the hearth. He took a long swig before addressing her.

"I'm going to keep you until that bastard fulfills his end of the deal."

She swallowed the lump in her throat and shifted into a more comfortable position. "So, you're not going to hurt me?"

Tomás rolled his eyes. "You're not my type, *muñeca*."

Relief washed over her, and she leaned against the wall for support. "Thank you," she said. She didn't know why she said it. This man came into her home. Scared her. Abducted her. Hurt her. But she was glad that was all he was willing to do.

"Whatever," he said and tossed the bottle back, taking a longer swig.

The liquid must have been strong because soon, he started to drift off into a drunken sleep. His head drooped, and his breathing grew heavy and slow until she was sure he had passed out.

She waited a few minutes before gathering her courage and walking to the window.

The moonlight cast an eerie glow on the cabin as dusk slowly turned into night. Bats flew around, screeching their eerie calls as they searched for their dinner. Crickets began to chirp in concert with each other, creating a melodic song that filled the air with peace and tranquility.

She moved over to the door and tried the padlock, the only thing in this place that wasn't old and rusted. But it was securely attached to the door. She didn't see where Tomás had hidden the key. She assumed he tucked it somewhere on him, but she was reluctant to go digging around in his pockets. He promised not to hurt her, but maybe he'd break that promise if he caught her trying to escape.

No. Waiting was the best thing Yari could do right now. Wait and hope that Arlando would come for her.

Sighing, she crawled onto one of the sofas and covered herself with a moth-eaten blanket she found in the corner of the room. Exhaustion took over her body, and she drifted into a blissful sleep filled with dreams of being home with Arlando where she belonged...was safe...happy...loved...

CHAPTER TWENTY-EIGHT

HEALING WOES

LUNA

L una sprinted toward Kiki, her best friend's name sailing from her mouth in a desperate plea. A strong pair of arms wrapped around her waist, pulling her back and knocking the breath from her lungs.

"Let me go," she screeched, her limbs flailing as she fought to get free.

She watched in disbelief as Kiki crumpled to the ground, her hands clutching at the gaping wound in her stomach. Blood oozed from four gashes along her chest, trickling down her battle leathers.

"Stop it," a familiar voice scolded.

Luna whipped her head around and came face to face with Solana.

"You can't help her," Solana said through gritted teeth, pulling Luna away from the fighting.

"No!" she yelled and shoved Solana off. "I'm the only one who *can* help her."

Solana grabbed her again, her arms like bands of steel, as she dragged Luna away. "Trust me!" she said, her strained voice betraying her exhaustion.

Luna's heart felt like it was cracking into a million tiny shards. "Let me go," she choked.

A feral roar ripped through the air, and Solana froze as they watched Erasmo and Bernat burst from their human forms and shift into bears.

Black shadows radiated from Erasmo's form and curled around him like the tails of many vipers. In bear form, he was larger than even Mauri, and his eyes glowed a brilliant azure, so piercing she had to avert her gaze.

Solana began to pull her again. "We have to get out of here."

"No," Luna protested, struggling against Solana's vice grip. "I have to help her."

Solana spun Luna, so they were face to face. Black demon ichor splattered her cheeks, and her leathers bore open slashes, red blood trickling down the material. "You *will* help Kiki. For now, we have to run. Before they see us."

"What?" Luna's brows furrowed into a deep crease.

"Just trust me," Solana said as she tugged Luna into the trees and pushed her behind one.

Together they stared out at the battle. Bernat had shifted in the clearing, and the black bear in his place was larger than Erasmo and Mauri combined.

At the sight, fear spiked in Luna's heart, and she sensed Solana stiffen beside her. Solana inhaled sharply, and Luna realized for the first time that she was seeing Solana's frozen exterior crack. Her mouth formed an "o" as she watched Bernat, in his bear form, his vicious claws tearing through the remaining demons.

"He warned me, but I didn't understand — " Solana said, her voice barely a murmur.

"Who warned you? What are you talking about?" Luna asked, but Solana seemed to be completely enthralled by the bears and demons.

Luna dropped the topic, seeing that she'd get no further answers from the distracted Commander. Kiki's body still lay in the snow, red blossoming beneath her like a macabre chrysanthemum.

If Kiki lost too much blood, Luna wouldn't be able to replenish the blood fast enough. Her best friend would die.

Her throat constricted painfully, and she balled her hands into fists. "I have to get back there. Kiki isn't going to last much longer without me," Luna hissed, pushing to a stand.

Solana grabbed her wrist and yanked her back down into a crouch. "Not yet. Wait until Erasmo gives the signal," Solana said. "Bernat isn't himself when he shifts. Erasmo told me to wait."

"I can't wait any longer," Luna said, ripping her wrist from Solana's grip and racing toward Kiki.

Sleet whipped her cheeks and stung her eyes as she ran, her lungs aching from the cold air filling them. She was several feet away still when Bernat caught sight of her.

His eyes blazed like sapphires in his bear form, and a spark of pure malice flashed within them that she had never witnessed before. His glare was so intense that it seemed to pierce her soul with an icy chill that shook her to her core.

But this was Bernat. The sweet and charismatic second-in-command. He'd never harm her. Feeling confident, she continued to sprint toward where Kiki lay.

Her confidence faltered when Bernat let loose a ground-shaking roar, sending her heart rate racing. Now, Luna understood why Solana tried to keep her away. Bernat truly wasn't in control anymore.

She pushed her legs to move faster, knowing that she'd never outrun him but determined to try. Kiki's life depended on her; she'd be damned if she let Kiki die on her watch.

A black and silver shape lunged over Luna, sending snow flurries into her face. She whipped around, recognizing Mauri's bear form as he collided bodily with Bernat.

"Mauri, no!" she yelled, her heart rising into her throat., choking her.

A deafening roar pierced the air as the two giant bears slammed together with thunderous force. The ground shook beneath them as their clashing bodies were locked in a savage battle, sending a shower of fur and saliva as they tore into each other with relentless claws and razor-sharp fangs.

Erasmo's bear form rushed forward and joined Mauri as they tried to hold Bernat back.

Luna steeled herself, knowing Mauri and Erasmo were buying her precious time. She couldn't stand around and waste it.

She wiped the tears from her eyes and raced to Kiki, dropping to her knees and quickly assessing the wound.

Four claw marks slashed across her chest, but the wound Luna feared the most was the fist-sized hole in the middle of her stomach.

Blood loss drained Kiki's face of all color, leaving it a pallid grey. Her chest heaved in slow, laborious breaths as if she had to fight for each and every one of them.

"I can fix this," Luna said aloud, more for herself than for anyone else. She pressed her palms into the earth to pull from its strength.

But the ground was hard and unforgiving, like a sheet of unyielding iron under her fingers. Even the life of the soil seemed extinguished, leaving her with nothing to draw upon for strength.

Her whole body trembled as she felt the weight of her situation pressing down on her. She was exhausted but knew that if she didn't act soon, there would be no hope for Kiki.

With a silent cry, she reached deep within herself and pulled on her own life force until it felt as if her very soul was being torn from her body.

It wouldn't be enough. But she didn't think about that for long because every second that passed was another iota of strength she didn't have to spare.

Gently her palms cradled either side of the wound. With a deep inhale, she closed her eyes and visualized strands of white energy radiating from her fingertips, pouring into the torn flesh, stitching together each shredded ligament as if they were patches on a quilt.

The grunts of the bears echoed through the clearing as they fought, and her heart sank at the sight of Erasmo taking the brunt of a powerful swipe of Bernat's paw, sending him sprawling across the white snow.

She quickly looked around and saw no more demons, for which she was grateful.

With all of her might, she concentrated on channeling as much energy as she could afford into Kiki's body. Her vision became blurry, and her heart rate slowed to a dangerous lull. She knew she had to stop, or else she'd pass the point of recovery.

There was only so much of her own energy she could take before she herself was in danger of standing at death's door.

Against her wishes, her hands fell to her sides, and she sank back onto her heels, her breaths heavy. The larger organs were restored, although a gaping hole still remained, and pieces of muscle were visible.

It was enough for now. She opened her pack and removed clean bandages, packing the wound with fresh linen and wrapping it tight.

She was almost done with her task when she heard a distressed sound coming from behind. She spun around and saw Erasmo in his bear form; head bowed down. Bernat had shifted back to his human shape while Mauri was kneeling beside him in the same form. Bernat gripped his head like he was ashamed of himself.

Luna's heart went out to Bernat, but she couldn't think about him right now. She could only think about Kiki.

Erasmo limped over, his body covered in sizzling wounds as his warm blood spilled along the white snow.

Once he was close enough, he shifted, and in human form, she could see the wounds he had taken more clearly. There was even a large bite mark on his shoulder, but it was already healing.

Erasmo bent over Kiki, his face twisted in anguish. "Can you help her?" he asked Luna.

"I've done all I can for now. I'm depleted. It was a fatal wound, but I managed to patch Kiki up enough for now," she said, her words slurring together as exhaustion pulled at her eyelids.

Erasmo placed his hand along the side of Kiki's face, and she couldn't bear the pained expression in his eyes. The way his lips were parted and turned down, the way his shoulders slumped like he was going to cave in on himself any moment. She turned her face away, or else she'd let his emotions overwhelm her.

"Stay with me," he said in a choked whisper, his blood-stained hand stroking through Kiki's midnight-black hair. "You can't leave me yet."

She heard footsteps and turned to see Solana helping Bernat walk while Mauri sprinted toward her.

He pulled her into his chest and held her by her face as he examined her. "Are you okay? Are you hurt? Is that your blood?"

"I'm fine," she told him and put her hands over his. "I'm not hurt. It's Kiki's blood."

He visibly relaxed, but when his eyes landed on his cousin, he stiffened again. "Erasmo — " he began.

"We just found each other," Erasmo continued, mumbling incoherently.

"Kiki is going to be okay, brother," Mauri said in a soothing voice.

Erasmo turned to face his cousin, and the look on his face nearly killed her. His face was full of so much desperate hope that she felt it would be her undoing.

"Yeah?" Erasmo asked. He looked back down at Kiki. "I don't know what I'll do if — She has to be okay. She'll be okay, right?" He turned his hopeful eyes to Luna. "You'll be able to save her? After you rest?"

Luna didn't respond right away because she wasn't sure that she could save Kiki. Her heart ached to admit it, but she'd sensed something dark crawling through Kiki's bloodstream. An infection that slowly poisoned the blood.

Mauri sensed her reluctance and clasped Erasmo by the neck, pulling him into a hug. "We'll do everything we can, brother. I promise."

She exchanged a glance with Mauri, silently thanking him for coming up with a response that didn't promise Erasmo the world.

Some wounds couldn't be healed.

CHAPTER TWENTY-NINE

A WILD PROPOSAL

LUNA

The Ozero princes built a fire and strung up tents in a semicircle around it, shielding them from the howling gale outside. Luna was too preoccupied to notice the tiny details of their work — Kiki's chest rose and fell weakly, her eyelids flickering as if trying to stay afloat on an ocean of exhaustion.

Once the first tent was put up, Luna and Solana took out fur-lined blankets from each of the packs and tucked them around Kiki's sleeping form until she was completely enveloped.

The minutes ticked by into hours with no sign of Kiki waking. Luna bit her lip in worry.

She ran yet another scan through her friend's body, placing her palms on Kiki's forehead, letting her magic navigate through Kiki's lungs, liver, spleen, and stomach. She detected the repaired organs, the replaced vessels, and the reconstructed sinews and ligaments. But something sinister lurked in Kiki's blood, sloshing through her veins with a thick, cloying presence. Something rotten and festering.

Solana gently squeezed Luna's shoulder and said, "She needs rest, Luna, and so do you. Why don't you lay down next to her, get under the blankets, and shut your eyes for a few minutes?"

Luna shook her head, her hands still pressed to Kiki's clammy skin. "No, something isn't right. I can feel it. When I touch her, there is something else. Something I can't heal is sucking at her life force."

Solana frowned. "What, like some kind of poison?"

"Yes, like a poison. It's leeching at her. I can sense it but can't touch it. I don't understand. I've healed lots of poisons. I don't understand!" she growled, shoving her hands into her hair, tugging at the roots.

Solana's eyes widened, and she quickly raised a finger to her lips. She leaned toward the entrance of their small tent before turning her serious expression on Luna as she whispered, "Shhh...they're still out there, and their hearing is better than ours. I don't want Erasmo to hear you."

Luna wasn't an idiot. She knew she couldn't tell Erasmo this news, especially because she didn't have any solutions to offer.

The last thing anyone needed was for Erasmo to go berserk, shift into a bear, and rampage around like a wild beast.

She had to figure this out before telling him. But she was running out of time, and the gnawing feeling in her gut warned her that so was Kiki.

The wind howled, and lightning cut through the night sky, illuminating the tent in a brilliant flash before fading to darkness. The tent's canvas walls hummed and trembled as though alive, straining against its rope-and-peg anchors.

Mauri pushed open the tent flap and stepped inside, a gust of snow blowing in behind him. Erasmo and Bernat followed suit, carrying a tapir and bundles of wood with them. Swiftly, they constructed a fire and skinned the animal to make a meal.

Once Mauri finished helping prepare the meat for roasting, she jerked her chin towards the tent exit. He understood her silent message and wiped the grease and gristle off his hands with a rag before following her silently into the raging storm. They navigated around a bramble of bushes, and once they were far enough away from camp that Luna was sure Erasmo wouldn't be able to hear, they stopped beneath some low-hanging branches.

Mauri's face dropped as he took in the serious expression on Luna's face. Mauri spoke hesitantly, "What's wrong?"

"I've done all I can," Luna replied, "but she won't wake up. Her breathing is shallow, and her color isn't right — she should have woken by now." She paused before continuing, "I think she may have been poisoned, perhaps something on the demon's claws. But I can't touch it. It's unlike any other poison I've seen."

Mauri stepped closer, apparently just as worried that someone might hear them, and asked in a quiet voice, "What are you saying?"

She looked into his deep, soulful eyes, and her composure crumbled. A strangled cry escaped from her throat as she tried to explain what she was feeling.

"She's dying, Mauri. I can't do anything to stop it. She's dying, and I'm supposed to heal her. That's what I do. That's what I'm good at. But I don't know what's poisoning her. It's like it's running from me. I can't help her — "

Tears clouded her vision as Mauri wrapped his arms around her and pulled her close. She sunk into his embrace, feeling the warmth of his body against hers and the gentle pressure of his hand on the small of her back.

"It's okay," he murmured. "It'll be okay," he said a second time; she suspected he was saying that more for himself than for her. Erasmo would be devastated, and there was no doubt that he'd lose himself completely.

"It's not okay. She's my best friend. No, she's my sister. We were all each other had growing up. She's never needed me for anything. Not really. And now, the one time she needs me, I'm powerless to help her."

A throat cleared nearby, and she and Mauri leaped apart as if caught doing something they shouldn't.

Solana stood a few feet away, snowflakes dusting her bright red hair and coating the heavy fur cloak wrapped around her shoulders. "That's not entirely true," she said with heavy emphasis.

"How long have you been standing there?" Luna asked hesitantly.

"Long enough." Solana glanced back at the tent and stepped closer so she was a hairsbreadth away. "I haven't mentioned it before, but there's something you need to see."

She slowly pulled her hand from beneath the sable furs, and they all leaned in when she opened her palm. A tiny spark appeared at first, but then a flame erupted in her hand that quickly grew before it burst into the air like fireworks. It illuminated the darkness with a flickering orange light before fading away.

Mauri and she both gasped in shock, their eyes wide with disbelief. They gaped at Solana for a moment before exchanging confused glances.

Solana tucked her hand back into her furs. "It started a few days ago. I can't control it very well, as you saw for yourselves. So I can't rely on it in a fight. That's why I didn't say anything before now."

"How is this possible?" Luna asked, slowly coming closer.

Solana shrugged. "I think it has something to do with the mate bond. Bernat and I — " She blushed, unable to finish her sentence, and Luna couldn't help but stare in shock at the red coloring blazing across the Commander's nose.

Was Solana Ramirez, the Commander with ice in her veins, actually blushing?

The Commander shook herself as if fully aware of her stare, and her cool mask slipped back into place. "We solidified the bond. I don't know what we did. But I felt something in me change."

Confusion and intrigue warred inside of Luna as Solana spoke, but try as she might, she could not make the connection between Solana's words and Kiki's current state.

She balled her fists in frustration as a hot spark of anger raced through her veins, and before she could stop them, the words slipped out of her mouth like molten lava. "That's great, but how does your little fire show help Kiki?"

If Solana was annoyed by Luna's tone, she didn't show it. Instead, she pursed her lips and took a deep breath before speaking slowly and deliberately. "Have the two of you sealed your bond?"

Now it was Luna's turn to blush. Her cheeks burned red as she averted her gaze.

Mauri stepped forward, his voice low and firm as he said, "That's none of your business."

Solana held up her hands in a gesture of peace. "You're right. It's not. But if it's the only way to save Kiki, I thought you'd want to know." Solana dipped her head in farewell before turning on her heel and returning to the warmth of the tent.

Alone in the cold, Luna allowed Mauri to wrap her inside his furs. "He probably had no idea what he was doing," Mauri muttered to himself.

"What?" she asked, pulling away enough to look at his face. He had a thoughtful expression, and his deep brown eyes seemed calculating. "Who had no idea?" she asked again.

"Bernat. Unless Guille told him, which that's also possible."

She pushed away from him, frustrated. "I have no idea what you're saying. Stop talking like I understand everything. I hate it!"

"Sorry, *chiqui*, I don't mean it," he said, pulling her in close again. "It's all I've ever known. I'm not good about this kind of thing."

His voice was so earnest and sincere that any annoyance she felt faded. "Can you please just tell me what was going on?" she asked, pressing her face into the warmth of his chest.

"It seems that Sol and Bernat have sealed their bond, which happens when a mated pair join together, and the male — " He paused and opened and closed his mouth as if looking for the right word. "There's no better way to say it — the male basically stakes his claim by marking the female. Sometimes, when the bond is sealed, the female emerges with magic that was laying dormant before."

There was so much wrong with that whole explanation that Luna remained silent as she chewed on the meaning of his words.

So she was meant to simply accept that Solana, the ice queen herself, possessed fire magic, and it had merely needed to be activated? And that it was activated once Bernat claimed her?

That was ridiculous. Laughable, actually.

A giggle trickled up her throat and burst forth with the force of an erupting volcano. Her breaths came in short gasps, punctuated by tiny hiccups, as she clutched her sides and bent over with laughter.

"If I'd known you'd find this so funny, I would have told you sooner," Mauri said seriously.

She choked down her laughing fit and wiped the tears streaming from her eyes. "It's not that," she gasped, still getting herself together. "It's that Solana, of all people, has fire magic. The irony!" She burst into another round of chortling laughter. "I'm sorry, I'll stop now," she said as she caught her breath. She heaved a deep sigh, and the reality of the situation came crashing down on her. "Here I am laughing, and yet not fifty feet away, my best friend is dying. I must be cracking."

"Don't apologize for finding joy when you're surrounded by darkness," Mauri said softly, tucking a strand of her dark hair behind her ear. "I, for one, am glad to hear you laugh again."

She smiled as she snuggled closer to him and leaned her head on his chest. "So sealing the bond could wake untapped magic. That's what I'm taking from everything you said. I'm going to ignore the whole 'marking' and 'claiming' thing."

Mauri chuckled, and the sound vibrated in her ear. "That's what people say, and if Solana is any indication, then I suppose it's true."

She chewed on the inside of her cheek as she considered the possibility that if sealing the bond could wake magic, it could be entirely possible to strengthen it. Deepen it even.

But the thought of sealing the bond meant that — she blushed just at the thought. Though Mauri was her mate, and she could feel that truth in her very marrow, she wasn't sure if she was ready to seal that bond yet. To share her body with him in such an intimate way.

It was not that she didn't want to, either. Because whenever he was close, like now, all her senses lit up. Her heart raced every time he smiled down at her.

"Your heartbeat is racing, *chiqui*," Mauri murmured. "I don't know how we're going to get through this, but we will. We'll figure something out."

She tilted her head to look up at him. "That's not what I was thinking about just now," she said sheepishly. He quirked his brow at her, and she continued, "I was wondering if — if sealing our bond might make my magic stronger — "

Mauri lifted his hand and caressed the side of her cheek. "There's no need for us to rush anything — "

"But what if it works?" she pressed. "What if we do this, and my magic is strong enough to heal Kiki? What if this is exactly what needs to happen to save her life?"

He ran his thumb along her lips. "I'm not going to say that I don't want that, to completely bare myself to you in every way. To forever solidify this bond between us. But the last thing I want is for you to feel rushed into something you aren't ready for. I would've waited an eternity for you, Luna. I'm not going anywhere."

"I want to," she blurted out.

His eyes widened in shock.

"I do. I have — I mean — want to. I just — I have never been with a man before."

"But you said — "

She blushed and hid her smile in the fur of his cloak. "I have. Just not with a man," she said again, placing emphasis on the word 'man'.

His eyes became circles as understanding washed over him. Then, a devilish smile tugged at the corners of his lips. "Now that's an image to revisit at a later time," he murmured as he leaned down and nibbled her earlobe.

Shivers of pleasure ran up her nape as his breath ghosted across her skin. She clung to him harder. "Is that a yes?" she asked as his lips moved down to kiss her collarbone. "Are we doing this? Will you help me?"

He drew back and stared her in the eyes. "I'll do anything for you, *chiqui*. Always."

CHAPTER THIRTY

HEALING BLISS

LUNA

Mauri gently took Luna's hand, leading her away from camp and into the woods. He found a large sycamore tree with a hollowed-out trunk. The space seemed made for two, so he turned to Luna, offering his hand in invitation.

Luna's lips pursed as she took in the cramped space. "How romantic," she said with false enthusiasm.

Mauri rubbed the back of his neck as he shifted from foot to foot. "It's not La Aguilera, that's for sure."

Luna sighed. This wasn't what she had in mind for her first time with Mauri, but the minutes were ticking by, and Kiki needed her.

"If a bug so much as crawls on me, I'm putting it on your dick," Luna joked, forcing a smile to calm the swirling nerves in her chest.

If sealing the bond with Mauri failed to deepen her magic, then —

No. She couldn't let herself think about the consequences. Because she couldn't let anything happen to Kiki. Kiki was more than her friend. She was family. Her sister.

Kiki had cared for Luna in ways that no one in the orphanage or the streets had bothered before.

Mauri shrugged off his cloak and hung the heavy fabric over the hollow's entrance like a curtain. Luna draped hers across the ground, flattening out the dead leaves to create a makeshift bed.

Mauri adjusted his position until he squatted on the floor, and she copied him. The air felt thick with the tension between them, and all she could think of was Kiki, which wasn't exactly calming her racing heart. Instead of getting into the mood, she couldn't seem to push thoughts of her best friend from her mind.

"I used to cry every evening," she admitted, her tone low and sad.

Mauri's eyes softened as he reached out and placed his hand against her cheek. She placed her own on top of his, savoring the warmth. "Why, *chiqui*?" he asked in a gentle voice.

A lump rose in her throat as she said, "I missed my mother. I'd sneak into the barracks where the Yearlings and Attendants slept and crawl into Kiki's bunk."

He stared at her, his hands balled into tight knots in his lap. "How long have you been in love with her?"

"I do love her, but not in the way that you're thinking," she uttered firmly, avoiding the temptation to scold him. "Kiki has always been so strong. Like a big sister to me. To Yari and me, actually. She made it her mission in life to look after us." Her voice cracked, and she shuddered as a sob bubbled past her lips. "I just — I can't imagine my life without her, which is stupid because she's a Slayer. Slayers die all the time. I think I just thought that she'd never be one of them. That she was invincible."

Mauri nodded in understanding, like he could feel her heartache. Luna could see the pain in his eyes as he spoke. "I know how you feel," he said. "I had a friend when I was a kid. We did everything together. People often mistook us for brothers. That's how close we were." He shifted closer to her and continued his story. His voice grew quiet and filled with emotion. "When the curse took me, he was there. Standing just a little too close." Mauri swallowed a lump in his throat and took a deep breath. His eyes became distant, as if he could still see those memories. "I killed him." He paused again, his eyes wincing shut as if he could rid himself of the image. "I shifted, and the beast took over. And I killed him." He laughs a humorless, derisive sound and adds, "That's why I only have my cousins now. They're harder to kill."

"Oh, Mauri," she whispered and placed her hand on his cheek, wanting to comfort him. His skin felt hot beneath her fingers, and he closed his eyes as he leaned into her touch.

Her heart raced as she locked eyes with him. His eyes were dark and filled with sorrow, his brows furrowed, and his lips set in a tight line. She felt an invisible connection between them that seemed to bridge the gap of sadness they both shared.

They stayed like that for a few moments, just searching for comfort in one another's presence. She felt Mauri's pain as if it were her own; she knew he felt her's in return. It was a strange feeling but one that was both familiar and comforting at the same time.

She made the first move, leaning in and connecting her lips with his. His breath caught in his throat as he responded, his mouth exploring hers slowly. When she opened up to him, he eased in, taking his time and savoring the moment.

The man she had first met at La Aguilera, who warned her he was a monster, contrasted sharply with the softly-spoken soul she now observed. Yet, beneath it all, she sensed the hurt boy who had lost his closest friend, shaping the man into a razor-sharp blade determined to shield those he loved. That was a sentiment Luna understood with absolute clarity.

She grabbed the back of his neck, and he let out a moan as she pulled him closer. She smiled against his lips as she deepened the kiss.

He cradled her face in his hands, lifting her up so she could straddle him. She ran her fingertips lightly across his shoulders, along his arms, then back up to his sculpted biceps.

He moaned into her mouth, and she shuddered in response. She had never felt such an intense desire to be with anyone before. His touch ignited a fire inside her that was unlike anything she had ever experienced.

She trailed her hands down his chest and over his abs, touching him with curiosity. His taut stomach and the light dusting of black hair that carved a path down past the waistband of his pants only added to the sensuality of his body.

She felt him groan appreciatively beneath her touch. When she looked up, he was already grinning at her. She gave a small chuckle and apologized for her boldness.

He laughed and reached out to brush her hair to the side, exposing her neck to him. "Don't be," he whispered. "My body is yours. To admire. To touch. To kiss. Whatever you want."

She shivered as he trailed his finger along the sensitive skin of her collarbones, his touch sending ripples of ecstasy through her until they settled between her thighs.

He pressed so close to her that she could feel his erection pushing into her stomach. She pulled back, their eyes locked, and she could see his need. And it made her wet. This gorgeous man melted beneath her touch. She did this to him.

Excitement ran rampant through her blood; she dipped her head down and kissed the skin right beneath his ear. He shuddered beneath her, and she couldn't resist the urge to nip at his earlobe.

His breath hitched, a desperate, needy sound, and she grinned against his skin. She continued down his neck, licking and biting, savoring the groans and moans she tugged from his lips.

She moved down his chest and over his nipples, already hard and waiting to be played with. She flicked the hardened points with her tongue, causing him to hiss in response. She grinned mischievously and took one in her mouth, sucking and biting gently.

He groaned, the sound deep and husky. He tugged at her hair, urging her to move lower. She loved how he was so vocal about what he wanted. It made her feel empowered.

She trailed kisses down his stomach, his muscles constantly rippling with need. She slid her hands over each muscle, stopping at his waistband to undo his belt and the buttons of his pants.

He lifted his hips to help her, his hands never leaving her hair.

She slid his pants and underwear down his legs and tossed them to the side. Her mouth went dry at seeing the hard evidence of his desire for her.

"You've got to be kidding me," she said dryly.

Mauri gave her a triumphant grin, clasped his hand around hers, and moved it up and down along the length of his shaft. "Are you afraid, *chiqui*?" he asked, his tone dark and dangerous.

She swallowed the lump in her throat, her eyes feasting on the way he held her hand wrapped around his cock, their hands moving in tandem. "Yes," she admitted.

"You should be," he growled.

A shiver of fear and delight swirled in her stomach in a heady mix of arousal. She liked the uncontrolled desire in his voice, it made her feel powerful, and she pressed her thighs together to ease the growing pressure.

"Take off your clothes and lay back on the cloak," he ordered, his voice husky.

She removed her hand from his dick and started to undress.

"Look at me while you do it," he said, his hand still stroking up and down, his eyes full of feral need.

The look in his eyes sent a tingling sensation rushing straight between her legs. Keeping her eyes trained on him, she slowly removed her dress, loving the way his eyes roamed over her body as she removed her bra and, lastly, the underwear that covered her pussy.

Air rushed from his lips as she stood before him, completely bare, and he groaned when she got on her knees and lay back on the cloak, spreading her legs so her pussy was bared to him.

"You have the most beautiful body," he said, his voice full of desire. He kicked off his pants and crawled between her legs, his cock pressing against his stomach as he neared.

She flattened her palm on his chest and slid it down to his stomach, running her hands down his torso and over his erection, loving the velvety feel of it. She wrapped her hand around it and squeezed gently.

She watched his face as she moved her hand up and down, his lips parted, and his eyes searing into hers. He swallowed loudly, his whole body tensing before grabbing her hand and stopping her motion.

"Stop. I don't want this to end yet."

He leaned forward and kissed her, his lips punishing as his hands moved to cup her breasts. His thumbs brushed across her nipples, and she cried out in response. He tortured her while he took her mouth, his expert fingers pinching and squeezing her nipples until she ached with desire.

"You like that?" he asked, his eyes drinking into her features like he was a man dying of thirst and she was the only source of hydration.

"Stop torturing me and fuck me already," she growled, wrapping her legs around his trim waist.

With a growl of his own, he responded by diving his hand between their bodies and stroked her clit.

Her hips jerked in response, wanting so much more than what his hand was currently giving her. "Mauri," she gasped, her voice full of need. "Please," she added, her breath ragged.

He smirked in response and slid another finger over her pussy. She moaned into his mouth and bucked her hips upward.

"So needy for me," he muttered against her lips before sliding two fingers into her wet pussy.

"Yes," she groaned into his mouth, and he pumped his fingers in and out of her.

He added a third finger, and she cried out, bucking her hips faster. Her whole body heated with need, her heart pounding, her breathing coming in ragged gasps.

She was so close...

Suddenly he pulled away, staring at her with heat in his eyes. "No!" she gasped.

Mauri grabbed the back of her neck possessively, sending a shiver of pleasure running up her spine. "You'll come when I say so," he said, his eyes full of fire.

She nodded, unable to speak. She felt just as unhinged as he looked, her body an inferno that could rage forever.

He chuckled and kissed her neck. "That's a good girl."

She shivered at his praise and clung to him, loving the look in his eyes.

"Open your legs wider for me," he said, his hands on her inner thighs, guiding her into position. "You're so wet for me," he said, admiring her slick pussy. "You're dripping for me," he added as he lined up his cock along her pussy.

"Mauri," she gasped, anticipation filling her to the brim. "Just do it, please."

He slowly breached her pussy, his size filling her, breaking down her barriers, a dull burning from the way he stretched her so fully.

"That wasn't so bad," she laughed shakily.

He arched a brow at her. "I'm not even halfway in, baby."

"What?" she squealed just as he slid out slightly, then thrust back in, giving her another inch of his length.

"Oh!" she cried out, the feeling of being so completely full washing over her.

He continued to do this until his hips pressed against hers, fully sheathed inside her. "Does it hurt, *chiqui*?" he asked, his voice strained.

She shook her head. "There is a slight burn, but it feels good."

He pressed his forehead to hers. "Good, because I'm going to fuck you so hard, you scream my name."

The threat in his words sent a thrill of arousal through her veins, and she captured his lips with hers, swallowing that promise.

He began moving inside her again, his thrusts gaining speed and force. As he angled himself between her legs, he hit a sensitive spot that had her panting.

His lips moved to her neck, and she threw her head back in pleasure. He bit down gently, and she felt the pressure build.

"Come for me, Luna. Come all over my thick cock."

His dirty words were her undoing. The orgasm hit her like a tidal wave, her body shaking and shuddering as it ripped through her.

A tandem wave of bliss cascaded through her, and she could feel her magic rising within to greet it. A hurricane of magic rushed through her veins, like a floodgate had ruptured, and golden threads extended throughout her body until they filled every fiber of her being.

She floated in that sea of pure bliss, her body filled to the brim with more magic than she had ever wielded before.

"Oh, Mauri, yes!" she cried out in rapture, and Mauri groaned in response, his thrusts hard, his hips slapping against hers. She gasped as he slammed in hard and held himself there, a growling roar ripping past his lips as he came undone. She felt his cock twitch inside her before he filled her with his warm cum.

He collapsed against her chest, the stubble along his jaw tickling her neck as he tucked his head.

"Fuck, Luna," he rasped. "You milked me so hard."

She felt a rush of pride at his words and wrapped her arms around him, wanting no space between their sweat-slicked bodies.

"I've never come so hard in my life," she mused, running her hand through his hair and down his back, feeling his muscles flex in response.

"Why am I taking that as a challenge for next time," he smirked, slowly sliding out of her and reaching for the cloak.

"Because you're twisted," she grinned.

"Only for you," he murmured, pulling the cloak around them as he wrapped his arms around her, pulling her tight to him.

They lay like this for a few minutes, and she enjoyed the silence. She never realized how comfortable silence could be, but with Mauri, it felt right.

She lifted her head and looked at him, a question on the tip of her tongue. "Do you think it worked?"

He grasped her chin and gently pulled her lips to his mouth. "Oh, I know it did," he said before planting a kiss on her lips.

"Why do you say it like that?" she asked, lifting up to see his expression.

He grinned. "You're glowing. Literally," he said, pointing at her.

She glanced down and noticed her own radiance. A shimmer of gold illuminated her skin as if the moon itself lived inside her and had finally decided to show its face.

CHAPTER THIRTY-ONE

ONLY FOOLS RUSH IN

YARIXA

Y ari awoke abruptly to a monstrous sound that shook the walls of the cabin. She leaped from her spot on the sofa, heart pounding, and raced to the window.

Her breath caught in her throat when she saw what awaited her outside — a massive beast with blue eyes that glowed like beacons in the pale moonlight. It stood on two legs, its claws digging into the snow below, and it opened its maw wide in another ear-splitting roar. Drool dripped from its razor-sharp teeth as it bellowed out into the night.

"What the hell," Tomás said as he crowded the window to look outside. His face turned ashen when he saw what was outside, and he scrambled back, tripping on the little table by the hearth. "No. He said — He promised."

Tomás frantically grabbed his dagger from his belt and unsheathed it.

A loud bang on the door made her jump.

"Where is she?" a booming voice called. "Tomás, you bastard, what have you done with her?"

Yari's heart stopped. She knew that voice. "Arlando!" she cried, rushing over and clinging to the door, tears streaming down her face.

"I swear, Tomás, if you don't give her back right now, I'm going to break this door down and rip your head off!"

Tomás shook his head and started mumbling incoherently as he took a few steps away from the door. He looked at Yari with despair, but she didn't understand why. What did he think would happen?

The banging on the door got louder, shaking the cabin walls. The sound of wood splintering filled the night air as Arlando broke through the door. He barreled through and stopped when he saw Yari, taking a moment to ensure that she was indeed unharmed.

His hair was disheveled, and his clothes were torn, but he had never looked more beautiful to Yari than he did at that moment.

Tomás stepped away and pointed his dagger at Arlando. "She's safe," he stammered, his voice trembling with fear. "I didn't hurt her, just like we agr — ."

A growl rumbled in Arlando's chest, cutting Tomás off before he lunged. Tomás dove for the door and scurried outside, scrambling in the snow toward his horse.

Arlando growled as he slowly turned. He pulled Yari into a quick embrace and pressed his lips to her forehead. "Stay here, *amor*."

Arlando peeled himself from her embrace and stormed out of the cabin. Tomás fumbled with his horse and then bolted for the trees.

She stood at the threshold of the cabin and watched in awe as Arlando sprinted after him, closing the distance between them with every stride. He closed in on Tomás and tackled him to the ground, grabbing his wrists and yanking them behind his back.

Tomás screamed and squirmed beneath Arlando's weight, but it did no good; Arlando was too strong.

He held Tomás down firmly and glared at him with a righteous anger that sent a chill down her spine.

"I did what you said," Tomás whines. "We had a deal!"

Arlando's eyes narrowed, and his face twisted with rage as he thrust his hand forward, fingers splayed, slamming it into Tomás' chest.

A scream split the air, and Yari only realized it was her own screaming when her lungs cried out for air. She clutched the door frame as she watched in horror.

Tomás's face contorted as he reached out to grasp Arlando's forearm. His breathing was ragged and desperate, his fingers digging into Arlando's arm like claws. Tomás's eyes were wide and glazed in shock as he weakened in Arlando's grip. Clenching his jaw, Arlando ripped his hand away, along with Tomás's still-beating heart.

Yari felt the breath leave her lungs as she slowly sank to her knees. Her entire body trembled in disbelief, and tears stung her eyes. This couldn't be real, she thought desperately. Arlando had never seemed to lean to violence, so why was he now holding the bloodied, shredded heart of another man in his hands?

Arlando slowly rose to his full height, spit on the ground, and glared at the man who had dared to kidnap Yari. He then clenched his hand into a tight fist, the sick squelching sound of flesh and blood squishing into a pulp before he dropped it to the ground.

Arlando then reached inside his vest and pulled out a white handkerchief, using it to wipe the blood from his knuckles.

Arlando slowly exhaled and then pivoted away from Tomás's lifeless body. His eyes had returned to their usual expression of cool control, betraying no hint of the rage that had been there just a moment ago.

Unconsciously, she stumbled backward until her spine collided with the wall.

"I'm sorry you had to see that," he said, still wiping away the blood on his hand.

She didn't even realize that she had started to cry until he wrapped his arm around her waist and wiped away her tears with his thumb.

"Don't fear, *cariña*. Everything will be alright now," he said as he leaned down and pressed his lips to hers.

She was still in shock over what she had just witnessed. How could the man she loved be the same man that she saw moments ago?

Arlando drew back with a frown on his face. "You're bleeding," he said with a frown, picking up her hand and examining the cut Tomás made.

"I'm fine," she lied and pulled her hand from his grasp. His very touch made her stomach roil.

Arlando's shoulders stiffened, and he reached for her hand again. This time, she couldn't hide her flinch.

He quirked his brow at her. "Are you afraid of me, *amor*?"

She inhaled a shaky breath and slowly nodded her head. She didn't know this man standing before her. She didn't know he was capable of such rage. Such violence. Such brutality and bloodshed.

He stroked the inside of her palm around the edges of the wound. "When I saw your blood in the snow, I feared the worst," he murmured as he leaned his head down and brought her palm to his lips. He kissed her wound, and she inhaled at the way it stung.

Before she knew what he was doing, his tongue darted past his lips and licked the cut.

She snatched her hand away and cradled it to her chest, her mouth open in shock. "What are you doing?"

The light around him seemed to dim, and the air crackled with palpable tension. As he stared at her, his eyes glowed with a sinister intensity that sent shivers of fear through her body and made her heart skip a beat.

"I'm helping," he said as he grabbed her hand and forced it open.

"Stop," she pleaded as she tried to wriggle away. But he was too strong, and his hands were like steel around her wrist.

He bowed his head once more, and she felt the wetness of his tongue against her skin.

Unable to witness such depravity, she turned her face away and winced her eyes shut.

After a few moments, Arlando stopped licking and said, "There. All better."

She peeked past her lashes to look at her hand, and the wound was gone.

Shock rippled through her as she stared at the spot where her skin had been split open. Now all that remained was some smeared blood.

Red stained Arlando's lips as he licked away the last of her blood.

"What?" she sputtered. "How?"

"I told you that I would always take care of you," he said as he wrapped his arm around her waist and pulled her to his chest.

"But how did you do that?" she asked, still staring at her palm.

"Magic," he whispered. He leaned his head down and brushed his lips across her throat.

"I don't understand," she said, feeling her stomach flutter with nausea.

"Just trust me," he murmured.

He kissed her hard, his mouth devouring hers. His hands caressed her shoulders and then moved down to her waist. He pushed her into the wall, trapping her under his body. His lips were feral against hers, and a deep rumbling growl reverberated from his chest.

She pulled back and breathlessly said, "Arlando, wait. Here?" She looked around at the shabby cabin and the broken splinters of wood.

Arlando's pupils were blown wide as he stared at her. "Here. Out there," he said, jerking his chin toward the outside, where Tomás' body lay cold and vulnerable to scavengers. "Everywhere," he growled before slamming his lips to hers once more.

She wrenched her face away. "No. I don't want to. Not here."

A storm clouded his face, and his eyes glazed over with ice. "You're ruining everything," he hissed. "I will have you when I want you, wherever I want you, however many times I want you," he snarled, before grasping her chin firmly in his hands, squishing her cheeks hard.

"Stop," Yari cried, trying to disentangle her legs from around his waist. "Please, take me home."

A rumble started in his chest and bubbled out past his lips in a humorless laugh. "Oh, Yari, my sweet girl. I am your home," he sneered and grinned wide.

His canines grew sharp and long, his lips pulling back in a vicious snarl. An eerie darkness seemed to spawn from the depths of his soul, surrounding him like an impenetrable fog. His eyes glowed a bright blue as the shadows around him gathered into a beastly form — towering tall with the body of a man and the head of a bear.

Arlando's jaws opened wide, exposing sharp fangs that glistened in the moonlight. He bit down hard on Yari's neck, and she felt a searing pain as his teeth punctured her skin, and blood gushed from the wound. She tried to push him away, but he was already transforming into a monstrous creature with thick fur and rounded ears.

Shock and fear coursed through her veins as her voice echoed shrilly through the darkness. Tears of terror streamed down her face as she screamed until her throat ran dry.

This couldn't be happening.

This wasn't real.

This was a nightmare.

She screamed until her voice gave out, and even then, she screamed. Silently. In the safe recesses of her mind. Where no one and nothing could penetrate. Not even a monster like Arlando.

Yari clutched the soft blankets around her battered and bare skin, fresh bruises coloring her flesh. She stared vacantly up at the rough-hewn wooden ceiling, listening to nothing but Arlando's ragged breaths in the small space. Her heartbeat thundered so loudly that it seemed to shake the very walls of the room.

With a groan, she slid off the mattress and stumbled onto the cold floor. Her shaky legs barely supported her as she hobbled to the wooden chair and held on for balance. She paused to catch her breath before shuffling over to the ceramic wash basin tucked into the corner of the room on a rickety wooden table situated in front of a frosted mirror.

In the mirror, she took in her reflection — her wide brown eyes seemed even wider against the discoloration of a large red and purple bruise along her right cheek. She lightly traced her fingertips around it, wincing as a sharp pain shot through her skin. Lowering her hands to the hollow of her collarbone, she could feel the raised ridges of a few half-healed claw marks from earlier, still faintly glowing red.

She swallowed hard and felt her throat constrict as she stifled the desperate cry that threatened to wake Arlando. Blinking away tears, she reached for a washcloth, dunked it in the icy water of the basin, and pressed it against her warm skin.

She winced at the shock of the cold before she began rubbing away Arlando's release from between her thighs. The cloth turned scarlet with each pass. She moved southward, wincing again when she wiped over five bloody puncture wounds left by his claws.

"What are you doing?" a deep, throaty voice rumbled from the darkness.

She gasped, and her heart seemed to stop for a moment before thudding wildly in her chest. She reached out blindly and felt the cool surface of the nearby table, steadying herself against it. Behind her, the bed creaked, and the heavy footfalls of someone approaching reached her ears.

She felt a chill run down her spine when Arlando stepped up behind her, blocking the moonlight that had been streaming in from the window. "I asked you a question," he said, his voice cold and distant.

The pungent smell of his soap invaded her senses, making her want to gag. She clenched her fists and looked away, trying not to make eye contact with him.

"I told you I would heal these later," he said, his calloused hand moving slowly up her arm, leaving a trail of stinging heat in its wake as he counted the bruises and scratches.

She trembled at his touch, desperately trying to keep herself from flinching away. Fear flooded her veins like ice water, freezing her in place as images of his monstrous transformation haunted her mind.

The churning in her stomach escalated, and though she wanted nothing more than to flee, her legs refused to move.

His fingertips brushed against the ridges of her skin, tracing the grooves he had left hours before. He kept his hand still and steady, his gaze locked on hers, as he asked in a low voice, "Have you learned your lesson?"

Her lesson. To submit to him in all ways. The one time she had denied him, and this is what he had become. And he wanted to know if she'd learned her lesson.

Yari closed her eyes tight and gave him a slight motion with her chin.

Arlando jammed his finger deep into one of the open wounds on her hip, and she gasped in agony. His eyes were cold and intense as he spoke through gritted teeth, "Say it out loud this time."

"Yes. I've learned my lesson," she cried.

He delicately removed his finger from her wound and brought the glistening red tip to his lips. His tongue flicked out, lapping up the slick rivulets of blood. "Good," he murmured. "As your reward, I shall heal you."

His hot, wet tongue flickered from his mouth as he explored each and every shallow cut that lined her delicate arms. Yari felt his arousal stiffening against her skin, and a wave of nausea washed over her. She held her breath and prayed that she would not have to endure the pain of being taken again.

After tending to every scraped and bruised inch of her body, he drew her back into the bed, cradling her like a fragile doll. His lips pressed into the top of her head as he sealed her in place with an arm around her waist.

She lay in bed, rigid and wide-eyed, her breathing shallow as though every inhalation might be her last. Her fear descended on her like a snarling beast, and she kept vigil all night, holding her breath until the first rays of morning light brought with it a sense of relief.

As they approached the looming, ivy-covered castle walls the next day, Arlando gracefully swung out of the saddle and offered his hand to help her down. His strong, calloused palm felt like an insult as she stepped gingerly off the horse.

She remembered the first time he did this. Had he always had this gleam in his eye? Did she just miss it? She couldn't be sure.

"I have a surprise for you," he said, taking her hand firmly in his and leading her up the stone steps.

She wanted nothing more than to rip her hand away from him, but she resisted the urge, fearing his detestable form of punishment.

"I don't need anything," she said softly, her voice still hoarse. "You've given me everything I could ever ask for."

She wanted nothing more from him but hoped that she could appeal to the part of him that had been kind and soft with her. That somewhere beneath the monster still lurked the man she had fallen in love with.

Arlando's mouth curved into a smirk as he stared down at her. The light glinting off his eyes made them seem cold and calculating. His words were like daggers; each one meant to make her fear him more. "I know I have," he said in a sickeningly sweet voice. "But I was feeling generous. You'll thank me later for it."

The heavy wooden doors of the castle creaked open as he pushed them, and a gust of cold air filled the room. In the dimly lit space, Yari could make out a fire crackling in the hearth, its warm orange light flickering across the stone walls. Near the hearth stood a figure, their face hidden by a cowl and their back to her.

Arlando's gaze flickered toward the figure near the fire. He put his arm around her waist and grinned, gesturing for the stranger to come closer. "Brother, come meet the love of my life. My mate."

Brother? She stole a glance at Arlando, taking care to hide the alarm on her face. And what did he mean by his mate? He'd uttered those strange words before, but she didn't know their meaning. Hadn't bothered to ask either.

Foolish. She'd been so foolish.

The figure spun around on their heel, and her breath caught in her throat. She knew the tall silhouette before he stepped into the light — his broad shoulders and confident stride were unmistakable. His bright blue eyes widened with disbelief as they met hers, a mix of surprise and recognition altering his features. He paused for a beat, taking in every inch of her.

"Yari?" he asked breathlessly.

Yari's mouth fell open in shock. "Turi?" she breathed, her voice barely a whisper.

Her eyes shifted to Arlando, standing proud and tall beside her – his arm an unyielding shackle around her shoulders. His fingers dug painfully into her arm as he flashed a smug smile.

"See? I told you that you'd love my surprise."

CHAPTER THIRTY-TWO

CAUGHT IN THE TALONS

ERASMO

"**P**lease stay with me," Erasmo said to Kiki as he placed his hand alongside her face.

He didn't want any of this to happen. This was the very reason he had stayed his distance. Because involving her would only endanger her.

With Mauri and Bernat's help, he may have slaughtered all the demons that attacked them, but he knew that there was one enemy out there that remained. His brother. Arlando.

Arlando was responsible for this. Erasmo didn't know how and didn't care to find out why. If there even was a why. When it came to his twin, sometimes he couldn't tell.

All he knew was this: Arlando was a poison. Sick and twisted with a cavity in the place where his heart should be.

Erasmo knew this truth deep in his bones. He had vowed to bring Arlando down but had let himself get wrapped up in her —

He glanced down at Kiki and gently stroked her midnight-black hair with his hand. His mate. His everything. His life. His love.

He didn't regret the day that Kiki came into his life. Not for a second. Every moment with her had been a balm for his cold black soul. She brought him to life in a way that he never thought was possible.

His only regret was that he left his brother to his own devices for so long. He regretted that Arlando was his blood. Erasmo's mirror image in every way.

He didn't know when they had stopped seeing eye to eye. He thought perhaps that, like most relationships, when the right amount of energy wasn't put into it and hurts were allowed to fester, the outcome was inevitable; a slow-decaying thing that no longer resembled its former beauty.

Then again, some people were just toxic, no matter how much love you poured into them. Like a parasite, they'd take and take and take until only a carcass remained.

Kiki lay sleeping in Erasmo's arms, her breaths shallow and steady. His eyes followed the gentle rise and fall of her chest, but then he noticed something else — her mouth twitched lightly, and her lips parted ever so slightly. He held his breath as he leaned down, placing an ear closer to her mouth in order to catch anything she might be saying.

"Erasmo," she whispered.

He ran his hand through her hair and nestled her closer to his chest. "I'm here, my love."

She parted her lips to say something, but the effort was too much, and her head sagged to the side.

It took every ounce of willpower in him not to let the shift consume him. He could feel the beast within, pacing back and forth as if waiting for someone to be foolish enough and come too close.

He wanted to murder everyone and everything. He would burn this world to the ground if that meant she lived to see another day.

"Brother," a deep voice called his name, forcing him back to the present.

Erasmo snapped his attention to Bernat, his arms outstretched, extending a canteen of cool water. But Erasmo didn't want the comfort and care his brother was offering. Not when the living embodiment of his heart was dying in his arms.

Erasmo shook his head vehemently as if refusing the offer would erase the situation altogether.

"You have to drink something," Bernat insisted. He crouched near Erasmo's feet and nudged him gently. "You're no good to her if you're not a full strength."

Erasmo winced because he knew Bernat was right. He hated that his brother was right, though. He just wanted to be left alone in his grief. Not be reminded of such mundane things.

"If I drink, will you stop trying to get me to suck at your teet?" Erasmo spat.

"No promises, little brother. I have to make up for missed time," Bernat said, his eyes growing tender at the edges.

Erasmo snatched the canteen from Bernat and guzzled it back, relishing in the coolness that trickled down his throat.

Despite his brother's outburst, Bernat smiled softly — a gesture that triggered a wave of shame inside Erasmo.

He handed the canteen back more carefully than he had taken it, accompanied by a muttered apology.

"She's going to be okay, brother. She's strong," Bernat said softly.

Erasmo shook his head at the useless words of comfort. Because he could feel that the opposite was true. He felt it in his blood, like he could feel her heartbeat fading under his palms.

Kiki was not okay. Her wounds might be healed, but there was something more at work here.

"Where the hell is Luna?" he snarled. "Why the fuck isn't she doing something?" Erasmo reluctantly pulled his gaze from Kiki, his eyes darting around the tent. His heart sank when he noticed that Mauri was also missing.

Anger curled in his gut. That bastard choose now to run off with his mate? If Erasmo weren't so afraid to lose a single second with

Kiki, he would chase Mauri down right now and tear him into shreds.

He couldn't believe Marui would abandon him at a time like this and only think about his dick. Erasmo stewed in his hate and fury for a few minutes before Mauri ducked into the tent, his hair slicked back with sweat and his cheeks flushed.

Rage flared in Erasmo's chest. He knew exactly what his cousin had been up to by the looks of him, not to mention the smell of sex lingering on his skin.

Erasmo stood in a rush to lay into Mauri right then and there, but Luna followed in after him, and Erasmo felt a shift in the air at her presence. Something had changed. Something he couldn't see, but the beast within him bowed its head in reverence.

Luna looked the same, but there was something about her now, something otherworldly that had him sealing his lips shut.

Her eyes zoomed in on Kiki, and without saying a word to him or anyone else, she brushed past Erasmo to kneel next to her friend.

She placed her hand on Kiki's forehead and closed her eyes.

Erasmo held his breath, waiting for her to say the words he feared the most.

That Kiki would die. That just when he found his mate, he was doomed to lose her. That life as he knew it would now cease to matter because, without her, he had nothing.

His chest constricted with each passing second until Luna's eyes snapped open, and she turned to him, her expression serious.

"I need everyone to gather around in a circle," she motioned to the area around Kiki.

Solana was the first to move, prompting Bernat to follow, Erasmo and Mauri right behind him. The group arranged themselves around Kiki as Luna instructed and waited with bated breath.

Luna grabbed Mauri's hand. "I need everyone to link hands. I'm going to need all of your strength to help me heal Kiki. This isn't an ordinary wound. There was some dark magic at work here, and it's going to take all of us to banish it."

It took everyone a few moments to get situated, but Luna didn't give them a chance to even settle in.

She closed her eyes and began to sing.

"From the earth, to the sky,
Let the magic flow and soar high.
With every word and every beat,
I summon forth the healing heat.
By the power of the elements,
By the power of the celestial sent,
I command the winds to blow,
And heal this wound, let it glow.
Oh, ancient spirits of the land,
Hear this call and lend a hand.
With your power, make whole again,
This body, mind, and soul of pain.
So mote it be, so shall it be,
The magic flows, and sets you free.
With every breath, and every beat,
This wound shall heal, complete.
And so it is, and so it shall be,
The magic flows, and sets you free."

She spoke with a powerful force coming from the depths of her being, and it echoed off the canvas of the tent, reverberating around them like an intense rumble of thunder. He had never heard anything quite like it before.

Erasmo and Mauri locked eyes for a moment, and he could see the fear in his cousin's wide pupils. He scanned the room and noticed the same anxious looks on Solana and Bernat's faces.

The magic in her words pushed and pulled on him, lifting him up and then sinking its claws into his chest. He felt a coldness seep into every part of him, like the kiss of death itself.

The air frosted, and icicles formed along the ground beneath their knees. His breath misted into white clouds in front of his face, and the more Luna sang, the deeper those claws of death sank into his chest.

Erasmo wasn't sure how much longer he could take the pressure in his chest. He felt like he hadn't taken a decent breath in a lifetime.

Just when he started to fear that this spell wasn't going to work, that he'd lose Kiki for good, blazing heat wrapped itself around his heart and pulled hard, sucking the air from his lungs, hollowing out his cheeks as if ripping his life force through his throat.

Just as quickly as it happened, it stopped, and he heaved a deep breath of ice-cold air.

Erasmo looked at the others and saw they hadn't fared much better than he had. Their faces were red and blue from the pressure on their lungs and the lack of air.

Erasmo quickly forgot all of that when Kiki squirmed in his arms. His heart leaped into his throat as he observed the color blooming along her cheeks, her eyes bright and glittering, and her heartbeat thrumming rhythmically against his palm.

He leaned in, inhaling her familiar scent. He barely made contact as his lips brushed against hers before lingering for a few perfect seconds. As he pulled back, their eyes locked, and his heart swelled with the realization that she was still here with him. His lips curled up into a smile as he felt her own smile pressing against them.

"You're not allowed to die," he said, breathless. "Not unless you take me with you."

"I'll keep that in mind the next time I get myself impaled on a set of demon claws," she said with a smirk.

"You let your guard down," Solana said, her tone matter of fact.

Kiki tossed her Commander an annoyed glare. "I'm seconds from the brink of death, and that is the first thing you have to say to me?"

Solana looked to Bernat as if for help. He smiled indulgently at her and turned to Kiki. "What Sol meant to say is that she's glad to see you're okay. We both are."

"Hmm," Kiki huffed, but she didn't press the matter further.

Tears lined the rim of Erasmo's eyes, and he reached across Kiki's body to take Luna's hand in his. "Thank you," he said softly, his voice cracking.

Luna smiled and glanced at Mauri. It was a look full of so much love and trust that it made him bend over to kiss Kiki once again, if only because he knew that feeling intimately, and it was one that he wanted to cherish with every fiber of his being.

Kiki fell back to sleep, but her breathing wasn't shallow anymore, and her skin was full of color. He felt safe to leave her side for a moment and join the others around the small fire in the middle of the tent.

As he settled next to Mauri, his cousin whispered, "We're not far from Arlando's castle, you know."

Erasmo eyed his cousin, fury already running rampant through his blood at the mention of his twin. "I'm well aware," he said, his tone darkening.

"Good," Mauri said. "Because I think it's about time we paid him a visit."

A few hours later, Erasmo and Mauri stood before Arlando's castle.

It was hard for Erasmo to believe that the last time he had been here, he led everyone who wanted to leave the madness for La Aguilera.

That had been a sad day for Erasmo. He and the rest of the family had lost faith in his brother. Unable to talk sense into Arlando, Erasmo took it upon himself to clear the castle — before anyone else could get hurt.

Only those deeply loyal to Arlando had remained. Old Sergio and a handful of servants and guards.

He wouldn't be here now after all this time if it wasn't for the love of a woman whose life was threatened only hours ago.

Mauri stretched his arms and braced them behind his head. "Look at this dump," he said with a whistle. "It's gone to shit."

Mauri was not wrong. What was once the glittering gem of Ozero, his birthplace and the home of generations of monarchs, was now a grey monolith of darkness.

"I never thought I'd see this place again," Bernat whispered, his mouth slightly agape. "For years, I thought maybe I imagined everything. That I'd made it all up as some kind of weird, messed-up coping mechanism."

Erasmo patted his older brother on the shoulder. "It may look like shit, and it may be home, but we should all remember why we have come here."

Bernat nodded, his eyes still taking in everything, and the trio ascended the grand staircase toward the main doors.

Erasmo didn't wait to knock upon arriving at the front door. He reared back his foot and kicked them wide open with a loud bang.

Snow flurries swept into the dimly lit hall, and he charged into the main hall.

"Arlando!" he roared. "Get down here, you bastard!"

A figure moved from the shadows and slowly stepped into the light. "Bernat?" said a soft feminine voice. "Is that really you?"

Bernat squinted his eyes to see in the dim light, but then his eyes widened. "Yarixa?"

A petite woman with soft brown curls flowing over her shoulders walked into the light. Her eyes were wary as she took in Erasmo and Mauri, but she smiled at seeing Bernat.

Her smile didn't reach her eyes, though, and Erasmo couldn't help thinking that a deeper sadness lingered beneath her expression.

Without warning, she launched herself into Bernat's arms. "It's so good to see you, Captain! Is Kiki with you?"

Kiki? As in *his* Kiki?

Erasmo's mind began to swarm with what Kiki had told him. About why she entered the Cicatrix in the first place.

He felt his cheeks drain of color at the realization that this Yarixa standing before him was Kiki's Yarixa. Her best friend. Which meant —

"Brother," said a smooth and cultured voice from behind Erasmo.

Erasmo whipped around and was confronted with his mirror image. Or rather, an inverted image.

Where Erasmo was the embodiment of darkness and shadows, Arlando was the embodiment of light and sunshine.

Arlando's hair had turned completely white. He wore a white tunic with silver embroidery across the chest and down his sleeves, and his blue eyes were bluer than Erasmo's. It was more than just his appearance that changed. Erasmo could sense the shift of darkness in his twin.

Warning bells pealed in Erasmo's mind at the visual representation of Arlando's descent into madness.

Arlando pulled Erasmo into a hug and planted a kiss on his cheek. "I'm so glad to see you."

Erasmo felt his stomach drop into his feet. Yarixa had been with Arlando this whole time.

Then his brother strode over to Kiki's best friend and tucked her under his arm. "Allow me to introduce my mate, Yari."

The small brunette looked up at Arlando, and Erasmo knew that look from anywhere. Complete terror.

He had to get them all out of here.

Now.

Things were much worse than he feared.

He opened his mouth to speak, but before he had the chance, a dark figure emerged from the shadows and let loose a metallic projectile. It hummed through the air and lodged itself deep in his neck, prompting a sharp sting.

He pinched the tiny metal dart between his thumb and forefinger, recognizing the straight line grooves around its circumference that marked it as Arlando's handiwork. It was identical to the one Tomás had used on Erasmo earlier; it made sense he'd keep a stockpile of them on hand – he was the one who hired the two-faced smuggler, after all.

Erasmo's eyes widened as he watched Turi slowly raise the blowpipe to his lips. With one strong breath, he sent another dart soaring toward Erasmo with incredible speed.

Erasmo gasped, feeling as if a physical force had knocked the wind out of him. As he dropped to his knees, he saw Mauri and Bernat sprawled on the cold marble floor; two darts lodged deep into their chests.

The last thing he saw was Kiki's best friend, Yari, her delicate wrist tightly held in Arlando's punishing grip, her quivering lip, and her sorrowful eyes overflowing with tears.

Arlando, you bastard. My blood and bone. How could you?

The End...for now.

Want more Solana and Bernat? Read their bonus scene!
https://BookHip.com/MRDKAXS

Continue The Ozero Curse series with A Curse of Fang and Sword (forthcoming August 22, 2023)!

Want to get the first updates on new projects, announcements, and bonus content?
Join Nicolette's Facebook Reader group: Nicolette Elzie's Fantastic Readers
Or sign up for her newsletter at nicoletteelzie.com/newsletter

A CURSE OF FANG AND SWORD

THE OZERO CURSE

NICOLETTE ELZIE

The final installment in The Ozero Curse series. See how it all ends August 22, 2023.

Also by Nicolette Elzie

The Ozero Curse Series
A Curse of Tooth and Claw
A Curse of Blood and Bone
A Curse of Fang and Sword

Acknowledgments

Thank you so much for making it to this part of the book! It's surreal that as I write this, I'm closing the metaphorical chapter of this book and writing my first sequel.

For some background, I've been writing since I was 11 but didn't start writing with the purpose of publishing until 2015. I didn't know what I was getting myself or my friends and family into when I started this journey.

I've written several first novels since 2015, but *A Curse of Blood and Bone* was the first time I've ever written a sequel. I was intimidated by the prospect, but I am delighted with how this story turned out and excited about where Kiki's story leads us next.

A lot goes into making a book come to fruition, and I feel very blessed to have a support system that allows me to pursue my passion.

I want to take a moment to express my gratitude to all the fantastic people who helped me make *A Curse of Blood and Bone* a reality. Firstly, my family has been an incredible support system throughout the entire process. It's not always easy to balance my full-time job, family, and writing, but their constant encouragement and unwavering support are invaluable.

A big 'thank you' goes to my daughter, Audrey, who reads every first draft and every proof. She reads them multiple times, takes them to school, brags about me unabashedly, and gets all her friends and teachers excited about my work. She's my sunshine, and I'm lucky to be her mom.

I also extend a huge thank you to my beta readers, Veronica and Rebecca, who put in countless hours of hard work to help bring my vision to life. Their honest feedback, insightful critiques, and encouragement were crucial in helping me improve this book and make it a reality.

Lastly, I want to thank my readers for their support and enthusiasm. Knowing that my stories have touched people's lives is a truly humbling experience. Every email, tag, post, Reel, and TikTok I see you make about these stories and characters bring so much joy to my heart. Thank you for trusting me with yours as I take you on this adventure of magic and romance.

I cannot thank everyone enough for their help in making this book a reality. I hope it brings joy and inspiration to all who read it.

ABOUT THE AUTHOR

Nicolette Elzie writes mythology-inspired fantasy romance with delicious, morally gray heroes and fierce heroines more likely to jump into battle mode with their swords blazing. She lives in Washington, D.C., with her swoony husband, two children, and three fur babies. She can usually be found reading, re-watching her favorite shows for the millionth time, playing board games, and reminiscing on her past life as a dragon.

Join Nicolette's Facebook Reader group: <u>Nicolette Elzie's Fantastic Readers</u>

Or sign up for her newsletter at <u>nicoletteelzie.com/newsletter</u>

Feel free to contact Nicolette on social media, tag her in a post or email her at nicolette@nicoletteelzie.com with your thoughts and concerns, or to rave about all the bookish things.

Nicolette's Newsletter

https://nicoletteelzie.com/newsletter/

Follow Nicolette on TikTok

https://www.tiktok.com/@authornicoletteelzie

Follow Nicolette on Instagram

https://www.instagram.com/nicolette.elzie/

Follow Nicolette on Facebook

https://www.facebook.com/nicoletteelziewrites

Visit Nicolette on the Web

https://nicoletteelzie.com

Ingram Content Group UK Ltd.
Milton Keynes UK
UKHW010053100623
423212UK00003B/9